Frequency Studios
presents

Haley Starr: Bad Kitty

by Ethan Sasportas

ISBN (Paperback): 978-1-7378949-0-2
ISBN (Hardcover): 978-1-7378949-1-9
ISBN (eBook): 978-1-7378949-2-6

Published by Frequency Studios

TABLE OF CONTENTS

CHAPTER 1
Another Harvest Begins

It was morning. The sun had been up for a couple of hours, and it was shaping up to be a beautiful October day. A few lines of scattered clouds drifted across the sky, but it was mostly clear with the direct light canceling out the chill nicely. The autumn foliage was on full display, and the occasional breeze would rustle loose a few more brightly colored leaves. The day before Halloween, StarrLight Farms had jack o'lanterns on bales of hay in a few spots of the front yard. A single-story house with a covered front porch, a barn, a few sheds and a field for potatoes, this little corner in the Town of Columbia was what Harry Starr and his daughter Haley called home.

It was Friday, and Haley usually would have been in school, but due to a strange earthquake the evening before, the district decided not to reopen until Monday, giving inspectors time to thoroughly check the building's structural integrity. While earthquakes are not unheard of in this area, they are very rare and mostly weak. The most recent, however, hit suddenly and hard yet was over as quickly as it started. The most unusual thing was that, despite its intensity, the quake was not felt anywhere beyond the town.

It was the day after Haley's tenth birthday and having fallen behind on a couple of chores she wanted to have done before the weekend, the young farmer seized her opportunity shortly after breakfast. Harvest was over, but the work was not. Even though the bumper crops of potatoes had shipped, the barn was in serious disarray. So, Haley had tied her long, vibrant blond hair back into a couple of pigtails, her usual preferred look, threw on a jacket and got to it.

She had been down quite a bit lately due to the passing of her mother, but the farmgirl was in better spirits today. She was in the moment and listening to Garth Brooks while she worked. Haley knew all his songs. Stacking crates and moving things back where they belong, she worked up a sweat quickly. The young farmer took off her jacket, hung it on a barn wall hook and used her brown bandana to wipe her forehead. She was wearing an orange and yellow striped T-shirt that matched the seasonal foliage and a pair of very well-loved coveralls. Taking a break and drinking some water, Haley's good spirits increased even more when her cat Hayseed came trotting through the barn and hopped up on the shelf next to her.

Haley giggled a little as she petted him, adoring the green color in his eyes. Hayseed was a black shorthair with a tuft of white fur on his chest and a bad habit of lounging where everyone else was trying to walk. Haley scratched the cat's head once more and then, with a warm smile, said, "Sorry, Hay. But I've got a little more to do."

It was just after ten when she was finished. Haley stood there with hands on her hips, inspecting her handiwork. She was quite pleased with the results of her efforts and even seemed to stand a little taller when she realized how quickly she had finished. With even more unplanned extra time, Haley began to wonder how she might like to spend it.

As if on cue, the two-way radio on the shelf where Hayseed sat earlier crackled to life with the sound of her father's voice. "Peeler to Bad Kitty, you still out in the barn?"

Haley slid the microphone off the side of the unit and pressed the key. "I'm here," she replied.

"How much longer do you think before you're done?" her dad asked.

Haley smirked and keyed the mic. "Two minutes ago," she responded proudly.

"Outstanding!" her dad exclaimed. "Why don't you go get the potato gun and meet me out in front of the work shed in a little bit. There's something I think you'd like to see."

"Okay, Dad," she replied, with her good mood apparent in her voice.

There was a ladder going up to the loft, but Haley instead preferred to climb up and down a few wooden crates she had arranged below the entrance. The barn loft was set up like a living room, and that's where the young farmer would often spend bad weather days. There was an old couch that somehow hadn't yet fallen apart, a giant wooden cable spool for a coffee table and a tube TV with a VCR, a game console and a stereo. In the corner was a bookshelf that was packed full, with more books stacked on the top and a few more on the floor. Her enjoyment of books surpassing even her love of sci-fi flicks, Haley had read every one of them. Most of them twice and a few others even more. She loved to absorb the words and let her imagination fill in the gaps. When she saw the images in her mind, she felt like she was helping to create the story.

Haley entered the loft and saw the potato gun on the couch right where she last left it. She walked over and picked it up. The appreciation she had for this device was easily apparent. Her dad designed it specifically for her. A one-of-a-kind, this potato gun attached to a gauntlet that strapped securely to her right arm. On the side of the barrel, her mother's badge number was engraved. When worn, the barrel mounted to the outside of her forearm, and it extended a bit past her knuckles. The triggering mechanism lined up with her hand, allowing Haley to easily rest her palm on top and squeeze.

The young farmer felt the giddiness in her sternum as she recalled assembling it with her father last year on her ninth birthday and the elation when the first potato was successfully launched. And the surprising kickback! She chuckled to herself a bit when she remembered falling over backward from firing that first potato.

Wondering what her dad had in mind, she leaped down from the loft and hurried through the barn. Haley slid the door open, looked left to the wall and smirked before exiting. There was an Indiana Jones poster she had hung there a couple of years ago. Looking at Indy holding the whip and the idea of exploring old ruins sparked her imagination. She had always wanted to go on an adventure.

It was warming up a bit more, and the shed doors were slid open. Inside stood Harry Starr looking down at his completed project on top of the workbench. The radio on the shelf was tuned to a classic rock station, and "Eye of the Tiger," one of Harry's favorite songs, was playing in the background. A smile of satisfaction made its way onto the man's face, and his eyes lit up as he thought about what the look on his daughter's face would be when she finally saw this.

Harry was a transplant from the south. After retiring from the Marine Corps when Haley was only two, he decided to stay in the region. His wife Heather, who had been a detective in Willimantic for a few years at this point, was thrilled with her career, and Harry was just bursting with ideas for the property on which they lived. Ideas that quickly became StarrLight Farms.

, The former marine was six feet tall and fit. In contrast to Haley's vibrant blond hair, his was dark brown, almost black. The color faded to salt and pepper along the sides but was barely noticeable due to his preference for keeping things high and tight. His drawl had muddled a bit but would come back strong whenever he heard the accent from someone else. This always made both Heather and Haley snicker because they understood that Harry never even knew he was doing it.

Haley came jogging in the doorway. "Hi, Dad!"

Harry turned around just in time to brace himself for the diving hug that Haley, when her mood was good, seemed to be so fond of lately. He grunted as he caught his daughter in mid-leap and prepared for the imminent squeeze. Haley wrapped her arms around him, laid her face on his shoulder and hugged him as tight as she could.

With a chuckle, Harry said, "Whoa, somebody's got a little extra energy today," relieved to see her more like her usual self. Yesterday, being Haley's first birthday without her mom, was particularly rough.

Haley, face still buried in his shoulder, went limp and said, "Actually, I think I might take a nap here."

Her words were muffled but understood as Harry laughed and suddenly let go. Haley started to drop but didn't even worry as her dad immediately caught her. Haley lifted her head and looked lazily into her father's eyes. The exact same blue. "You know I'm never gonna fall for that prank again, don't you?" She asked with a playful smile and hopped down.

"That's quite alright, Honey. I've got plenty more tricks up my sleeve," he said cheerfully as he pointed to the workbench.

Haley looked to the table and saw what appeared to be a wood-carved backpack with a sturdy but flexible tubing attached to the right side. She noticed clips on that same side of the pack that was just like the ones on her gauntlet. She sometimes wondered why there were clip brackets on both sides of her gun barrel but now, seeing what was on the workbench. She realized that her dad had planned this from the beginning.

Haley's jaw dropped, yet the corners of her lips turned up to smile once it all clicked together, resulting in a giant open-mouthed grin and that giddy feeling in her sternum once more. Her expression was exactly the face that Harry had hoped for.

Harry picked up the pack and held it so his daughter, still sporting the big grin, could slide her arms through and pull the straps tight. He then attached the loose end of the flexible tube to the back of the potato gun. "Let's try out those clips first," he said to his daughter. "Might be a bit awkward but try to move your arm back and get the gun to attach to the side of the pack."

Haley rolled her arm and shoulder back a bit and, without much effort at all, managed to connect the potato gun to the new accessory. The pack clips engaged while the gauntlet disengaged. "Wow, Dad! You're a genius!"

"Thanks, Darlin', but you can shower me with praise after we make sure it loads the gun properly."

The farmgirl laughed, "If you made it, it probably works."

He dropped a hand on her shoulder, looked into his daughter's eyes and said, "I wanted to give this to you yesterday, but I was still working out a couple kinks. Happy birthday again, Darlin'."

Haley looked up at her dad and smiled while squeezing his hand.

"Why don't we launch some potatoes?" Harry asked.

"Wicked awesome!" Haley exclaimed. She was having so much fun, she could burst! She couldn't imagine how her dad did it, but the trigger was working with the pack. She'd squeeze it once to load a potato and again to launch. The pack was a bit heavy, but the young farmer was used to work and stronger than her four-foot ten-inch frame would suggest. She noticed that the air cartridge had run down quicker than usual, so she pulled a fresh one from her gauntlet and changed it out. Before taking her next shot, she turned to see if her dad was watching and found something else entirely. Harry was there, but a strange glow was appearing around him as she felt an odd sensation in the air.

Harry began looking around, confused as he was also noticing the light. The light brightened in a flash, causing Haley to squint, then it was gone just as quickly. Harry was standing there, looking straight ahead.

"Dad! Are you alright?" she asked. "What happened?"

The man looked down at Haley. With an unusually cold expression, he cocked his head as if he was surprised to see her there. "Go. Play."

"But Dad, you just…"

He cut her off, "Go. Play." And with that, he walked to his pickup truck, started the engine and drove away.

Haley, utterly stunned and confused, made her way back to the barn. Her breathing became faster and sharper as an unsettling knot grew inside her stomach. "What just happened to Dad?" she wondered aloud through partially labored breath.

Her mind reeled as she tried to understand what had just occurred. This, now coupling with thoughts of her mother, swirled together faster and faster, leaving her momentarily lightheaded. She reached up and grabbed the handle of the barn door, intending to close it but hung on to it for stability instead. Finally steadying her breath, she looked up and began to slide the barn door shut as a car was pulling up the drive.

In no mood for any further surprises, she went and stood below the poster on the adjacent wall as she looked out the northern window. Four men stepped out of the vehicle. Three of them were identical to the one of the town plow drivers, and the fourth looked like Hank, who worked at the store. A sudden thump startled Haley from her focus, but to her credit, she did not make a sound. She slowly turned her head in the direction of the sound to see her cat. "Hayseed," she sighed in relief. Relief that was far too short-lived.

"You're in danger and must escape. Now!" said a woman's voice from Hayseed's mouth.

Haley's eyes went wide, and her pale skin seemed to become even paler still as she felt the blood drain from her face. She was visibly shaking as she chattered out the words, "My cat is talking to me!"

"I'm not your cat," the voice from Hayseed's mouth claimed. "And there's no time to explain. It's time to run!"

Haley looked back out the window to see the group of men walking with an air of determination and purpose. Straight for the barn.

She was petrified. The hairs on the back of her neck stood up as she felt strange vibes and hostile intent radiating off the approaching group.

"Run!" the voice from Hayseed shouted, snapping Haley from her stupor. Her mind kicked into gear as one of the men grasped the barn door handle. Haley pivoted and ran for the back door, hearing the front door slide open as she went. Hayseed leaped at the first attacker. The unexpected impact to the side of the knee caused the man to stumble, tripping up the second man behind him. The third man, without missing a beat, hopped over the first two and sprinted straight for Haley. The fourth man pulled one of the first two up as he came by.

As she neared the back door, she could hear the feet of the third man coming up behind her. In desperation, Haley spun around, leveled her arm and let a potato fly! The potato whizzed by the man's face, thudded against an eight-by-eight support column and landed on the floor. The man stopped and looked to see what almost hit him. Upon seeing the potato, he slightly smirked, betraying his otherwise stoic demeanor.

"This spud's for you!" the man heard Haley shout, causing him to look up in time to see another potato just before impacting the bridge of his nose.

"Arrrgh!" he blurted out as he staggered backward while grabbing his face. His nose was broken, and a yellow viscous fluid dribbled out from both nostrils. Despite this, he instantly regained his composure as the other three men came up alongside him to see an open back door.

Haley was gone!

CHAPTER 2
Happy Trails

"Hey, Mom! Can I call Haley?" Elizabeth asked her mother.

Elizabeth Guerreiro and Haley met four years ago at a horseback riding lesson and became the most unexpected of friends. Haley was typically well behaved, while Elizabeth had quite the rebellious streak. Elizabeth, taller than Haley, had tried to intimidate her. Haley didn't know what to do, so she just stood there.

And she wouldn't back down.

Awkwardly, Haley tried and did a horrible job at suppressing her nervous smile. The facial expression looked funny to Elizabeth, which caused her to try and stifle a laugh. The two both stood there holding their lips tight with their cheeks steadily puffing up in an attempt to hold it back and maintain control. Together, they burst into uncontrollable giggles, and the girls had been inseparable since.

Elizabeth, who turned ten three months earlier, was just over five feet tall. Her brunette hair, which was tied back in a ponytail and hung down between her shoulder blades, would get blondish streaks every summer from her time in the sun. Thanks to Portuguese ancestry, her skin had a subtle hint of bronzing color to it that could quickly and easily turn into a beautiful tan whenever she spent time outdoors. This was sometimes a point of jealousy for the pale-skinned and easily-burned Haley. The farmer's friend had a slightly thicker build and was physically stronger due to her size combined with tomboyish, rough and tumble ways.

She was often restless and had a tendency to wander. Having an odd sense that something was missing, Elizabeth always felt like she was searching for something but had no idea what, leaving her unfocused.

Maggie looked and saw that the breakfast dishes were done, and the kitchen counter was clean. Elizabeth had actually completed her chores. She then looked to the clock, which read 10:34.

Maggie smiled and said, "Sure, Honey." She knew that her daughter was excited to talk with Haley about the previous night.

Elizabeth and Haley would both sense things that they couldn't quite explain. The feeling of a presence, or a sudden something in the air that just felt different. The two girls referred to these sensations as the 'spookies' and would both notice these vibes, but Elizabeth seemed more sensitive to them. They also both seemed able to sense the emotions of others, but Haley, in this case, was far more in tune. Elizabeth had wanted to talk to her parents about those sensations but was always apprehensive.

Elizabeth's mother, Maggie, was thought of by most to be a bit of a hippie. She worked as a yoga instructor in Mansfield and was all about those positive vibes. She was known for her interests in the metaphysical and was also a devout Christian, which many in town thought of as an odd combination. Everybody loved her due to her genuinely warm, social nature, and even though she often seemed to have her head in the clouds, Maggie was also able to pull her mind into a laser focus when necessary.

She practiced mysticism but never discussed it with Elizabeth. She was worried that if she pushed the subject with her daughter, then Elizabeth would have no interest, just like what happened with the yoga lessons. But if Elizabeth came to her asking, then she would be ready to listen. Maggie had constantly wondered if she was making the right choice but was thrilled last night when her daughter finally came to her wanting to discuss the spookies.

Elizabeth picked up the phone and held it to her ear. "Mom, there's no dial tone," she said.

Maggie looked out the window and said, "Hold on a second, Honey. Harry's here."

The bright light faded, and Harry's eyes adjusted. Disoriented by the strange experience, He looked around at the very large and dimly lit, rectangular room in which he stood. Two of the walls that appeared to be made of concrete reflected the pale fluorescent lighting, giving everything a bleak and washed-out look. One of the end walls appeared to be made of metal and across it, about eight and a half feet up, were three square openings. The openings looked like the bottom ends of large utility chutes. The fourth wall was made of prison bars. He was in a ballroom-sized jail cell, but where, he had no idea. And he wasn't alone.

"Harry, is that you?" Harry turned around to see Trooper Ed Weathers.

Trooper Weathers was down to earth and genuinely cared about people. The townsfolk considered themselves lucky to have him as he was a very personable man who was firm but always kind and fair.

Standing beside him was Mary Saddler, Columbia's First Selectman. With them also was Frank, a Windham County Public Works employee, Hank Cranston, owner of the town's general store, two men from the fire department and Ellen, a school bus driver.

"What's going on?" Harry asked.

"No idea," Ed replied, "We've been here a while. You're the first new face we've seen since last night."

"We all came here the same way a few moments after the quake," Hank added.

Suddenly, there was another flash of light, and there stood a confused-looking Joey, the man who ran the coffee shop.

Then more flashes occurred. Sophie, the town clerk, Dr. Scott Patel, the pediatrician, school bus drivers, a security guard, and everyone else from the fire department. On and on, it went for the next minute until there were about thirty of the most prominent and trusted faces from town, all standing in this large cell.

Maggie watched Harry get out of his truck while a couple of busses pulled up and parked outside. Trooper Ed Weathers also pulled up to the area and stopped his cruiser. A fire truck with flashing lights but no sirens came onto the street next as Trooper Weathers addressed the neighborhood over his PA system.

"Everybody, I have some troubling news, but stay calm as I deliver it because we have prepared a plan to ensure everyone's safety."

The hairs on the back of Maggie's neck stood up. Everyone who was home was now either standing outside their house or by an open window giving the Resident State Trooper their full attention.

"I'm afraid that the quake last night was deliberate. I've been in touch with the National Guard, and they said that we might soon be under a full attack," the Trooper told the people as a few gasps could be heard from some of the houses.

Maggie immediately began to worry about her husband Ryan, who was out to sea. But it wasn't the words that made her neck hairs stand. Something felt very wrong about this entire scene.

Trooper Weathers continued, "We have a shelter beneath Town Hall. It's big enough for everyone and very well stocked. To keep the roads free for emergency personnel, we need you to get on the bus, and we'll take you to the shelter, but we need to move quickly!"

"Mom!" Elizabeth said in a hushed voice.

Maggie turned and saw just how terrified her daughter looked. She guessed that Elizabeth's fear was also not about what they were hearing. This was confirmed when the ten-year-old said, "Spookies!"

Maggie then looked back out the window to see everyone hurrying out to the buses. She then turned and immediately took Elizabeth's hand and said, "C'mon. We need to get away from them."

They moved through the kitchen toward the back door, and Elizabeth grabbed her gray hoodie off the chair as they went by. Maggie grabbed her windbreaker off of the coat hooks by the back door as Elizabeth zipped up her hoodie. Maggie reached to open the back door but then came to an abrupt stop just short of the handle. They both felt it.

Maggie stepped to the side and slowly leaned over, trying to inconspicuously look out the back window. As she did, the back door was kicked in.

Their neighbors were already rolling down the road in the school buses, so no one heard them scream.

Two men, both of whom looked exactly like Frank, charged in the back door. One went for Maggie and the other, Elizabeth.

Maggie put her hands up and forward, trying to keep her attacker at arm's length, but the man just grabbed her wrist tight and restrained her.

Elizabeth, looking to the man's right, charged straight at him. Last second, she turned her body sideways and lunged to his left, between him and the back wall. He almost pinned her, but the fake-out threw him off just enough, allowing her to squeak by.

"Run!" Maggie yelled as her daughter booked straight out the back door and into the woods.

The Frank look-a-like ran out the back door after Elizabeth, while a man who looked just like Harry Starr came in the front door to help the other man restrain Maggie. He came in behind her as she struggled with the other man and locked his arm around her neck until she passed out. Then they brought her out to Harry's truck.

Her mind was reeling as she sprinted down the path through the woods. Haley had witnessed a string of impossibilities in a span of fewer than five minutes. She had no idea what to make of it. So, she kept running. Running down a path she knew so well. A path forged over the last three years by her very own feet.

She always enjoyed playing in the woods and had often used them to make her way to the park in town. As time went on and she wore the trail into the ground, this path became somewhat of a sanctuary to her. She would unwind with an enjoyable walk during pleasant weather or use it to pace away those occasional pesky butterflies in her stomach. And sometimes, her mother would come on walks with her.

"Mom!" Haley said as she trotted to a stop. Her eyes welled up, and tears streamed down her cheeks as she dropped to her knees. She tipped forward and put her palms to the ground for support. "Mom," she again choked out softly through the tears. Haley wanted nothing more at that moment than to be able to hug her mother again.

Back in January, Detective Heather Starr was working on a kidnapping case. After locating where the child was being held, the police moved in to rescue the four-year-old and apprehend the suspect.

During the operation, the young boy saw his chance to get away and took it. He crawled out of a window into the backyard and tried to run. With a thin layer of snow on the ground, he had no idea that he had left solid land and ran out onto the thinning ice of a small pond. Heather was coming up behind the boy when he fell through the ice, but she didn't even hesitate and went in after him.

The frigid water stung as the heat was rapidly being pulled from their bodies. Heather knew she had no time as the numbness was immediately set in, and she was losing control of her arms and legs fast! She took hold of the boy and, with every ounce of willpower she could muster, pushed him back up onto the thicker ice for her approaching partner to reach the young one and pull him to safety.

But the courageous detective was now in serious trouble. Even though she was tall enough to reach the bottom, she couldn't feel it. Heather's limbs would no longer respond to her mental commands as she started slipping below the surface. Then suddenly, her partner's hand had a firm grasp on her collar, and he pulled her out as an ambulance team arrived to help, but despite their best efforts, many hearts were broken that night when the hypothermia claimed her life.

Haley's thoughts settled slightly as her mind went through a few memories of her and her mom here on her favorite wooded path. The detective quite often used the woods to teach Haley about situational awareness and connecting dots. "Always take note of what's around you," her mom would say. Heather would often lead her daughter to an unfamiliar area and then suddenly place a hand over her eyes and say, "Describe the area around us."

"Always take note of what's around you."

The memory of those lessons snapped Haley back to the present. She pushed herself back upright and climbed to her feet. Strong as the young farmer was, she was really feeling the weight of the rig on her back. Using her brown bandana, Haley wiped the tears from her face and then reached down to dust off her coveralls.

The cool breeze blew against her skin, and she knew her T-shirt wouldn't be nearly enough when the temperature dropped in just a few short hours. Haley took a good look around to make sure she wasn't still being followed and removed the rig from her back to take a rest. After a couple minutes, tired though she was, Haley put the rig back on, tightened the straps and started for town.

Nearing the halfway point, she saw a cat just up ahead, sitting in the center of the trail, illuminated by a sunbeam.

Haley stopped.

Normally, she would have been thrilled to see such a beautiful cat, but due to the earlier events, Haley was taking nothing for granted. The cat was gray in color with slightly darker lines of gray creating just a hint of stripes. The fur was about medium length and got lighter, almost cream color, around the snout from where the whiskers extended. The eyes were a gorgeous and mellow yellow with specs of vibrant green.

Haley made eye contact with the cat. Considering what happened with Hayseed, she was not sure what to make of the feline before her now. Keeping eye contact, Haley could sense nervousness coming from the cat as well as what felt like…concern?

The mysterious cat stood up, and the sunbeam faded as another line of clouds made its way across the sky. With the sunlight gone, Haley suddenly noticed that she could see right through the cat. *I should be scared*, she thought, *but I'm not.*

Even though she detected no malice from the translucent feline, the young farmer was far from at ease. She looked to the ground, sighed and looked back up. "Are you gonna talk to me, too?" she asked with a hint of both curiosity and irritation in her voice.

"Yes," said the cat in the same voice that came out of Hayseed. The gray cat sauntered down the center of the trail toward Haley, and as it came closer, it began to glow. The more that it illuminated, the less definition Haley could see until the cat looked like it was made of nothing more than a swirl of gold and purple light. The glowing silhouette then began to elongate and change shape, taking on a humanoid appearance. At this point, the glow died back, and the definition returned. The cat was now a beautiful woman standing before Haley.

The woman, although just a couple inches shorter than Haley's dad, looked quite tall from Haley's perspective.

She appeared to be Egyptian in heritage with long black hair, high well-defined cheekbones, beautifully bronzed skin and those same tell tail eyes as were seen on the cat. Soft yellow pupils with specs of green. Haley thought that looking into them was like gazing into a gemstone.

"I'm sorry," the woman said, "I know this is all very disturbing, but we don't have much time."

Haley stood in awe at the sight of the ghostly figure. She couldn't believe this was real. Or that anything she had seen in the last fifteen minutes was real. She was drained, exhausted, and now, she was getting fed up! She closed her eyes and shook her head as her adrenals kicked back in, and that flame just below the ribcage began to burn hotter once more. Haley opened her eyes.

"Who are you, and why do you look like a ghost?" she demanded with her usual spunk starting to return.

"I'm trapped," the woman began, "and cannot fully manifest into this plane. I am the goddess, Bast."

"Goddess?" Haley scoffed. "Am I supposed to bow or something?"

"No," Bast replied firmly. "I am not The Creator. Do not worship me."

"Well then, what do you want? Who were those weirdos chasing me, and most of all, what's wrong with my dad?"

"That was not your father but an imposter. I cannot maintain this projection for long, so we must be quick. Our sphere is being invaded by people from beyond our own universe. Reptilian beings with unspeakable appetites and intentions. They came with advanced knowledge of both mysticism and technology. They used this to bind all the Earth gods who would have posed a threat and are now replacing people with strange copies, empty shells that they project their consciousness into and control from another plane of existence. I do not know what they are planning to do next, but they must be stopped before they gain too much foothold."

Haley threw her arms out wide with her palms up as she leaned forward slightly. "You gotta be kidding me!" she exclaimed. "This has got to be a Halloween prank or a bad dream!"

"I'm sorry, but no. This is very real," Bast went on. "Many of your fellow townsfolk have already been taken. You are going to have to stop the invaders."

"Me!?" Haley responded, unable to believe her ears. "What am I supposed to do? Scare them with more potatoes? I hardly got away from them to start with."

Bast said, "Your vibrations resonate well with that of felines. I will lend you my energy, awakening abilities within you."

"You'll lend what?" Haley started to ask, but Bast's eyes suddenly began to glow with a soft golden light.

The farmgirl felt her fatigue beginning to fade. The hairs on the back of her neck stood outward as a tingle made its way up her spine, but in place of a chill that would normally be expected with such a sensation, warmth was instead present. She began to feel the world around her. Like an extension of herself, feeling it beyond her own skin, similar to how she would sense the emotions of others or strange energies around her, but much stronger and much more intense.

Then it all pulled inward.

She suddenly felt like her body was made up of millions of tiny electric bubbles. After a few seconds, the fizzy sensations died down, and the young farmer felt more like her solid self. She took a couple of deep breaths and began to feel comfortably lighter on her feet.

"What was that?" she asked.

"You are now in tune with your energy field," Bast explained. "You can use it for accessing abilities that few others are yet able. Try it. Feel your vibrations. The essence of who you are."

Haley, going with it, closed her eyes and focused. She began to feel a tingle in the center of her being, and it became much like the fizzy sensation from before.

"Yes!" Bast exclaimed. "Now increase it. Raise it and direct it."

The young farmer felt those fizzy sensations expand. It seemed to become magnetic. She immediately found that she could spread this sensation throughout her body by her very whims. Haley willed it up her torso and into her right arm. As if on instinct, she mounted the potato gun to her gauntlet, raised her right arm and funneled the energy into the gun. A blue glow began to emit from inside the barrel.

Fixated on the sight and her mouth partially open, Bast looked mesmerized. The goddess was thoroughly impressed, stunned even, by how quickly Haley was able to grasp the concept. "Now release it," she said breathlessly.

Haley, who truly was mesmerized by the experience, did just that.

They both watched as a blue plasmatic-looking orb with streaks of purple, shaped much like a kitten, rocketed ahead from the barrel of her potato gun. In a fraction of a second, the blast hit a tree about twenty feet away, giving the maple a shudder as a small but potent concussive burst was released from where the strange small ethereal kitten contacted the tree.

Some leaves fell loose, Bast smiled in satisfaction, and Haley's jaw dropped in astonishment as they watched a few small bits of bark fall from the point of impact. Haley looked up to see an unhappy squirrel dangling from the end of a tree branch. The squirrel pulled itself up, chattered angrily and turned to scurry off.

"Sorry," Haley called out sheepishly to the squirrel as Bast began to laugh.

With a warm smile, the goddess said, "I suppose it's best to be mindful of who and what's around you before doing that again," as a hint of her Egyptian accent slipped out.

Haley looked down as she let out a small chuckle. The farmgirl then looked up at Bast and matched the goddess' warm expression with a smile of her own. After a couple of seconds, Haley's face went from peaceful to worried as she noticed that Bast was beginning to fade from view.

"We're out of time!" The Egyptian goddess began to speak faster. "There is a wizard somewhere in your town. Find him! I believe him to be an ally. Look to my cats for help, learn from their experience and may The Creator watch over you."

The voice trailed away, and the apparition of Bast was gone.

Haley just stood there a moment. All of a sudden, she once again felt utterly alone. Her eyes began to mist up a bit as they dropped down to the custom-made potato gun strapped to her forearm, looking at her mother's badge number. The young farmer closed her eyes tight for a moment and then opened them, looking down the trail before her with new determination.

"I'll find you, Dad," she vowed and then continued south toward the park.

CHAPTER 3
Reinforcements

Elizabeth was moving as fast as she could, running between the trees and bushes. Hopping and maneuvering around the rocky, hilly landscape, she could still hear the man chasing her and was looking around frantically for anywhere to hide. She thought that she felt an odd wave of energy from the north as she continued to search for cover.

Many leaves were on the ground, and the bushes did not obscure nearly as much view as they had just a month earlier. As she crested the slope and began to go down the other side, she came by an old, dead tree that had been lying on the ground for the last couple of years. With the top of the slope blocking her attacker's line of sight, she dove behind the rotting tree and hoped he wouldn't see her.

The man came to the top of the hill and stopped, looking around to see which way the girl might have gone.

Elizabeth tried not to make a sound. She could hear him up there, just fifteen feet away. She could feel his unnatural presence. Elizabeth figured that the jig was up as this old tree was one of the very few decent hiding options.

Why wouldn't he look here? she thought. Elizabeth was feeling lightheaded, almost like she could pass out. She looked down and saw a rock, quietly picked it up and waited.

After a couple more seconds, Elizabeth glanced down the wooded slope to see a white cat that everybody called Snow.

Snow was often seen lounging on the front porch of Goldman's Woodworking Studio, which was on the town's main road just a couple of minutes to the west. This stray would regularly come to her neighborhood's backyards in the evening, and he was very well fed.

Elizabeth suddenly got a sense of peace from the cat as he turned his head up to her and then back down toward the bush in front of him. She then started to feel the energy around her more clearly while the cat started rubbing his sides against the bush, causing it to rustle.

The man immediately caught the movement but couldn't see the cat from his angle. He headed toward the bush as the cat went further down the hill and toward the south. Just as the man got to the bush, the cat rustled another. This continued until the man was headed south and gone from sight.

Elizabeth couldn't believe her luck. Still extremely shaken, she looked up at the sky and mouthed the words, "Thank you," and then continued down the slope toward the west.

After the initial shock, the new arrivals to the large cell calmed right down and looked at Mary and Ed.

"Last night, seven of us arrived here the same way as the rest of you," Mary told the group, "That's all we know at this time.

Ed turned to Harry, "You're an engineer. Do you have any idea how we were all…" He struggled to state the obvious, but it just seemed so absurd. "…Teleported?" he finished.

Harry shook his head and said, "No."

There were a couple of thumps heard from the chutes up near the ceiling in the meta wall. The group looked over in time to see one of their fellow townsmen slide out of the left chute, land and stumble to the floor, shouting, "Ow!"

Two of the firefighters and a medic immediately ran over to tend to him when they again heard thumping sounds from the left and center chutes. "More are coming!" one of them shouted, and the rest of the firefighters and medics ran over to help and, in many cases, actually caught the people sliding out of the chutes and got them out of the way managing to prevent any serious injuries.

Only about twelve people came down the right chute, mostly women and crying hysterically. A few moments and some sore backs later, there were a little over one hundred people in the cell.

Maggie began to open her eyes. She was groggy but getting her bearings. She was being carried by a couple of EMTs, and it looked like they were in the Town Hall.

In the floor was a new hole. A big opening that sloped down to a tunnel below the building. As they carried her down the slope, she could see a few people up ahead. Along the northern wall, there were two big openings that looked like utility chutes and to the left of those was a set of double doors.

Maggie saw firefighters helping people into the chute. She also saw Dr. Patel standing by a different door in the adjacent wall, directing some children through. Maggie heard one of the mothers say, "I need to stay with my son."

"Understood," said the EMT and walked with her to Dr. Patel.

Dr. Patel smiled warmly and took the hand of the apprehensive toddler. The EMT tapped the mother on the shoulder.

When she turned to look, the man had a grave expression on his face as he said, "There's something you need to see," and he turned and walked through the double doors next to the two chutes. He motioned for her to follow as he went. She stepped in, and the doors shut.

Firefighters helped the last couple of people into the chutes, and Maggie was carried over behind them. The next thing she knew, she was sliding.

They heard the thumps of Maggie, and the real firefighters were there to catch her. Then suddenly, thick metal panels covered and sealed the chute openings as the medics and Dr. Patel tended to some bumps and scrapes.

Despite the sheer terror many of them were feeling, they all settled after just a few minutes while Trooper Weathers tried to gather everyone's attention. As they all quieted, the Trooper was about to speak when they all heard his voice from outside the bars.

"That should about do it," a man said as he approached the cell.

Everybody turned and looked to see a man who looked exactly like Ed Weathers, but while the real Ed was six feet and two inches tall, this man was about six feet even.

Then a Mary look-a-like, along with a few other copies of people known in town, joined him. The townsfolk were all getting a nasty, sinking feeling, and it seemed to be invigorating the fake Ed, who began to speak. "I would stick around to talk, but I have to go tell a news crew why all the town's roads are barricaded," he said with a smug smirk. "Something about a gas line. The press eats that stuff up."

"Where are the kids!?" one of the women demanded.

The false trooper got an evil-looking smile as he said, "You'll find out, but first we must wait."

"Wait for what?" the real Ed asked.

"For the rest of my people to arrive," said the imposter while gesturing with his arms out wide in a cheerful, almost eccentric manner. "More of us are coming and once everybody has arrived…" a wicked smile slowly spread across his face as he spoke the next words, "…you're all coming to dinner."

High in the atmosphere above where most other aircraft travel, a spark appeared. Little blue-white arcs spread out from this spot, forming what looked like a horizontally spinning ball of electricity. It then opened at the vortex, growing wider as the sky around the portal looked as if it were flowing into the airborne hole like water. A small ship sped out of the hole and into the atmosphere of Earth. The vortex collapsed in on itself immediately after.

The ship seemed akin to a large, triangular jet and probably would not look too out of place sitting amongst some of the newer aircraft of Earth. Not that anyone would have noticed because as soon as this ship was in the planet's sky, it flickered from view. With cloaking engaged, it was undetectable to any instruments that the people on the surface would be using. After just a moment, the craft was over New England and descending toward a town called Columbia.

The jet-shaped ship slowed down to a hover over a level clearing atop a wooded hill near a picnic area, just large enough for the ship to set down. An impressive find, considering that almost nothing about Columbia's landscape was flat. As soon as it landed, the soft low hum of the engines faded to silence. After a few minutes, a doorway opened. It looked as if a drawbridge was opening out of thin air. The ramp continued to lower until it touched the ground, and two men descended from inside the ship to the small grassy field below.

They stopped once they set foot on the soil to see the world before them. Both men had a human appearance, were about six feet tall and physically fit. One had a full dirty blond beard but was bald on top. He had a blue buttoned flannel tucked into his black jeans and a pair of cowboy boots.

The other had long dark-brown hair tied back and a goatee. He wore a gray T-shirt tucked into blue jeans and a black vest overtop an unbuttoned green flannel.

They stared ahead, looking in the direction of the town. The long-haired man had a determined expression on his face, while the bald one had the look of a predator on the trail. They were hunting. And they started for town.

As they walked, the ship's ramp closed, making it once again completely invisible. Inside were two more men. One with a buzz cut staring intently at a display panel and the other with a greenish tint to his skin, operating some controls. Silently walking through the area and unnoticed by both men was an orange and white cat. The cat hopped onto a nearby surface without making a sound, licked his paw, settled in and watched the man with the green skin.

Haley, continuing down the trail, was absolutely amazed by how much easier it was to move. The rig on her back, although she could still feel the weight, was almost as manageable as an empty school backpack. And the ease with which she walked! She was always light and nimble on her feet, but now Haley felt like she was almost floating.

She neared a maple. Haley had been trying to jump up and reach a branch on this tree for the last couple of months but so far has only been able to brush the bottom of it with her fingertips a couple of times. She stood underneath the tree and looked up.

A playful smile made its way onto her face as she said, "I'll bet I can do it now." She squatted down and then jumped as hard as she could. The effort was more than needed as she easily grabbed the branch. Haley had a big open mouth smile, and her eyes were wide with wonder as she hung from the tree's limb.

Even with the rig on her back, she had a freedom of movement that she had not known before. Haley pulled herself up onto the branch as easily as climbing a ladder and had no trouble standing to her feet.

She was amazed yet again as she found balancing and walking along the branch to be just as easy. The farmer let out a long whispered, "Whoa," as she was beginning to feel like she could go anywhere. She walked up and out along the branch a bit to where it started bending under her weight.

"Hmm," Haley was about fifteen feet up. She thought about jumping straight down but then decided instead to squat, grab the branch and dangle first. The farmgirl hung there for a moment, still apprehensive about the height. Finally, she went hand over hand down the branch a bit more to about eight feet and let go, landing lightly into a crouch on the ground and standing up straight with a huge smile.

A smile that dropped when she realized that she had no idea what to do next.

She was almost to the park. And then what? Haley wanted to find her dad but didn't know where to begin. Bast said to find a wizard in the town. A *wizard!* Even after all that she had witnessed, Haley thought the idea sounded ridiculous and also presented with the same problem. She didn't know where to begin.

Haley slowed as she neared the exit from the woods by the park. Despite how nimble and light on her feet she was, walking quietly wasn't much of an option with all these leaves on the ground. Trying, and failing, not to make any extra noise, she came to the wood's edge. Haley looked out from behind a tree to the playground about three hundred feet away.

It was a basic playscape with swings, a slide, a carousel and a couple of sandboxes.

Everything was quiet. On a nice autumn day like this, the park would usually have at least a couple of families taking advantage before the snow flies. Especially if school was closed, but there was nothing except for the gentle sound of an inconsistent breeze.

Taking another look around before exiting the woods, Haley began to get an overwhelming sense of fear and anxiety. She stopped, wondering why she was suddenly so shaken. After a moment, she realized that it wasn't her. She was no stranger to sensing the emotions of others, and this is what she was doing here, but it was strong, and she was beginning to feel from where it was coming.

The feeling grew as she turned toward the carousel. Haley became nervous as she wondered who or what could be under there. She surveyed the area and then stepped into the park, heading toward the fear. Once within thirty feet, she took another look around to make sure there was no one else, knelt to look underneath the carousel and saw a silhouette of someone huddled under the center. Haley waved. The shadow underneath waved back, and she felt the anxiety dissipate slightly.

Haley looked around again, stood up and made her way to the carousel. As she arrived, the shadow from underneath moved outward to just under the edge. Haley felt a wave of shock and relief as she saw Elizabeth with mist in her eyes and a rock in her hand.

CHAPTER 4
Park It

Elizabeth stood up, dropped the rock and threw her arms around Haley. Sobbing, she said, "These people almost took me. They got Mom!"

Haley nearly teared up again herself. "They almost got me too," Haley said as they both squeezed tighter, granting them a slight but much-needed morale boost.

They released their hug, and Elizabeth asked, "How did you know to look under there?"

"I felt how scared you were," the farmgirl replied.

Elizabeth's eyes widened with excitement as she forgot the current circumstance, "I finally asked my mom about that," she enthusiastically began, "and she called you an empath!"

"What's that?" Haley asked.

"Somebody that feels what other people feel."

"Did you ask your mom about the spookies yet?" Haley inquired.

Elizabeth sharply inhaled while her eyes lit up. Haley felt the excitement and could tell that her friend had been bursting to have this conversation. "Yeah! She said that I…"

Her words were cut short when they both felt the hairs on the back of their necks stand right up.

"Spookies," Elizabeth whispered in fright.

They had both gotten lost in the conversation and forgot to pay attention to their surroundings. Elizabeth, visibly shaken, reached down and picked up the rock she dropped a moment ago. Haley mounted her potato gun to the gauntlet.

The farmer's fear resurged, but knowing she now had a means to fight back helped her hold it together. Elizabeth was obviously terrified, yet there she was, ready to defend. The young rebel had always been a bit of a brute when compared to the other girls. In fact, she would usually be the one to stand up and protect Haley during the occasional schoolyard 'disagreement.' But Haley's best friend was more shaken here than she had ever seen and still seemed ready and willing to jump between her and any opponent with nothing but that rock.

The girls heard the rustling of footsteps on leaves coming from a different area of the woods, looked over and saw two plow driver look-alikes. The imposters stepped out of the woods and locked eyes with the two young ladies. Elizabeth tapped Haley on the shoulder and pointed in the other direction. Haley turned her head to see three more people coming their way from the road.

She turned back toward the two from the woods, who were closer. Elizabeth gripped her rock tighter and hunched down a bit. Haley felt the electricity build within her again, and as soon as she did, Elizabeth's head snapped toward the young farmer.

"Spookies?" Elizabeth asked Haley, looking very confused. What she felt coming from her friend here seemed the same as that strange wave of energy she felt back in the woods.

Haley looked down, sighed, looked back up to Elizabeth with a sheepish shrug and then seemed to gaze off into the distance as she let out a long, slow, "Yeah."

Her expression suddenly shifted back to one of determination as her gaze darted to the men by the trees. She raised her right arm, and the blue glow began to emit from the barrel.

"Whoa!" Elizabeth breathlessly whispered.

The farmer's friend was not the only one caught off guard by the sight. The two coming from the woods immediately stopped. They both had shocked expressions and, in unison, said, "How so soon?"

Haley didn't know what they were talking about, but she recognized all too well the sinking feeling of an unpleasant surprise. She felt it strongly radiate from four of the five shells approaching the girls.

The two men from the woods burst into a charge toward the girls, and Haley let loose with a blast. Her aim was true, and the ethereal kitten struck the man on the left in the center of his chest. The resulting concussive burst knocked both men to the ground. The skin of the one who endured the direct hit seemed to be changing color.

Haley spun around and launched a blast toward the three men from the road. The blast hit the ground in front of their feet, knocking the lot of them over. Elizabeth just stood there wide-eyed, with her jaw dangling as Haley pivoted back toward the woods and shot another round. The man on the right, who was now back on his feet, took a kitten to the face, and the burst made his head snap weirdly as his skin became yellow and the body gelatinized. The skin of the man on the left had turned yellow, and he was struggling to get up on his knees.

"Ewwww," both girls said in disgust.

Haley spun back toward the road and found it was her turn to deal with an unpleasant surprise. The three men had closed the gap.

Two men grabbed Haley as the other reached for Elizabeth. The scrappy girl dove between the man's legs, rolled over, and kicked the back of his knee. She then rolled out of the way and onto her feet as the man fell over backward. Elizabeth bolted.

Haley had enhanced strength and could put up a good struggle, but the ten-year-old still wasn't about to outmuscle two grown men. She was held off the ground, face up. One of the men had her by the shoulders and was trying to pin her arm, while the other had her feet and was trying to stay away from the end of that arm cannon. Haley saw Elizabeth breaking away from her assailant as he got back up to give chase, and she took the opportunity to fire a blast at him. All that time launching potatoes paid off as she landed a perfect headshot, causing the man to instantly gel out.

"Run, Beth!" Haley shouted to her friend.

"No matter," said the man at her feet, a nasty grin on his face. We'll get her very soon." Haley felt the stomach-turning vibes of intentions most foul as she tried to fight back, but the man by her shoulders had managed to pin her arm right after that last shot. Then she felt a familiar rage from the direction of the man at her feet as Elizabeth dove into the back of his knees.

The man fell down, bouncing his head hard off the edge of the carousel and landing partially on top of Elizabeth, but the commotion caused the other man to lose his grip altogether. Haley landed on her butt in a sitting position, looked straight up and saw the man leaning over her from behind. He reached down as Haley reached up. She was quicker.

Although her leg was pinned under the man, Elizabeth could reach the man's face and was still holding that rock. She went to work.

Haley's blast flung the suddenly gelatinizing man backward. She then shifted her aim to the man by Elizabeth to find her friend repeatedly slamming a rock into a quickly dissolving puddle. She was practically growling while tears streamed down her face.

Haley approached her friend, who seemed to quickly be running out of steam. "Beth…?" she gently asked.

Elizabeth stopped slamming the rock on the pile of clothes that were left. She grabbed the shirt off the ground, stood up and let out a frustrated grunt as she threw it away. She then turned and grabbed Haley in another hug as she sobbed. Haley squeezed her friend back. Elizabeth then stood up straight, wiped her eyes, furrowed her brow and said, "We gotta go."

Haley, as usual, was amazed by her friend. Even with the new superpowers, it was still 'Beth to the rescue.' They heard a rustling and turned to see the last man still struggling to crawl toward them. Haley thought it surreal. Like that Army of Darkness movie that her father finally allowed her to watch. She snapped to her senses, raised her arm and launched a potato into the man's destabilizing face, turning him to gel.

Both girls curled their lips back in disgust once more at the odd sight and then turned to leave.

'Ed' walked down the dimly lit corridor accompanied by 'Hank and Mary' and two other people.

"Your new shell should be ready for use soon," 'Mary' was informing 'Ed' as they neared an elevator.

"Excellent!" 'Ed' exclaimed. "It'll be nice to walk around here in something a little more comfortable."

"Yes," agreed 'Hank and Mary' in unison. The other two men remained silent as they all entered the doorless elevator, and it began to descend.

The car stopped at their intended level. They stepped out to the corridor and turned to the left. 'Mary' pulled out a small bag, reached in and pulled out a piece of bacon. "The generators are functioning at full capacity…" she began and then put the bacon in her mouth while 'Hank' finished, "…and the cells should be fully charged well before our window opens."

'Ed' nodded with a smirk. He then turned his head to one of the other men behind him, "How are you enjoying your new freedom of movement, Kone?"

"Very much, as a matter of fact," the man replied. "Being able to walk this plane remotely will certainly accelerate our plans."

"Starr is surrounded as we speak, and Gentry is with her," 'Hank' said gleefully.

'Ed' began chuckling. "Two less potential problems to deal with. Make sure you take them alive," he said. "I think we all would like to enjoy some retribution for what they could have done."

'Mary and Hank' both let out an identical, sinister laugh.

Kone looked to 'Ed' and remarked, "These young ladies must have been quite the thorn in your side, Ahnk-Hume."

"Among a few others," 'Ed' said. "There are five men we must find and eliminate after the transfer. And then, the rest of those thorns won't even be born."

Again, 'Mary and Hank' began laughing, then stopped abruptly, jaws dropping in unison. "Starr has her powers!" 'Hank' exclaimed in shock.

The usually chatty 'Ed' suddenly had no words, but his face silently screamed, "How?"

"Are you certain?" Kone asked, his expression skeptical.

"Yes," said 'Mary and Hank' with conviction.

"With all the diminishers, it's rare for humans to discover that they have abilities at all, let alone access them. And rarer still for one so young. I understand quite well the allure of payback, Ahnk-Hume, but it sounds to me that these two should be eliminated immediately," Kone offered.

"They've escaped," said 'Mary and Hank.'

"I'm starting to begrudgingly agree," 'Ed' responded. He turned to 'Mary and Hank.' "If we're unable to apprehend them the next time, then execute them."

"Agreed," they said.

"And the Hunters?" 'Ed' inquired.

"Two are already in town. More will be joining very soon as the shells become ready," they said.

Kone spoke up, "I'll have Sahmbo on standby. He'll be awaiting your call." 'Ed, Hank and Mary' all nodded in agreement. Kone then turned to the man on his left. "Inform him that he may be needed. Also, make sure he has all the Archon's information on Starr and her band of thorns that she calls friends."

The subordinate nodded and stopped walking. By the time everyone else was a couple of steps away, he had turned to gel.

Kone then turned back to 'Ed.' "If we nip this in the bud now, then we should have no problem moving things onto a very different path than the one you experienced. My men are preparing a shipment of pistols. When they arrive, we'll port them into this plane."

'Ed' chuckled gleefully as he said, "I do enjoy having options."

They all stopped at a door in the eastern wall of the corridor. 'Ed' opened it up, and the group walked through into a lab where the shells were being grown.

A huge, well-lit room with rows of large clear cylinders, many of them contained shells in the form of people from town. But many others were growing something different.

'Ed' was pleased to see these newer shells, which were akin to their actual bodies. "These look much more comfortable, but they are a bit small."

Archons often varied in height, anywhere between five and eight feet, but seven and a half feet was the average. The Archon-shaped shells seen here were all a uniform six feet.

"This *was* as large as we were able to make the bodies while maintaining structural integrity. Any larger, and it couldn't consume enough lipids to sustain itself," 'Mary' explained.

"Was?" 'Ed' asked, noticing her emphasis on the past tense. 'Mary and Hank' both smiled and motioned to continue.

They continued walking along the many jar-like vats and turned the corner to see a larger vat that held a very different shell. Ed, or Ahnk-Hume, was not just a regular Archon, but a Drakel.

Drakels, due to their physiology, were the elite warriors. Like all Archons, they possessed six digits on their hands and feet, had innate psychic abilities and were natural mystics, but a Drakel was usually larger than the common type as all were above seven feet tall, had four arms and a long powerful tail. Many were near ten feet! Some were also blessed with large leathery wings allowing them to glide.

And Ahnk-Hume had it all. He was the tallest and physically strongest, measuring in at ten feet and four inches. His battle prowess and tactical skills brought the Hive far in their efforts, and he was feared by all who would stand against them.

But then came that wretched woman Haley Starr and landed a devastating head injury, cutting him off from his natural psychic abilities and his precious Hive.

Ahnk-Hume wanted nothing more than to rejoin his Hive. And he wanted to make Haley pay!

The Archons could all share their thoughts and experiences instantly and in real-time. The combined minds could coordinate to solve problems, and this allowed them to make incredible progress technologically. But as time went on and the Hive grew, they used less imagination, and their emotional range decreased. Their species stagnated.

Then one day, they encountered an immensely powerful being. So powerful that if the entirety of the Hive's might had been brought against him, the Archons still could not have prevailed. This being, however, had not come with hostility but instead offered to share knowledge. He showed them how to increase their mystical prowess. This being used his teachings to, in very slow and subtle ways, manipulate and corrupt them over time.

Under the direction of this being, the Archons went on to almost take over the Earth in another universe, but their master somehow fell to a group of mortals. With their leader gone and plans ruined, the Archons returned to their plane where resources were dwindling, and their extinction was all but assured.

Then Ahnk-Hume had made a breakthrough!

Necessity being the mother of invention, Ahnk-Hume was searching for a way to rejoin the Hive. It was he who found a way to make a device with which he could project his consciousness. And he also came up with the idea to modify cloning technology in order to quickly generate shells into which they can project their minds, eliminating the need for a willing host as the Archons' physiology would not allow them to stay manifest on the human plane without aid.

However, they could not remain as the Humans were now wise to them.

But Ahnk-Hume came through once again. Their port technology was modified to open not just to different planes within their universe but to another universe. They ventured into a very close parallel and met a new ally, the Cetatians.

The Cetatians, a humanoid marine-mammal species, seemed to have served the same role in this universe that the Archons had served in their own. So much so that the Cetatians were playing out the exact same plan that Archons had tried…and failed. With this new information, they got to work on modifying their plan to achieve a different outcome.

Mary and Hank informed Ahnk-Hume, "This is the same method from which the hunter's shells were made. It's much more durable, and this is what we will be using forward. And we have a second shell growing for you as well," Hank said.

Ahnk-Hume's face lit up as he said, "Excellent!"

Haley and Elizabeth were walking down the road but not saying much. Their attention was outward, watching and listening for anything or anyone that could be nearby. They had been walking for a couple of minutes, heading from the park toward the strip mall in town. Not that they had plans beyond that, but they couldn't think of anything else. So, they began heading to other familiar grounds, hoping that they could find someplace safe to hide and figure out what they should do.

The girls heard the sound of a vehicle rolling down the road and immediately ran into the woods. They jumped over an old stone wall that ran through so many of the wooded areas in New England, indicating that this was likely a farmer's field just a couple hundred years earlier.

Ducking down behind the wall, Haley began to muster the electricity within when Elizabeth grabbed her arm and quietly stressed, "No!"

Haley dissipated her energy as a public works truck drove by. After it was a short distance away, Haley turned to Elizabeth, who began to answer her question before it could be asked.

"If we can feel spookies, maybe they can too," Elizabeth explained.

Haley's eyes dropped down, and her eyebrows rose as she said, "That's a really good point." She then lifted her head and turned her ear outward. No longer hearing the vehicle, she said, "C'mon." They hopped over the stone wall and went back to the road, continuing toward the mall.

With no other traffic interrupting their travel, they arrived at the mall a couple of minutes later.

It was a rectangular building with an overhang covering the walkway in front of the shop doors. One unit was a pizza restaurant. The next was a packy. The center unit was currently available for rent, followed by a barbershop. In the fifth and final unit was The GamePort Arcade, a place where the two girls had spent many Saturdays and had a couple of birthday parties.

Not seeing or sensing anything nearby, they quickly made their way around the side and to the back so they wouldn't be seen from the road. The parking lot pavement continued along behind the building. There was a back door for every unit with concrete steps coming down to meet the asphalt. About fifteen feet away from the mall's back wall, the pavement stopped, and the ground began to rise up into one of Columbia's many wooded hills.

The girls found a spot at the foot of the leaf-covered hill, sat down and tried to think.

What a morning!

The two friends had much they wanted to tell each other, but neither had any idea of where to begin. Then Haley happened to look up and across the back of the mall, toward the arcade that operated in the end unit. There sat a long-haired calico cat in the middle of the paved way.

"It's Trinket!" Haley said, surprised to see her here.

Elizabeth looked over, also surprised to see the arcade manager's cat. Trinket was only here when the manager was working, and he normally wouldn't arrive for another half hour as the arcade didn't open until noon. If he even could have gotten there.

The two friends looked around once more, then began approaching the cat. Trinket immediately walked up the back steps to the arcade and sat down by the door as if expecting the girls to let her inside.

As they came to the end unit, Haley began to feel someone's anxiety. She turned to Elizabeth and said, "I think Neil's in there," and Elizabeth hoped that Haley was right.

Haley took a deep breath and exhaled, walked up the steps and knocked while Elizabeth kept watch. A few seconds later, the feeling of anxiety moved closer to the door, and Elizabeth started to notice it a bit too, but there was no answer.

She knocked again, and still no response. Feeling the anxiety right on the other side of the door, she finally got fed up with waiting. After another look around, Haley said as loud as she dared, "Are you at least gonna let Trinket back in?"

The door opened immediately, and Neil saw the two ten-year-old girls with cheesy grins and waving sheepishly as if they were sorry for disturbing him. He leaned his head out, looked around and then back to the two friends. "What are you waiting for?" he asked. "Get in here!"

They were moving before he even finished his sentence.

CHAPTER 5
This is Not a Game

Leaves rustled under the boots of the two men as they exited the woods. They looked ahead to the park before them and saw five piles of clothes on the ground, three of them near the carousel. The men from the ship approached the scene and seemed to be taking careful note of the discarded clothing.

The long-haired man turned his head and noticed an odd small lump in the third furthest pile from the carousel. He raised his left arm and opened his fingers in the direction of the object, and as he did, the object levitated as well. The item then moved through the air into the man's waiting grasp. The long-haired man turned around and held up the potato for the bearded man to see, both their expressions grim. The bearded man nodded, and then the pair continued toward the road.

Trinket and the girls ran inside, and Neil immediately locked the door. The arcade manager turned around to see the two exhausted girls slumping into the break room couch together.

Neil Portman was thirty-five years old and owned two businesses. The GamePort Arcade in Columbia and Problem Solders in Mansfield, where he lived. He was a slender six-foot-three with a knack for computers and electronics. His wife, Sandra, would often be with him, but lately, she had been staying home with their infant son, Neil Junior.

He had started off by repairing television sets for people he knew. Then folks started referring others to him. As his skills improved and his customer base expanded. He ended up opening an electronics repair shop that, over an eight-year period, became a full-blown tech support company.

Portman, being a good judge of character, hired the right people, and the business flourished. The employees knew what they were doing, and the managers handled everything else. Neil didn't even need to be there.

And he rarely was.

Even though the Arcade barely profited and the last couple years had been a loss, that is where Neil spent most of his time. And that's where he met Haley and Elizabeth about three years ago.

Harry used to have a language problem until one day. He heard his words repeated out of a very young Haley's mouth. He cleaned up his act and made sure to teach Haley not to use those words. It worked.

In fact, Haley seemed able to catch when someone was about to curse and would cut them off with a loud, "Hey!" Even the rebellious Elizabeth, who had been expanding her vocabulary in recent months, bit her tongue around Haley.

And that's how they became acquainted with Neil. He was fixing a coin jamb in one of the game cabinets when he sliced his finger. "Son of a…" he began when he was cut off by a shout from an almost seven-year-old girl by the Skee-Ball machine.

The arcade manager looked up from his interrupted slip to meet who would become two of his favorite regulars. A Saturday rarely went by without Harry and Heather bringing the two young ladies to play games for about an hour and chat.

"Are you two okay?" he asked, their distress evident.

Haley began shaking her head while Elizabeth said, "No."

"What happened?" Neil asked. "And does it have anything to do with everybody suddenly being rushed off by the town workers?"

Elizabeth said, "Yeah. The two men who tried to take me looked just like Frank, the plow driver," Elizabeth stated.

Haley added, "And three of the people that showed up at my house looked like him too."

Neil looked confused. "Really?" he asked.

"Yeah," Elizabeth replied as Haley nodded. "Like twins."

Trinket jumped up into Haley's lap as she started to get that knowing smirk. Elizabeth looked at the cat sensing something different. Neil looked down at the cat and got an odd look on his face. He asked, "And exactly how did you get outside?" never expecting such a direct answer.

"I let myself out," replied the hollow voice of Bast.

Elizabeth's eyes went wide, and her jaw dropped, unable to tell if she should have been excited or frightened. Neil stood there, trying to keep a neutral expression, but the surprise on his face was evident. As soon as he realized his mouth was open, he shut it. Haley suppressed her laughter and took the opportunity to enjoy their expressions. The empath could feel their shock, but neither seemed to be afraid.

After a couple seconds, Neil's expression shifted to one of curiosity. He tilted his head slightly and then asked, "Bastet?"

"Correct," she replied through Trinket's mouth.

"Like the cat figure that my mom has on the end of the mantle!?" Elizabeth asked.

"Yes," Bast confirmed once more.

Haley's eyes went wide as she suddenly thought about what happened earlier, "Is Hayseed okay?" she asked.

"He's sleeping comfortably on the couch in your loft," Bast assured Haley. "I had him rustling bushes in the woods to lead your would-be abductors in the wrong direction just before our first meeting. He's been home ever since, although I would not suggest going there. Trinket then turned around to face Haley directly. "They are definitely looking for you." Turning to face Elizabeth, Bast continued, "You as well. I don't yet know why, but they fear you both."

Elizabeth asked, "Are you why Snow did the same thing for me?"

"Actually, no," said Bast. "I saw you being chased as I was fading from this plane after my encounter with Haley. I tried to ask Snow to do what he did, but I was too weak at the moment to reach him."

"So, how did Snow know to do that?" Haley asked.

"I don't know," Bast replied.

Trinket then stood up and walked to the arm of the couch, turned to face everyone and sat down. "They won't be able to detect you in here. The bindings on the walls are quite potent and will keep the invaders from sensing your energy." Trinket turned toward Neil. "Nicely cast, by the way. But it's also wearing me down, so if you'd be so kind?"

"Oh, right!" Neil said, immediately catching on. He closed his eyes and focused on the wall bindings, adjusting them with his intention, allowing Bast's energy through.

"That is much better, thank you," said Bast, her voice now sounding full.

Haley looked at Neil with an expression of surprise, "You're the wizard!?"

"Wizard!?" Elizabeth exclaimed with both confusion and excitement.

Neil put his hands on his hips and sighed as he looked at the floor. "Mystic, actually," he said, sounding a little embarrassed. "I don't use spells."

Then Haley looked confused as she thought about it and asked, "How come we've never noticed? And if the walls are protected, why was I able to feel the butterflies in your stomach from outside?"

"As far as your empathic senses, I don't think that can truly be blocked except by maybe another empath. I also noticed you two were sensitive to energy right away," Neil explained, "So, I never did any energy work whenever I knew either of you were around."

"Why not?" Elizabeth asked.

"Because I wanted to avoid the topic altogether," said Neil, "I think such things are better discussed with parents."

Haley turned to her friend, "You said you finally talked to your mom," she mentioned.

"Yeah!" Elizabeth began, turning a bit to face everyone. "We talked about exactly this last night! And she's gonna start teaching me…" The steam appeared to instantly drain from her as she looked down to the floor. "…if I even ever see her again," she finished, trying not to tear up.

Bast said, "I believe your parents and the rest of the townspeople are underground. They were brought to the Town Hall down the street. When I was able to look inside, everyone was gone. So, I tried to peer below the Earth's surface, but there were mystical barriers in place. They were also quite active at the warehouse earlier. There seems to be no more activity there, but the Town Hall is too dangerous to enter at this time."

Trinket then turned a little toward the farmgirl, "Haley, will you go to the warehouse and see if you can discover anything that will help us find out where they took everyone? Then come back here, and we can decide how to proceed."

Haley felt the butterflies in her stomach at the thought of going back outside, but she was itching to do something useful.

"No way!" Neil shouted. "We are not sending a ten-year-old girl into who knows what. No disrespect, Bastet, but that is completely insane! I'll go."

"That would be preferable, but I have a different request for you," Bast said. "Could you start working with Elizabeth on how to harness her energy?"

Elizabeth fought hard and successfully hid her excitement, although Haley and Bast were definitely aware, and Neil could feel it a bit as well.

Looking to Trinket with great apprehension in his eyes, Neil said, "That should be reserved for parental guidance." To his thinking, that was crossing a major boundary.

"I agree," Bast replied, "But her mother has been taken, and we need to find them. Perhaps we should find out why these invaders fear her."

"But you still can't send Haley out alone," Neil said in response. "How would she defend herself…"

Right before he finished the sentence, Neil felt a swelling of energy from Haley. He turned his head and saw she had her rig back on and her potato gun mounted to her gauntlet once more. The inside of the barrel was glowing with blue light.

"With this," Haley said, sporting her mischievous smirk.

"Wow! You look kinda like a ghostbuster!" Neil exclaimed, making Haley laugh.

"The energy blasts she can release are quite potent," Bast said.

"Yeah!" Haley excitedly added. "Just like the Hadouken move in your fighting game!"

"But this is the real world," Neil responded. "With real consequences."

Haley suddenly had an idea. "Hey, Bast! Can you give Elizabeth powers like you did me?" she asked.

"No, I cannot," said Bast. "It takes a great deal of concentration just to do what I'm doing now. It took a great deal more to manifest and interreact earlier. Your natural vibrations resonate closely with mine. That, coupled with your unusually keen empathic senses, allowed me to help you tune to your own field. And for clarification," she continued, "I did not give you powers. They are innate to you."

Trinket turned to Elizabeth, "Now let's see if Neil will help you find yours."

Neal folded his arms across his chest, sighed and shook his head, "Without her mother's okay…I don't know, I don't like it," he said.

"Nor do I," said Bast, "But our sphere is in danger, and our options are few."

The three could feel the energy weakening around Trinket. Bast said, "I must rest, but I will try to find more help. I will also be in communication when I am able. Please consider what I've said, pray to the Creator and make your choices…" The energy faded, and Trinket was her regular self again.

Haley was nervous but also a little excited. She wanted to see if she could find out what was going on. She wanted to find the entrance to whatever was underground. She wanted to find her dad. Haley stood up and was about to announce that she was going when her stomach suddenly rumbled. Having relaxed a bit, her appetite woke back up, and she realized that it'd been a while since breakfast. Elizabeth had worked up quite an appetite as well.

Neil heard the rumble and stifled a laugh as he turned to the break room fridge. He had picked up a couple of pies the night before, and one was still untouched. He opened the door and pulled out a three-meat pizza.

It didn't last five minutes.

The two men from the ship walked just inside the woods along the west side of the road, somehow managing to not rustle the leaves on the ground as they moved. There was a strip mall just up ahead on their left. As they neared, the two men paid careful attention. They slowed their pace and ducked further into the woods on the side of the road, watching for any sign of activity in the windows.

The bearded man had something in his hand. It looked like clear glass or plastic and was about the size of a cell phone. He turned to face the building, held the device up and looked into it as if he were reading something.

Haley and Elizabeth were leaning back on the couch, letting the pizza settle. Neil was sitting on his work stool with his right elbow in his left palm and his chin resting in his right hand.

The arcade manager wasn't sure what was the right thing to do here. He certainly didn't agree with letting Haley go out on her own, but if he went out, then he'd be leaving both the girls alone. And he knew that there was no way a combination of Haley and Elizabeth would stay put. Even if he unlocked every cabinet in the arcade for them to play while he was out, it wouldn't even be fifteen minutes before curiosity got the better of them.

Sure, Haley could get lost in a good video or puzzle game as she had a tendency to stick to just a few particular interests, but Elizabeth, on the other hand, would get bored with them very quickly as she was always restless. She could become engrossed in a good strategy or volleyball game, but Neil had nothing that would fit the bill. He knew that Elizabeth would venture out and where she would go, Haley usually followed.

And then there was the matter of instructing Elizabeth. In truth, he would love to do so, but not without the blessing of her folks. However, Bast was right. People were missing, and the three of them needed any advantage they could get in order to find the others.

But what could he possibly teach her that would be advantageous in any useful amount of time? People practice and meditate their entire lives without ever coming close to any kind of ability like Haley. Or any special abilities at all. Most people don't even believe these types of things are possible anymore.

Then he wondered, why *do* they fear her…

"There are people outside!" Haley said suddenly, her tone urgent, but her voice hushed.

The only windows were on the front of the building. Neil immediately glanced over toward the door between the break room and the arcade floor to ensure that it was shut.

"Have you fixed your cameras yet?" Elizabeth asked, hoping to see outside via the monitor on Neil's work desk.

Neil had resurrected the cheap cameras many times but eventually got fed up and decided to replace them. He called a security company and ordered better quality replacements. The manager shook his head and said, "Not yet. The guy is supposed to come on Tuesday to install the new system."

Haley closed her eyes and tried to focus on any feelings from beyond the walls. "I think it's two people," she began. "One of them is…focused…like a runner about to start a race. The other is…" She paused as she tried to think of the words to describe the odd sensations. "Everything…?"

"Huh?" said Elizabeth while Neil sported a puzzled look.

"Everything," The farmer stated, sounding a little more comfortable with her description. She wasn't completely unfamiliar with this sensation as she had felt similarly this morning when her father was taken, and nothing made sense. "It's like being happy and mad at the same time…mixed with everything else. But it all feels…small…" She turned to Elizabeth, "It's all fuzzy…I can't tell them apart. None of it seems very strong, and it's all…fading."

A feeling of anxiety shot up, and it was compounded by that of the others. She tried to keep her focus outside.

For a moment, they were all on edge, practically holding their breath. Then, Haley sighed and said, "They're moving away." The fuzzy jumble seemed to shrink and disappear altogether while the sense of focus moved further south.

After a couple moments, the three of them breathed much easier, and Neil even dared to go onto the floor to grab some cans of soda out of the vending machine. "What do you two want to drink?"

"Cola," said Elizabeth.

"Any cream soda?" asked Haley.

"No," replied Neil. The guy hasn't come yet to refill it."

Haley did her best to mimic the cadence of William Shatner's voice as she said, "Let me guess…Tuesday."

Neil, catching the Star Trek reference, snapped his fingers and mirthfully said, "Haaaaaa!" as he pointed at her.

Elizabeth rolled her eyes with a scoff and then muttered, "Nerds," under her breath. Of course, the other two both heard it. As Elizabeth had intended.

CHAPTER 6
On the Road Again

The townsfolk were all terrified. Trooper Weathers had taken a headcount and every adult, except for those who were known to be out of town, was in this cell. Worse, they had no idea where their children were.

The EMTs started making regular rounds, checking on everybody. Most were quiet and somber, while a few were crying. Every now and then, somebody would just start laughing hysterically. None of this made sense to anybody.

Harry was leaning against the metal wall, trying to work the present situation in his mind. He was worried sick about Haley. He hoped that his daughter could have somehow escaped whatever this absurd nightmare was. But how? With the technology to teleport people, what hope would a little girl have of escaping? How does that even work? If they can teleport people, why did they trick everybody else into coming here?

Harry's eyes snapped open wide with an epiphany. He stood up and looked for Trooper Weathers.

"Ed," he called as he made his way through the crowd.

Ed turned and began making his way to Harry. As they approached each other, Ed said, "You look like you've got something."

"More like a piece of something." Harry said, "I think they have a power problem."

"What do you mean?" Ed asked.

"They can teleport people, yet they still rounded most of us up physically. I think either their batteries are running low, or they're saving their juice for something."

Ed replied, "That does sound like something to keep in mind. Hopefully, we'll learn some more pieces so we can start putting them together."

Neil still couldn't believe that he had let Haley walk out that door. Elizabeth was sitting on the couch, and Neil was sitting on his stool opposite her. The arcade manager was trying to stop fretting about what he could not control and focus on the task at hand.

Neil took a deep breath, held it for a second and then exhaled. He then looked at Elizabeth and asked, "When you feel the energy, how would you describe it?"

"You know when you're in a swimming pool, and someone swims by under the water? They don't touch you, but you can feel them swimming there. It's like that, but not so…noticeable." Elizabeth explained.

"It's subtle," Neil said.

"Yeah!" responded Elizabeth. "That's the word my mom used."

"Okay," said Neil. "Now, close your eyes and just tune in to those senses."

The aspiring young mystic did so. A moment later, she was feeling the little subtleties in the air all around her. "Okay, got it."

"Good," said Neil. He held his hand vertically in front of him and then began moving it from side to side.

"Whoa!" said Elizabeth. "It feels like the air is moving back and forth."

"Excellent. Although it wasn't the air you felt, it was the energy," Neil said. "Now that you're definitely tuned in, cup your hands and bring them together as if you were holding a ball."

Elizabeth had seen some girls in a clique doing this at school and wondered what it was about. *Perhaps this might be it,* she thought. But if so, the aspiring mystic never sensed anything from them. She cupped her hands and held them close, feeling the subtle vibrations.

"Now feel your own energy gather in your hands," Neil said.

"I do feel it," Elizabeth replied.

"Yes, but gather it. Focus on that feeling where it's all coming together. Stay focused on that spot and keep pulling it in. Let it build." Neil saw a look of pure concentration on the young girl's face. She began to squint her eyes tight.

"Wait," he said with a bit of a chuckle. "Take a breath. You might be trying a little too hard."

Haley was between the back of the arcade and the hill, looking to the south at the gas station on the other side of the shrubs. The corner of the mall building was at the turn of the hill, allowing flatter and more usable land behind the gas station. Unfortunately, it was used for a parking lot that left no trees for any practical cover between the steep hills and the road.

On the other side of the gas station's parking lot was Goldman's Woodworking Studio. There were some trees around the studio and some space between the building and the steep hill, giving her more cover options. Haley figured that if she could get over there, she could duck behind something.

About to make a break for the studio, she heard a vehicle coming down the road, so she crouched down behind the shrubs and waited.

The public works vehicle pulled into the gas station and stopped at a pump. A Hank and a Frank got out of the vehicle. Hank went inside while Frank grabbed the pump handle. A moment later, Hank opened the station door and shouted, "It's on," and went back inside as Frank began fueling the truck.

Haley tried to sense these two empathically and thought that they felt different than the people who were chasing her earlier. In fact, they felt more…normal.

The Hank came back outside the station with some sandwiches from the cooler and some pork rinds. Frank hung up the handle, and then they both went to the hood of the truck and started eating.

Haley was beginning to wonder if these two might be real people, but something still felt a little off. She stayed quiet and watched.

"I love these sandwiches, but I'd rather eat them in person," Hank said and then took another bite.

"I hear ya," said Frank. "I hope we can get back soon. My *real* body's getting hungry."

"Yeah, but I've gotta admit, these projectors are something else! And just think, all the Archons can do this without the tech," Hank said.

"I've tried that kind of stuff but just couldn't get it," replied Frank. "I guess some of the Proctors were able to. I never did quite take to telepathy or magick."

"I never took to those things either," Hank said back. "I guess these guys are gonna use this town as a bit of a base once the rest of them get here."

"Don't know, don't care," said Frank. "I just do what the Podmen say, and I'm left alone. And that's the way I like it."

Hank nodded along with those last words as he was chewing.

They finished their food, and Frank threw his wrappers in the trash while Hank just tossed his on the ground. They got back in the truck, started it up and drove away.

Archons? They must be the reptile people, Haley thought, then focused back on what she was trying to do. *But who are the Podmen?*

Haley picked her point, stood up and looked around while listening for any more vehicles. Satisfied that there was no one else, she ran for the studio.

"That's more like it," Neil said, sensing the energy between Elizabeth's hands started to intensify. "Hold your focus and hold your energy."

Elizabeth was in deep concentration yet relaxed. It was the same mental state that she called 'the sweet spot.' She sometimes reached it when playing volleyball. A switch would just flip in her mind, and when it did, she was practically unbeatable by her peers.

She felt her energy building between her palms. It was warm at first, like nothing more than her own body heat. But then it started to tingle just a bit. The longer she held her focus, the stronger it became, and the tingling started to intensify with a bit of an electrical feeling, like a magnetic field.

"Wow!" the hopeful mystic said, and then she excitedly opened her eyes and looked down at her palms to see…nothing?

Neil saw the disappointment on her face and asked, "Were you expecting to see some special effects?"

Elizabeth looked up at Neil feeling a little foolish, and with a shrug, said, "Kinda?"

Neil chuckled and sighed. He then said, "You're catching on a lot quicker than anyone I've ever seen, but these things take years of practice and discipline. You're actually doing extremely well. Let's take five minutes and then try something a little different."

Feeling more secure once she got to the studio property, Haley sat down behind a couple of thick shrubs and listened for a moment. While sitting there, she looked up to the covered porch and thought about the many times she'd been here before.

Yesh Goldman was in town sporadically. His craftmanship was always top-notch, and Harry even came here for some pointers when making Haley's rig.

Mr. Goldman looked to be around thirty and usually had long hair but would cut it short every now and then. Last week, while in town, was one of those times. Long or short, it was always neat and tidy, as was the beard. Yesh had that olive skin tone common to the Mediterranean and always seemed so full of life.

He was known for being an incredible storyteller. Fiction, fantasy, history and even Bible stories. When the craftsman started going, anyone in earshot would buckle up for a wild ride. He would get into the narrative and really made it feel like you knew the people in the stories. The guy just knew how to deliver. Even Elizabeth, who had heard Bible stories ad nauseam, would love to sit and hear them from Yesh.

And the carpenter always seemed to be able to help folks think through a problem, often by leading people into answering their own questions. For that reason, Haley's father would sometimes compare Goldman to Wilson from the show *Home Improvement*. Harry often said that "Goldman could do more good as a bartender than all the shrinks on the east coast." Goldman, to the core, was a people person.

Haley smiled while the memories from here quickly ran through her mind as she always felt at peace in the studio. Even in her circumstance, being here helped her calm down.

She began to think about where to go next. The road continued up a slope and leveled out just before the grocery store. From there, it continued on to the warehouse, a short way further to the Town Hall and then the church.

Right before the warehouse, the road forked to the right and went down to a lower step and ran parallel to the upper road. Along this lower step were the hardware store, the diner, and the fire department.

Unfortunately, the road came in closer along the steep hillside after the studio, leaving no cover until after the grocery store.

The other side of the road would probably be better, she thought. The ground was much more level and had plenty of trees, but there were no buildings, and the foliage was getting thin. Still better than against a steep hillside that was mostly rock near the bottom.

After the grocery store, the steep hill starts to level out, which would allow her to walk behind some trees. *I could cross back to this side after the store and use the woods to get to the warehouse from the back*, Haley thought.

No sign of anyone around, Haley stood up and prepared to cross the road. As she stood, she noticed a letter on the deck boards of the porch. She ran up the steps and picked it up to put it in the slot but was interrupted by the sound of a car engine coming up the road.

After a glass of water and a stretch of the legs, Elizabeth sat on the couch again and was tuning back into those subtle frequencies.

"Now think of the energy you feel around you. Think of it as an extension of yourself," Neil said. "Remember how it felt when you thought the air was moving. Work with it and make it happen."

Elizabeth concentrated on how it felt when Neil made the energy flow earlier. She felt the energy around her and imagined it moving in the same way. After a moment, she seemed to fall back into her sweet spot and felt everything start to shift a bit.

Neil smiled in surprise as he felt the vibes flowing back and forth. "Very good!" he said. The manager couldn't believe how quickly she was catching on. "Keep flowing with it."

As Neil sensed the energy that Elizabeth was moving, he began to notice that it was getting stronger still. He felt it more easily. Too easily. The arcade manager's eyes popped open wide when he realized that he wasn't just feeling the energy. He was feeling his hair shifting back and forth.

He was about to comment but changed his mind, letting her continue. And continue, she did. Elizabeth herself was rocking back and forth just a bit with the energy movement for about another ten seconds until a paper swept off of Neil's desk and to the ground.

Elizabeth opened her eyes when she heard it land on the floor in front of her. She looked up at Neil, who couldn't even begin to suppress his smile. The excitement in the young mystic grew as she asked, "Did I just move that paper with my mind!?"

Neil stood up off his stool, the excitement obvious on his face. He threw arms up and out as he happily and enthusiastically exclaimed, "No!"

Elizabeth's face went from excitement to utter confusion. "Then why do you look how I'd think you'd look if I had?" She asked at a total loss.

Neil blinked a couple of times as his mind caught up to the quickly spoken words. "Because you were moving the air!" he said smiling.

Neil paid close attention to Elizabeth's face as what he had just said slowly sank in. Her eyes widened as her jaw sank into an expression of utter shock and astonishment. She sat there for a moment with that face until Neil, who just remembered something he had on his shelf, interrupted it with a flash and click.

Elizabeth looked over at him, holding an instant camera that was making a whirring sound while a new photo rolled out. He said, "Unlike my security cameras, this old Polaroid still works."

CHAPTER 7
Measure Twice Cut Once

Haley turned from the door just in time to see the car come into view. "Oh no!" she gasped. She reached up, grabbed the door handle and to her surprise, it turned! She opened the door, dashed inside and shut it.

Haley wondered if the people in the car had seen her. She was oddly calm while she stood by the door and listened to the vehicle come closer, pass the studio and continue toward the south. Confident that nobody was stopping, she looked down to the floor and realized that she was standing on more than a dozen envelopes. Haley picked them all up and put them on the counter where she had seen Goldman place the mail before.

The studio looked as if it used to be a residence at one time. Most of the bottom level had been converted to an open floor, and this is where Goldman did the work. There were a variety of workbenches and table saws. There were many types of both power and hand tools around the shop, all placed neatly and awaiting their next use. The walls were white, and the hardwood floors had a light natural finish. With the sun a little lower in the sky this time of year, the natural light spilled in and reflected off the surfaces, illuminating the room nicely. If Goldman were working here today, the overhead lights probably wouldn't be needed.

As Haley stood there for a moment, she was surprised at how peaceful it still felt in the shop, as if the problems outside couldn't come in here.

She suddenly remembered the water bottle she had left the last time she was there. Sitting down with Elizabeth to listen to another story, Haley set the unopened bottle down somewhere and forgot about it.

Looking to the bench that she and her friend frequented, Haley sighed. "So much has happened today," she said aloud as the weight of everything began to catch up with her.

She walked over to the bench, took off her rig and sat down.

Haley would sometimes tell her troubles to the kindhearted carpenter, especially about how her mother was taken from her, and she surely wished she could do so now. "It's all way too much," she continued as if someone were there to listen.

The tears began to flow as Haley recounted the unbelievable events she had witnessed and the things she had been through. This went on for the next couple of minutes, but the crying felt a little different to Haley. The streams running down her cheeks were almost like a purge as the tears flushed away much of the stress.

The young farmer leaned back and rested her head against the wall. With a slight smile, she wiped the last of her tears away and said, "Thanks, Yesh. Even when you're not here, it's like you're still listening."

Haley was now feeling a little thirsty. She sat up straight, looked to the right and actually laughed a little when she saw the water bottle that was forgotten last week, sitting just to the side of the bench.

After a moment or two of dancing, jumping and squealing, Elizabeth finally calmed down enough to see what Neil would have to say next.

Neil laughed a bit and asked, "Are you done now?"

Elizabeth looked up at Neil with a big smile and slowly shook her head as she said, "Nooooo." She then launched into one more happy dance and ended it with a twirling jump. She landed facing Neil and happily stated, "Now I'm done."

"Okay," Neil said with another chuckle. He sat back down on the stool and thought for a moment. He lifted his head suddenly and said, "I wonder…"

He hopped up and went over to a cabinet, opened it up and pulled out a candle. He went to another and pulled out a small bowl, set the items down on his desk and then went to the back door. He opened it up and looked around outside, then ran down the steps, picked something up and ran back in. He quickly closed and locked the door, then put a rock on the desk. Next, he cleared off a small end table and pulled it to the center of the break room.

"Are you thinking earth, air, fire and water?" Elizabeth asked.

"Exactly," replied Neil, and he took the bowl to the breakroom sink to fill it with water. He then put the bowl on the table with the candle and the rock.

Haley walked to the front door and grasped the handle, took a deep breath and exhaled, preparing to venture back out. She was actually feeling more confident and a little invigorated. While everything still weighed heavy on her mind, she didn't feel afraid. Haley turned the handle and opened the door.

She cautiously stepped out onto the porch and looked around. Everything seemed calm at the moment, so she walked out to the railing and looked south. The road went uphill and leveled off right before the grocery store, and she could see the sign by the parking lot entrance from where she stood.

As Haley was preparing to cross the street once more, she again heard the engine of a vehicle. She looked back up the road and could see a car pulling into the store's parking lot, followed by another car.

A few seconds later, she could hear the sound of a diesel getting closer, then saw a couple of school buses follow suit.

Haley couldn't see anything beyond the vehicles turning into the store entrance. *Great*, she thought. *I can't cross the road up there without being seen from that lot.*

Haley went back inside the studio and closed the door. She walked to the back and looked out the window, wondering if there could be a better way past this obstacle. She stepped out the back door and started looking around. There were a few small trees in the back and a very tall oak.

She looked up at the tree and wondered, *Is it tall enough to see them?*

While the branches of this oak were too high, the smaller trees could easily reach them. "I guess it's worth a try."

Haley climbed onto a smaller tree and effortlessly made her way up to the lower branches of the oak. She was again smiling about how much easier she found movement and balance. She hopped and climbed from branch to branch, quickly making her way up the tree.

As she neared the top, Haley found that the tree wasn't tall enough, and even if it was, there were still lots of trees growing out of the steep hillside that was blocking her angle of view. But as she looked around, Haley realized that another path might be available to her.

Some of the oak's higher branches reached the branches of another tree growing out from the hillside. And that tree could reach many more. She once again got her mischievous smirk and said, "Looks like I'm taking the high road."

She felt so free jumping from branch to branch. It was easier than when she last walked on the playground balance beam. There were rock ledges about the hillside, and Haley saw that she could make her way to them by some of the lower branches. As she neared the store, Haley jumped onto a ledge and looked down to the road below.

Not wanting to be seen, she crouched down. This high up from the road, the hill wasn't quite as steep, and she could stay back further, giving her a somewhat decent vantage point. But Haley knew that she still needed to be very careful because here, she was about level with the grocery parking lot and could be seen by cars coming down the hill.

She stuck her head out a bit and peered through the thinning trees to see a few cars, a couple of trucks and two school busses. Haley saw people moving around in the lot but couldn't make out what they were doing. After another look around, Haley took back to the trees and began making her way closer.

She neared the parking lot and looked ahead, becoming more confident that she could make her way around the back of the store through these trees. Maybe even all the way to the warehouse.

Haley found a decent point where she could see the lot without being noticed and stopped to watch what was happening. There must have been about thirty people down there. Many Hanks and Franks and Joeys and…

The young farmer choked up when she saw that many of them looked like her father. She knew that none of them were Harry, but the sight was like an ice-cold knife to the gut. Haley steadied herself and continued to watch.

The people were bringing shopping carts full of food out to the buses. There were multiple people around each bus, unloading carts and handing off the contents to people inside. Both buses and a couple of box trucks were looking about full.

They were moving quickly. It hadn't even been ten minutes since Haley saw those buses pull into the parking lot. After another couple of minutes, they finished their task. The diesel engines fired up, and a moment later, the buses pulled out of the parking lot and headed south, bearing left at the fork and continuing past the warehouse, followed by the box trucks. Everybody got into the other vehicles, and they all began to leave.

Most of them took a left out of the lot and went south, following the bus' route, although some of those cars turned right at the fork. The remaining four cars turned right from the lot and headed down the hill, back toward the park to her north.

With everybody gone, Haley continued to make her way around the back of the building. While moving along the rear lot, she looked down to the ground and saw a gray and black cat. This cat was often seen around the store for the past year. Both of her front feet were double pawed, and the feature became her namesake, Paws.

The cat was playfully pouncing at some leaves that were stirring in the breeze, and Haley thought about going down to the cat but knew she had more important things to do.

She began hopping to lower branches as she continued. The hill wasn't as steep here, so Haley made her way down to the ground, where the colored leaves of the trees growing near the bottom of the hill were now providing some nice cover.

As Haley approached the back of the warehouse, there was an oak tree growing out from a rocky area of the hillside, and she noticed a fairly large opening just beneath. She stopped to take a look.

The cave opening was big enough for her to easily crawl inside. Haley took a peek inside, but it was dark, and she could see nothing. So, she turned toward the building to see what could be found.

Neil couldn't believe it. He'd never seen anyone pick things up this quickly. And he really couldn't believe how much she could do. Over the last half hour, Elizabeth was playing with the air currents. She had manipulated the candle flame and even managed to make the water in the bowl ripple a little bit.

Neil spent months practicing meditation and training his focus with a candle before he ever got so much as a flicker. And months more before he could do it consistently. Many of those who practiced tended to not even get the flicker.

Elizabeth was looking at the candle and slowly breathing. As she inhaled, the flame expanded, and as she exhaled, the flame contracted.

After a moment of that, she looked at the bowl of water. Elizabeth connected with the energy. She could clearly feel it. After some deep concentration, the water began to slightly ripple with her breathing.

She next looked to the rock. This rock has been puzzling her. Elizabeth tuned her senses to it. She could feel it more keenly than the other three. The young mystic figured that if she could feel it so strongly, then she would see more obvious effects from the result of her connection, but the opposite seemed to be true.

Elizabeth could feel the connection with the water more than with the fire or the air, but she would barely get a ripple. Am I doing something backward?" she suddenly asked Neil.

"Uh…what do you mean?" Neil asked in response.

Elizabeth explained, "I feel the rock and the water strongly, but I don't see them do…stuff, like with the fire and air." she said.

"It feels stronger because the energy is far denser," Neil said.

"Sooo, what does that mean?" Elizabeth asked.

"It means you're gonna have to practice," Neil replied. "More density means more energy in one spot, and it takes time to get used to." He then added, "I've gotta say, you're already performing way beyond anything I could've expected. Ever!"

Neil continued. "Some people spend their entire lives practicing the piano. And they're really good," he said, gesturing with his hands as he paced, "but every once in a while, someone comes along, sits down, picks it right up, and they're fantastic!"

He then turned to face her directly, "You…have a knack." After a brief pause, he added, "And a half! I've never seen or heard of anyone outside of myth that's picked things up like this, and you definitely seem to be wired toward the four elements," he finished.

Elizabeth was getting excited. "I might be able to help Haley!" she practically shouted. Then her expression dropped to one of worry. "It's been a bit. Do you think she's okay?"

Haley had been gone for about a half-hour, and the warehouse would usually be a five-minute walk. Neil, who has been second-guessing himself ever since he let Haley leave, tried to shift Elizabeth's attention back to what was before them. "I certainly hope so," he said. "The best thing we can do for her at the moment is keep practicing."

Haley carefully made her way across the back of the warehouse. Having never seen the building from this side, she now looked at the older building made of brick. The parking lot was wrapped around the front and both sides, and the back had a ten-foot clearing between the wall and the wooded hill. There was a utility shed on the back wall next to some ductwork and a shiny black bulkhead for stairs.

Haley turned to her right, went to the corner of the building and looked left around the side. The door was on this side near the front, so she carefully took in her surroundings and didn't see anyone. Not hearing any cars or sensing any presence, Haley made her move.

She sprinted toward the front of the building, reached the door, grabbed the handle and pulled, but it wouldn't budge. She quickly looked around, gave another couple of pulls and then ran back to the rear of the building.

After a moment of making sure she wasn't seen, Haley started making her way to the other side. On this end were the overhead doors into the loading docks. A moment later, she dared to run down the side, pulling up on all the doors. All of them locked. Haley swiftly returned to the back of the building to think.

She considered just blasting a door but decided it would be far too risky. She wandered toward the other end, coming to the ductwork where she stopped to take a closer look.

It was a box made from sheet metal with some thin vent slots. Wondering if she could get in through the system, she grabbed on and gave it a bit of a shake, finding it to be fairly sturdy and attempts at pushing it loose would not be practical.

But it was the back of the building.

Haley, using all her senses, checked but couldn't detect anyone around. She returned to the ductwork, gathered her energy and blasted it.

The box broke free of its fastenings and tumbled to the side. It was loud, and Haley worried that she may have just given herself away.

She quickly looked at what she had uncovered before running back into the woods and taking to the trees.

Haley was hoping to see an air duct that went into the wall through which she could fit. She got part of her wish. There was a vent shaft big enough for her, even while wearing the rig, but it went straight down.

After a couple of minutes, she felt secure that no one was coming and returned to take a closer look.

Peering down the cylindrical shaft, she could see only darkness. Haley did not like the thought of sliding down into the unknown and began looking for more options.

The utility shed was unlocked, so she went inside. But it was just a shed with no connections to the larger building.

Stepping back out, Haley looked over to a bulkhead. *That looks brand new,* she thought and walked over to grab the handle. It, too, was locked.

After another check of the area, she mounted and raised her potato gun. Haley fired a blast, giving the bulkhead quite a shake, but held it up just fine. She fired two more blasts but stopped when she realized that making noise and some useless dents was all that she was doing.

It was time to make her way back to the arcade and let them know everything she's seen and heard.

CHAPTER 8
Shipping and Handling

Elizabeth was still making unbelievable progress. She had decided to go back to cupping her hands and feeling her own energy, focusing and letting it coalesce, while Neil could sense a denser collection of energy than her last attempt.

That electrical feeling returned, and she continued to let it build. She felt like her hands were buzzing. She opened her eyes but, unlike before, continued to hold her focus. The young mystic could still feel it. She continued to maintain it for a few minutes before letting it dissipate.

She then tuned into the air. Elizabeth started off as before, shifting back and forth. After a moment of this, she changed it up and tried shifting it in different directions and did so with little effort.

She then smiled and held up her index finger. The mystic began twirling her finger while looking at the candle. The air circled around the flame, causing it to twist. "I can't believe it's working," she said with a slight chuckle.

Next, she turned to the water bowl and tuned in. Elizabeth now had no problem making the water ripple, but not to any greater extent than her previous attempt.

Then there was the rock. She felt it. So clear. So strong. But all she could do was feel its presence.

Elizabeth began again. She cupped her hands, the energy built. Not even closing her eyes at all this time as the young mystic was learning to focus with great ease.

She was looking at her hands while focused, letting them become stronger. Her hands again tingled with the energy, and then, she fell into her sweet spot.

Both Elizabeth and Neil shouted, "Whoa!" when an orb of sparkling amber light appeared in her hands.

Elizabeth immediately dissipated the energy as she whipped her hands away from each other, and Neil, after a couple of seconds, started laughing.

Elizabeth, after looking shocked for a couple more seconds, joined in with his laughter. "I scared myself." She giggled.

Haley went back into the woods and up a tree. After watching and listening for a moment, she figured nobody was coming and began to head back.

The farmgirl was becoming much more oriented to her balance and agility. Now, she could practically run along some limbs, provided they could support her weight. But having spent much time in the woods and climbing trees, Haley had a pretty good sense of where she could step. Within a minute, she was behind the grocery store parking lot, where the slope of the hill began to steepen.

"Meow," Haley heard and looked down to see that Paws was still there. The cat was looking up directly at her. "Meow," Paws said again, maintaining eye contact.

Haley couldn't sense anything unusual, but the adolescent feline looked as if she were trying to tell her something.

Haley took another good look around, then began her descent as the cat pounced at another leaf. When she set her feet on the ground, Paws came over to her and rubbed against her shin.

"Good to see you too, Paws," Haley said as the cat suddenly pounced on another leaf.

The farmer gave the friendly cat a quick scratch on the head but still felt nothing unusual. "I gotta go," Haley said.

As she turned to leave, she heard Paws say, "Meow," followed by a soft trill. Haley turned back toward the cat.

"Meow," said the cat as she sat down.

Haley squatted down and looked in Paws' eyes.

The empath inhaled sharply as her eyes widened and her senses kicked in. Haley could feel the experience of jumping into the air, of falling back to the ground and landing on top of the scurrying leaf. The exhilaration of the leap and the thrilling satisfaction of landing powerfully on the object.

Haley could feel the playfulness of the pouncing and began to giggle. As she did, she felt that electricity and magnetism building within her once more.

Paws pounced on a wrapper as it blew by. Haley's energy built even further, and she just wanted to join in.

Another leaf blew by, and Paws went at it!

As Paws leaped into the air, so did the young empath, and at the apex of their leap, Haley's energy propelled her back to the asphalt, and she slammed feet first into the ground. A quick small wave of blue light splashed out from where she landed.

Haley slowly stood up straight from her crouched position and looked down at the ground. She took a step back and couldn't believe her eyes. It was slight, but her feet had actually indented the parking lot pavement.

The farmer, with her mouth hanging open, stared at the ground for a moment in disbelief.

Paws had backed away when Haley made the impact, but the cat was somehow already over it and rubbing against the side of the farmer's leg.

Haley looked down and smiled as she petted Paws on the head. She looked back to those slight foot-shaped indents where she landed, and her eyes lit up. Then, Haley got that tell-tale smirk.

"Thanks, Paws!" she said with a final pat on the head and turned back toward the warehouse.

She began to run but immediately stopped. Haley was so excited about her idea that she almost forgot to look around. And she was glad she did. Haley, hearing a few cars coming by, immediately returned to the trees. She climbed high enough to see a couple of cars as they continued past the store and warehouse toward the Town Hall.

Stepping down from the trees behind the warehouse, Haley again went to one corner of the building and then all the way down to the other, verifying that no one was around. Next, she turned and looked at the defiant bulkhead, narrowed her eyes and smirked.

Haley hopped on top of the metal cover, excited to try her idea, but was suddenly a little nervous. She had no idea who or what could be waiting beneath the barrier or if doing this was a good idea at all. Haley didn't even know if this would work.

Her father would sometimes say that there's a fine line between daring and stupid, which made Haley wonder where she was at the moment in relation to that line. "Am I daring or stupid?"

Haley took a deep breath and exhaled, jumped up as the energy coalesced and then she pounced.

The amber glow reflected in her eyes from an orb of sparkling energy between her cupped hands. Elizabeth couldn't believe that she was able to do this.

Neil was doing the same thing alongside her. This took him years to do, and he still had to really focus, yet Elizabeth, within an hour, had gone from nothing to doing this almost casually.

They took a break to drink some water. Neil leaned against the breakroom counter and took a swig. He then looked at Elizabeth and said, "I've always known that you were sensitive to energy, but it's like you were already completely in tune and just needed to be shown what to do. I've been thinking," he continued, "Bastet said she was able to help Haley tune into her field and that's why she can do her…potato-gun-cat thing."

Elizabeth laughed a little.

"So, when did you suddenly become this tuned in?" he asked.

"What do you mean?" Elizabeth asked back.

"Well," Neil replied, "If you were always this connected, you would have probably seen signs here and there of what you're able to do. Have you that you can think of?"

Elizabeth took a moment but couldn't recall anything she's done that would hint toward any of this. She began to slowly shake her head as she said, "No…nothing that I can think of…Snow!" she said as her eyes popped wide. "Right after Snow lead the man away, energy just felt stronger. Could that have been it?" she asked.

"I don't really know, but sounds likely," Neil replied, nodding slightly. He then pulled his cell phone out of his pocket, flipped it open and said, "Still no bars." He thought of Sandra and Junior, hoping that they wouldn't try coming to town.

Elizabeth sighed and looked at the phone on the desk. She shrugged, picked it up and held it to her ear, "And still no dial tone," she added.

With a crash, Haley broke straight down and through the bulkhead. In a splash of blue light, she tumbled down some concrete stairs and, at the bottom, landed in a crouched position on her feet.

The bulkhead doors were crumpled down and inward, letting some light down the stairwell.

Haley stood up straight, surprised that she was not hurt from the spill. She looked herself over, but all she had to show for this stunt was a light scrape on her left forearm. "Woah," she said quietly.

Now beneath the warehouse, Haley took a good look around. Where she could see, the walls were dirt and stone, but they were absolutely smooth. The ceiling was concrete and also appeared to be just as smooth as the walls. Along the ceiling and walls were one-by-three inch metal bars, spaced about twenty inches apart. They crisscrossed in a grid pattern that formed a cage that appeared to support the concrete above.

Haley could see another light source coming from the ceiling down the other end. This wide underground room looked like it ran the entire length of the warehouse, and there was a ramp going up and into the building above.

I'll check it out, she thought, *then I gotta go back to the arcade.*

The pickup truck pulled into the Town Hall parking lot, shut down, and both doors opened. The driver 'Hank' and passenger 'Frank' exited the vehicle. These two shells were piloted by Cetatians. Unlike the Archons, the Cetatians had the same physiological proportions as humans and were quite comfortable in these shells.

Without the shells, they could put on clothing and walk around unnoticed, but a direct look at their necks might give away that something was different.

They shared the same facial features as humans. This included ethnic distinctions around the regions of the world from which their ancestors hailed, but the skin coloration was different. Cetatians had the same skin tones as humans in the front, but along the back, their skin colors varied. The pigment on their backs was usually, but not always darker and could present in a wider range of colors. The two tones blended down the side of the neck and back into what they called the color line. Now, with the use of the shells, they could interact with the humans unnoticed to all except those already in their pockets.

Hank, whose real name was Gary, was looking forward to ending the workday and returning to his real body. Frank, whose real name actually was Frank, had complained about his true stomach needing food a couple of times.

The Cetatian culture had many similarities to the human cultures, as the unseen cohabitants of Earth had been slowly influencing their human neighbors for generations. Especially through means of entertainment and education systems. They would introduce ideas that were in a certain direction, stifle opposing ideas and slowly nudge and shape the opinions of others just a little bit. Then they would do the same with the next generation, but just a bit more. Slowly and subtly corrupting society with another "new normal." Things that, on their own, were not a problem but collectively pushed at particular times, these issues were used to sow division amongst people and to shape the direction of human society. This, used in concert with control of financial institutions and media networks, allowed them to manipulate humanity into being a collection of unwitting cogs in the Cetatian machine.

As the two men walked up to the Town Hall entrance, they heard a crashing sound to their north.

"Sounded like it came from near the warehouse," Gary said.

Frank sighed and shook his head as he pulled a flip phone out of his pocket. "I'm calling Podman Serrin," he replied.

The farmer walked slowly into the darkness, heading for the light spilling down onto the ramp in the southeastern corner. As she neared, more details became visible. The ramp, also perfectly smooth and made of the earth, went right up to the opening in the concrete ceiling, granting access to the warehouse floor. In the corner of the western wall across from the ramp was a large sliding metal door.

With no idea how to open the door and figuring that she had pressed her luck far enough, Haley decided that it was time to head back to the arcade. She turned back toward the cement stairwell and stepped into the dark once more but then stopped.

Haley could see shadows moving on the floor at the bottom of those stairs. Somebody was coming down, so she immediately turned around and ran up the ramp to the warehouse floor.

The ramp came up through the floor near the southern end of the building just inside the warehouse proper. The floor was cement, and the room was huge. Rows of shelves filled the area and held a variety of boxes and supplies. A metal staircase along the eastern wall made its way up to a skybox-style office room in the center of the storage facility. It had large windows, allowing for an excellent view of the warehouse floor.

The southern wall had an open overhead door on the left for forklifts to access the loading docks. A larger overhead door, big enough for a truck, was on the right side and closed. On the northern wall was a door that went to the administrative office.

Haley went through the forklift door. On the other side were four bays. The floor went out about seven feet and dropped off, making a ledge for loading and unloading trucks. The fourth bay to the right was level with the warehouse floor. Haley had seen the ramp going to the outside of this bay door from the road over the years, but this was the first time that she had seen the inside. She didn't know how to operate the overhead doors and had no time to figure them out. She turned and began to run across the warehouse to the other side.

As she passed the opening in the floor, Gary and Frank came running up the ramp.

"Get the door," Frank shouted while pointing toward the loading docks and then turned to chase Haley.

Gary ran through the forklift doorway and hit a button on the other side of the wall. The first bay door began to open as a vehicle approached. He then turned back into the warehouse to go after Haley.

There was a metallic cylindrical object about two and a half feet wide and a foot tall in the center of the floor. Haley jumped over it, spun around when she landed and launched a blast at her attacker.

"Whoa!" Frank exclaimed as he dove down an aisle, successfully dodging the blast.

Haley saw the door to the office as she neared the other end of the warehouse and began heading for it but stopped abruptly as someone opened it from the other side.

Her stomach dropped as two Harry look-a-likes came running through from the office. She turned to run and was face to face with Frank.

He smacked her right hand aside with his left, pushing it out to keep her potato gun pointed away while reaching with his right to grab her by the collar, but the quick and agile farmer turned with the push and ran down an aisle.

"Hey!" Frank shouted as he ran after her, not letting her get enough room to turn and aim.

She could hear more footsteps all around and sense the disharmonious vibes of two Archons among them. In a moment of either panic or brilliance, Haley jumped as high as she could and fired a blast straight down.

Frank ran right into it. "Ah, c'mon!" he shouted as his shell was blasted back. He stood up and wobbled from the damaged leg, but the farmer let loose one more blast before turning the corner to the next aisle.

Frank removed the visor to see his relief standing before him. He handed it to the other Cetatian and said, "She's all yours, Pal."

Haley was running back toward the center aisle when she heard a voice on the intercom system say, "She's in aisle five."

A Joey shell, inhabited by an Archon, was in the skybox office watching Haley's location.

Gary and another Joey, also piloted by an Archon, came in the aisle with her. She turned to see a couple of Harrys coming in the other end.

Even though the farmer knew it wasn't him, she felt sickened as she let blasts fly at these people who looked like her dad. She then quickly turned, releasing shots at Gary and the Archon, knocking them both back. She pivoted back to the Harrys and turned them to gel.

Haley lept forward before turning to fire, as she could feel that horrible energy from the Archon coming too close. Her blast took him out as she followed it up with another, ending Gary's shift.

"She hasn't come out from aisle five," announced the Archon in the skybox, and the sound of more footsteps could be heard in the rows around her.

Haley began to quickly climb up the shelves as a couple of Hanks came in from one side and a Joey with two Harrys on the other. They ran beneath her and also started climbing.

The sight of these people using her father's appearance was sickening to Haley. It angered her. It infuriated her! She looked down to see three of the five directly below her and had had enough. A scowl found its way onto her face as the energy coalesced, and she pounced.

The Archon in the skybox saw flashes of blue light as the shelves rattled a bit and a stray blast even shot upwards, shuddering a support beam. A few seconds later, an angry Haley climbed to the top shelf, stood up and glared at the Archon in the skybox window.

"Cleanup, aisle five!" she screamed as she blasted the plexiglass. The first shot rattled and cracked it. The second blew it clear out of the sill. Haley started across the shelf tops toward the skybox and could feel the aggravation from the Archon growing as she got closer. Then, it suddenly shifted to anxiety as his eyes popped wide, and he said over the speaker system, "We're out of time. We must end her now! Get the Hunters!"

As more people came around the shelves, they began to pull out strange-looking metal pistols. Her eyes widened, and she began leaping across the aisle tops as bolts of yellow energy zipped by. She jumped from one top shelf to another, quickly making her way toward the office.

The Joey shell started to call out her position again when feedback squealed from the speakers throughout the building, and the sound of fiddles started to play. As the music began, Haley noticed a sudden increase in the Archon's anxiety. She didn't know where the music came from, but at least he could no longer call out her position.

She saw a Joey climbing up the shelf ahead, so she stopped and sent a blast before he could raise his pistol.

He was knocked down as a Frank came up, and Haley didn't give him an opportunity either. Then more attackers came into the aisle above which she stood, and Haley had to hop down behind the shelves as they opened fire.

What are those space-laser things? she nervously wondered as she dropped to the floor.

The vocals in the music started, and it was the voice of Garth Brooks, but she didn't recognize the song. Haley ran to the end of the aisle and turned right toward the northern wall. She sent blasts down the remaining aisles as she ran, knocking over and gelling out some of her attackers. Haley made it to the corner and turned along the wall, sending blasts ahead while running for the office door. Her blasts hit their targets while Haley grabbed and turned the door handle. She opened, went through, then shut the door and turned the lock.

Haley turned to see another door across the office that went out to the lobby and moved quickly, knowing that the people chasing her would break through the lock any second. Then, the chorus kicked in, and so did the lobby door. With that kick came a wave of terror that washed over Haley as before her, radiating that intensity she sensed back at the arcade, stood a bald, bearded man.

CHAPTER 9
Interruptions

Haley went cold. She couldn't move, paralyzed by fear. The look in the man's eyes was intense. He began to move his right arm, and Haley glanced at his hand to see no energy pistol or imagined space-ray but a very real-looking Glock. She then looked back up into his eyes as the door behind her broke open. The bearded man lifted his eyes to the people coming in behind her and said, "Duck," while bringing up his arm.

Haley hit the ground and covered her ears as the bearded man fired shots at the shells coming in from the warehouse floor. She immediately noticed that this man's gun was much quieter than the one with which her dad would practice at the range. He made quick work of the invaders who were bottlenecked in the doorway as another man with longer hair and a goatee also came in from the lobby. He fired shots back out the door and went to shut it. He noticed the busted latch, grabbed a folding chair from next to a desk and wedged it under the handle.

"Clear the floor," said the bearded man, and his partner ran into the warehouse. He then got between Haley and the lobby door, holding up his gun as someone began slamming it from the other side.

Haley heard some commotion out on the warehouse floor and felt the nasty vibe of the Archon disappear. "Who are you guys?" she asked, but before any answer could be given, the lobby door split.

The old wood door cracked along the grain, and the chair buckled. Half of the door fell to the floor while the other half swung loosely on its hinges.

The man who broke through looked like a seven-foot-tall and very muscular version of Joey, followed by a similarly altered Hank.

The bearded man opened fire, but the bullets only lodged into the surface level of their skin. Some even fell back to the floor, leaving nasty-looking yellow welts. The two large men did not seem at all bothered by them.

Hank smirked and laughed a little, turned to Joey and said, "This might actually be fun."

"It's always fun," Joey enthusiastically said in return.

Haley stepped alongside the bearded man and let out a blast, landing a direct hit on Joey. He was knocked back a bit and grunted as he said, "I'm going to break that…" His words were interrupted by a blast to the face accompanied by another to Hank's. Now Joey was irritated. He and Hank began moving forward.

Haley turned her head to look up at the bearded man and noticed that his firearm began changing shape, seemed to move like fluid and merged into his clothing.

He clenched his fists, and Haley felt a swelling of energy from the bearded man when his hands suddenly erupted with blue and orange flames. The man jumped forward, closing the gap in a single leap and landed a wicked blow across Joey's face.

The punch added more to the damage left by Haley's blast, but Joey quickly countered with a powerful right jab. The bearded man turned to the left while leaning back, dodging the unexpectedly fast counter. He then grabbed Joey's arm and went to twist it into a lock, but this Joey shell was superhumanly strong and just hoisted the bearded man into the air. Joey threw his opponent across the room, and as soon as he did, ethereal kittens began slamming into him and Hank.

The blasts were doing damage, but not enough to stop them before they got within reach. She was about to turn and retreat when the bearded man came running back.

He threw a softball-sized orb of blue and orange light at Joey's face. Joey raised his arms to block it while the man closed the distance and kicked Joey hard in the solar plexus.

Haley fired again at Hank, doing more damage, but he was getting too close. She leaped backward onto a desk and let out another blast as Hank rushed forward. Then an orb of green and purple light zipped in, impacting Hank's throat.

Hank grabbed his own neck and stumbled, seeming a little disoriented, but quickly regained his senses in time to see the man with the longer hair flying toward him. In a splash of green and purple light, Hank was tackled into the wall.

Joey was absorbing enhanced blow after blow from the bearded man. He was a Hunter and no stranger to combat, but he could not keep up with the skill of the newcomer before him. The false body was worn, and Joey still tried to fight back, but the shell would no longer respond to his mental commands, and the Hunter had to reach up and remove his visor.

The long-haired man held up his arms as he turned, almost as if he were holding a baseball bat, and Haley felt a small surge of energy from him. A green orb of light, with swirls of purple, appeared and elongated from his hands. It shaped into a plasmatic-looking sledgehammer, and with a hard swing, he knocked Hank over near the desk. As soon as the Hunter hit the floor, Haley pounced.

In a burst of pale blue light, the farmgirl rebounded off of Hank and landed about six feet away. The fallen Hunter had turned to gel.

Just before the music faded out, Haley realized that she was hearing it come from the two men as well. When it seemed as if no one else was coming, the bearded man spoke, "Haley Starr," he said.

She looked at him and asked, "Who are you?"

He held out his identification and continued, "We're U.S. Marshals. I'm Chuck Gentry, and this is my partner, Logan O'Connor."

O'Connor nodded.

"Were you guys playing the music?" she asked.

"Yeah," Gentry replied. "It annoys the Archons and seems to keep him happy," he said, pointing at O'Connor. "And we need to go before more of 'em show up."

"That was definitely Garth Brooks, but I don't know that song," she said as they headed through the lobby.

"'Tearin' It Up.' It just came out," Logan said.

Haley shook her head, "No, it didn't. I would have known."

Logan looked into a clear rectangular object in his hand. "Oh…Umm…just wait eighteen days."

"Hey," started Gentry with a taunting smile, "Aren't you the one who insisted on no time-inappropriate music?" He looked through the main door, opened it up and checked the area. The Marshal then motioned for the others to move.

"It came out in ninety-eight," O'Connor grumbled as they stepped outside, "and the year's almost over. It's October here. Gimme a break."

Haley's eyes went wide, and she said, "Oh, no. You guys reek of a flux capacitor."

Logan's eyes seemed to light up a bit. He smirked and turned to Gentry, "Now I get it."

"Yeah," Gentry said with a slight laugh.

"Get what?" Haley asked.

"Never mind," both Marshals said in unison. Serious expressions had returned to their faces as they could hear a car rapidly approaching.

O'Connor said, "Looks like we gotta deal with a little more bull…"

"Hey!" Haley interrupted. Both Marshals turned toward her, looking stunned at her angry expression. "No swearing," she firmly stated.

No time for debate, the normally foul-mouthed Marshals turned back toward the parking lot entrance, guns drawn, as a Crown Victoria pulled in and chirped the tires, coming to a stop between them and the road.

Haley could feel the nasty Archon vibes emanating from the vehicle. She felt Gentry snap right back into that intense focus, and O'Connor was…very difficult to sense.

The car door opened, and a State Trooper calmly stepped out of the vehicle.

The Marshals did not lower their firearms.

He stood up straight, set his left hand on top of the open door and locked eyes with the Marshals as a smug smirk appeared on his face. "You two hillbillies are way out of your jurisdiction," said the false trooper.

Suddenly, Haley could clearly sense O'Connor's emotions, but they were hard to pin down jumble for just an instant. Then they all settled, and he seemed more in focus like that of Gentry.

"Ahnk-Hume, is that you?" O'Connor asked.

The false trooper's smirk widened into a big prideful grin. "In the flesh…almost," he answered.

"So, are these discount clones your idea?" Gentry asked.

"Yes," Ahnk-Hume answered. "And we have a great many of them at our disposal," he said with his usual smug smile.

O'Connor scoffed and glanced toward Gentry, "I told you we should have brought Remy and Gus."

Gentry shot him an aggravated look accompanied by a harsh shushing sound, and an embarrassed O'Connor dropped his eyes to the ground.

Haley felt Ahnk-Hume get giddy at the slip. But right after he did, O'Connor had a sense of satisfaction.

Chuck asked, "So who's The Hive answering to these days?"

Ahnk-Hume's smile widened once again as he said, "I now lead The Hive."

The empath noticed the sinking sensation in both of the Marshal's stomachs at the statement. But then they unexpectedly started laughing.

"You!?" O'Connor asked, chuckling in a bit of genuine disbelief. "Somebody lied on their application," he taunted.

"Yeah," Gentry said with a grin and looked directly at Ahnk-Hume. "Whose scales did you have to lick to pull off this con job?"

Haley could feel Ahnk-Hume becoming irritated from the Marshal's quips. Even more so, she could feel an intense hatred every time the Archon looked toward her. It felt…personal.

The Archon narrowed his eyes in anger but maintained a sinister grin. He said, "You two idiots came to this universe alone. You're in way over your heads."

"Maybe so," said O'Connor as they could hear more vehicles approaching, "but you know that annoying wait time to respawn during a video game?"

"No," said a confused-looking Ahnk-Hume.

"You do now," said Gentry, and he squeezed the trigger.

The bullet went right between the eyes, and the false trooper was instantly turned to gel. As they turned to move, O'Connor said to Gentry, "He's getting more unstable." Then the Marshal's emotions again faded from Haley's senses.

They all turned to run behind the building as a truck and two cars hopped the curb coming into the parking lot.

Everybody in the vehicles, ten altogether, immediately threw their doors open and came out with pistols raised.

Haley and Gentry went behind the building as O'Connor turned around and held up his left hand.

They ran past the broken bulkhead to see more opponents coming around the corner of the southern end.

Haley felt an intense gathering of energy from the Marshal when he shoved her toward the wall. The maintenance shed now shielding Haley from any fire. Chuck released a giant burst of blue and orange flames. The large orb of fire flew down to the other end, taking out the first two in one shot.

The attackers opened fire, sending bolts of yellow energy zipping toward O'Connor. Then the bolts all slammed to a stop against the protective energy field the Marshal had manifested. Green and purple light rippled out from where the bolts impacted the otherwise invisible wall.

This afforded O'Connor a couple of extra seconds to observe the scene. He detected no Archon energy but made certain that the rest of these people were all shells. Once he confirmed that none of them were truly present, he lifted his left hand a little higher. When he did, the ten assailants lifted about twenty feet into the air. The Marshal then closed his fist, and the group all pulled together into a mid-air heap.

He then lifted his right hand, and the two cars levitated, one on each side of, and level with, the group. O'Connor then opened his left hand and turned his palms toward each other. Some of those in the group were already turning to gel while, in the Second Density, Cetatians were removing their visors, understanding what was about to happen. The Marshal clapped his hands, and the group was crushed between the two cars.

Gentry moved quicker than they expected as he dodged their shots, and then he threw a rapid series of fiery blasts in return. The Marshal took three of them down while he and Haley heard the crash of the cars landing in the parking lot, accompanied by a shake in the ground. A shot then hit Gentry in the chest. He grunted as it staggered him back a step, but he seemed to absorb it without too much trouble.

The sleeve of his shirt started to ripple, and nanobots extended outward and around his right hand, forming back into his gun. He fired off some shots as O'Connor came around the corner. The bullets hit their marks, but more vehicles were heard approaching the building.

Then, more attackers came around both corners. Two enhanced Hanks were among those on the southern end and an enhanced Joey with some Franks and Hanks on the northern end, to which they were closer.

Gentry opened fire, but the two enhanced Hanks could absorb the gunshots and stayed to the front, shielding the others as they all moved forward.

O'Connor threw a hand up, and Haley felt the energy coalesce around them, but she did not know that it was a protective field. So, when Joey and the others raised their pistols, Haley panicked and looked for cover. She saw the vent opening in the ground that she had uncovered earlier and jumped in.

"Haley, no!" Gentry shouted.

O'Connor turned his head just in time to see her drop below the surface.

Haley threw her feet forward and the back of her rig against the shaft walls to stop her fall, but she couldn't get enough traction and only managed to slow her descent. "Oh, no," Haley cried as she slipped away from the daylight.

The Marshals kicked into high gear. Gentry released a massive stream of fire. Everyone on his end went down, except the Hanks, who sustained heavy damage. O'Connor telekinetically hoisted the Joey, Hanks and Franks off the ground and slammed them into gel smears on the brick wall. Gentry, with a couple large and fiery bursts, finished off the Hanks.

They both ran over to the ventilation shaft and saw there was no way their shoulders would fit. "Haley," they shouted down the shaft, but there was no response.

O'Connor attempted to figure out how far down she went, but a mystical barrier was in place and blocking his energetic senses. He could, however, detect a nervousness. A faint sense of isolation and dread, deep below where they stood. "She's scared," he told Gentry, "but I don't think she's hurt."

"Let's find another way down," he replied. Then he said, "Gus, Haley went underground. We're going in after her. No idea how long we'll be out of contact."

Just below the ears were little speakers in their collars, from which a baritone voice with a thick Texas accent responded.

"Copy that," Gus said. "For now, I'm gonna keep working on those strange readings."

"Sounds good," Gentry said back. "Remy, scout the area for now. And try not to engage."

"No promises," they heard Remy quip.

They then went to the broken bulkhead and started down. When they got to the bottom of the stairs and saw how dark the tunnel was, a slight hissing sound could be heard as the nanobots that made up their clothing began to reconfigure themselves and formed what looked like full-face motorcycle helmets. The insides of their visors went into a night vision display, allowing them a view of the area. They saw the cage-like lining along the tunnel walls and ceiling. In the center of the ceiling was a cylindrical object like the one Haley had jumped over in the warehouse. They could also see the ramp and the door at the other end.

The Marshals made their way down and went to the door. It had no handle or any obvious way in which they could open it. They began running a scan, and the head-up displays in their visors showed that their coms were attempting to sync into a system. A few seconds later, 'access acquired' read inside their visors, and the door slid open to reveal a cargo elevator lift. They stepped inside, the door shut, and the elevator began to descend.

The inside of the shaft was lit, and the Marshals' helmets receded. They both took a deep breath and exhaled, worried about the young farmer trapped alone.

O'Connor suddenly said with a bit of a smirk, "All her blasts look like kittens."

Gentry laughed a little and said, "I know, right?"

CHAPTER 10
Brave New Underworld

She was sliding straight down, and it became too dark to see. Then there was a bend in the vent, and Haley continued sliding at a forty-five-degree angle. About ten seconds after that, she slid into a sitting position at the bottom. Haley couldn't see a thing, and all she could hear was the humming and rushing of the air that was pumped through. Her heart was beating faster while she tried not to panic.

As her breathing became rapid and shallow, Haley reached out to grab anything to steady herself. Her hand came in contact with the shaft wall and slid forward a bit to find some kind of edge. She wanted to grab on as she tried to steady her breath, but the edge was sharp, and she almost cut her hand. Her eyes moistened with tears, and she wiped them with her left forearm. She then opened her eyes to find that they had adjusted a bit.

Haley's breathing steadied as she became more focused on the hint of light she could see. Although very dim, she could tell that the sharp edge she had grabbed was a circular opening from the bottom of this shaft into the side of another, which ran horizontally. Haley leaned forward, turned her head to the left and found the source of light. It was coming in through a vent on the side of the shaft.

The farmer, though still frightened, pulled her work gloves out of her front pouch. After fumbling with them for a moment, she got them in the correct hands and then crawled forward to investigate. It was a little cramped, but she was able to make her way to the vent opening without any trouble.

Haley found that the opening had no cover, and she slowly peeked her head out to look around.

The building structure, from what she could see, appeared to be made of concrete. She was near the arched ceiling, and a catwalk ran along the outside of the vent shaft. A large pipe and various conduits ran the length of the long room. When Haley looked down, she could see that she was in a large industrial corridor.

The empath couldn't sense anyone around, so she climbed out onto the catwalk to get a better look. The walk extended ten feet to her right and about twenty to her left. The pale lights, some of which were mounted beneath her walkway, would flicker sporadically and add to the uneasy vibe. Haley walked to one end and then the other. It seemed as if the walk had continued further in both directions at one time, but now the only path available to her was down to the corridor floor.

Isolated in a strange place, Haley had never before felt so alone. She again found herself struggling to keep calm. She had no direction, no one to tell her which way to go or what needed to be done next. No one to let her know what particular problem to solve. No one.

Haley was on her own.

Two Cetatians in Joey shells were standing on either side of a cargo elevator door. They were wearing uniforms that looked like that of law enforcement, and the two Proctors were assigned to this post just a few moments ago due to an incident that was taking place in the warehouse above. A control panel was on the wall next to the elevator door, and one of them noticed the change in display.

"Hey," he said and pointed to the panel. "The elevator's moving." He then started tapping the panel's surface.

They were both informed that no one was to be coming down. The Cetatian tried to stop the elevator but quickly found that he was locked out.

One of them punched their code into a wall-mounted intercom and reported what was happening, then they leveled their pistols toward the door and waited.

As the elevator descended, a tone sounded from Gentry's phone. He held up the clear rectangular object and the surface of it became a display. He then looked back up and said to O'Connor, "They know where we are. Someone just tried to shut down the elevator."

O'Connor closed his eyes for a second and then said, "Yep, picking up a couple bits of tension right below us."

The nanos in their clothing began to move as the Marshals conjured their firearms, and they both aimed toward the door.

Haley was overwhelmed and felt hopeless. Tears were streaming as she sobbed. *I can't do this*, she thought. *It's not fair!*

She continued to think about all the events leading up to this moment. The look-a-likes that had chased her in the barn and then more in the park. They almost got her both times. Then the crowd in the warehouse. Thinking about this added to her sense of dread as they were actually trying to kill her.

Then a simple thought came, *But they didn't.*

This prompted Haley to start looking at the previous events a little differently. Many foes had attacked her today and, though they came close, couldn't stop her. In fact, she had defeated many of them.

Haley was still frightened, but a new feeling started to grow inside. A feeling that maybe she could handle more than she thought. A sense of confidence.

After a moment, Haley again managed to collect herself. She wiped her eyes and realized that, despite how overwhelming this was, she needed to figure this out herself. "What would Mom do?" she silently asked.

She then looked to the floor below, took a deep breath and let it out with a long sigh. There was no sign of anyone around, so she hopped off the catwalk and down to the floor.

Haley landed lightly on her feet and stood up straight, taking a good long look around. The corridor walls and the floor were concrete, and the pale, bleak look of the place was downright depressing. A little way down in one direction, it looked like the floor just stopped, but the walls continued.

Curious, she walked over to the odd sight and slowly approached the edge. A twenty-foot section of the floor looked as if it were just cut out and removed. There was a square lift platform that rode along a track, which was attached to the wall on her left and reached the corridor below.

Another lift was on the same wall but at the other end of the opening. Both lifts had a control panel mounted next to them on the wall, but Haley had no idea how to operate it. Also jutting out from the same wall were some chunks of the old floor. Haley looked down to the lower corridor. It was also dimly lit and missing a section of the floor just up ahead. Haley, taking a good look around, tried to figure out which way she should go.

The elevator doors opened, the two guards fired their pistols, and the bolts smacked harmlessly into O'Connors protective field. Once the guards stopped shooting, Logan dropped the field, and both Marshals squeezed their triggers.

As the shells gelatinized, Gentry walked over, picked up the bolt pistols, one in each hand, and fried them.

The Marshals looked around to see the corridor in which they stood. It was made of concrete. Some sections were metal, and they stretched off in either direction.

"They know where we are right now, so we gotta move," Chuck said. He then asked, "Can you sense her right now?"

"Yeah. She's further down a bit. Not sure how far," O'Connor answered.

They looked back and forth at the two ways they could go. "Let's each take a direction and try to rendezvous back here in two hours," Gentry said.

O'Connor nodded and began to glance around as he said, "More are coming."

"Then it's time to go," responded Chuck.

Things calmed down around the warehouse. Although there were still some Cetatians in the building, there was almost no activity outside.

Almost.

Stepping out from the woods was an orange and white cat. This cat had seen thirteen years and many close calls. His tail was crooked, there was a scar on the left side of his head, and he favored his back left foot.

As the cat approached the ventilation shaft where Haley slipped away, he was met by another cat. This one was a black short-hair who wore a pink flea collar.

The two cats looked at each other and then turned their heads when they heard the rustle of leaves to see more cats coming their way.

The orange cat then turned toward the shaft and jumped in. About fifteen seconds later, the black cat jumped in. One by one, the felines made their way into the shaft and then spread out through the ventilation system.

Elizabeth was a little tired. She was moving bursts of air around the room when she started to feel light-headed. The young mystic had never deliberately manipulated energy before, but now she had been doing it for over an hour.

Neil had her sit down while he went to the counter and got a Snickers bar. "Here ya go," he said when he came back to the break room.

"Thanks," Elizabeth replied as she reached up and accepted the snack.

"Relax for now," Neil said, "and we'll see how you're feeling in about twenty minutes."

Then, they both felt the energy shift a bit as Trinket hopped onto the arm of the couch and sat down. Neil and Elizabeth both looked at her, and Bast began to speak. "How are you two doing," she asked.

Neil shook his head with a bit of a chuckle as he replied, "I've never seen anything like it." He and Elizabeth then enthusiastically told Bast all that the young mystic had so far accomplished. The Egyptian goddess' surprise was evident on Trinket's face.

Neil then asked, "Any word on Haley?"

Bast could feel the nervousness emanating from both of them when Neil asked. The goddess was not happy with the news she now had to deliver.

"Haley has gone below ground through a warehouse vent," she informed the pair.

They both felt sick at the news. Elizabeth began to visibly shake in fear for her friend. Before either of them could respond, Bast continued, "But she has found allies."

"Who?" Elizabeth asked.

"Four men have followed the invaders to our universe, and they are law enforcement. Two of them had come to Haley's defense and have now gone underground in search of her."

This news did offer a bit of hope to the mystics, but it did not make them any more comfortable with what was happening. Bast then informed them of the battle she was able to observe in and behind the warehouse, but she still could not look beyond the barrier just below the building.

As she told the story, the other two listened while going through a rollercoaster of excitement, fear and hope. They probably would have enjoyed such a telling if Haley's life wasn't on the line, but they were extremely thankful to learn that she was not completely on her own.

"Is there any way we can contact them?" Neil asked.

"After I rest from this interaction, I'll try to communicate with them directly, but for now…" Trinket then turned toward Elizabeth, "how are you feeling?"

"A little better," the young mystic said.

"Good," Bast replied. Trinket then turned a little to face both of them. "When you start practicing again, I suggest focusing on protection."

Neil nodded in agreement.

"I must rest. After that, I'll speak with one of these Marshals and see what more we can learn." Bast said.

"Anything we can do for Haley?" Elizabeth asked.

"Keep practicing," both Bast and Neil said in unison.

Derek Sahmbo entered the office earlier to research the Archon's information on Starr. This man had earned the position of Hunter-Ralt, and as such, all other Hunters are subordinate to him. No one disputed his title as his skill and ability had elevated the Hunter's status amongst his peers to that of a legend.

Hunters varied widely in their skill sets, but all were excellent trackers and very proficient fighters. Sahmbo had focused on and sharpened four skills in particular. The lead Hunter's expertise in physical combat, investigation and strategic planning carried the man far in his career, but his true talent, the thing that made him so feared, was his mastery of profiling. The other Hunters, often with great respect, would whisper to each other that "Sahmbo knows what you're thinking before you do."

He sat down at a glass top desk. It looked simple enough but with the tap of a finger, a holographic display emitted from the surface. Researching this woman from another universe, he could see that this alternate-future version of the young girl was quite formidable. The Archon that had tried restraining Starr in the park said she struggled against them with the strength of an adult man.

According to the Archon records, Starr was superhumanly strong. She had easily thrown people twice her size and ripped a car door off its hinges. He watched a recording of her as she, with a loud grunt, rolled a very large pick-up truck onto its side.

The strain on her face was evident, but it only took her about three seconds to accomplish. She was able to use her energy manipulation abilities for a variety of effects and was a competent hand-to-hand fighter, especially with a staff. She had also been known to sometimes move in bursts of speed too fast for the eye to follow. For a brief time, this was thought to be teleportation.

As Sahmbo combed through the information, he began to look at those she had worked alongside to get a better idea of who she was or who she may become.

Starr and Gentry started a private detective agency called Mystified Investigations. They worked alongside three others, all of whom had energetic abilities, and they operated primarily as consultants to a team of Marshals. He found it strange that the Archons had no information on Haley or Elizabeth that predated their year of 2018. Sahmbo continued through the information and found his curiosity piqued.

"U.S. Space Force?" he read aloud. A few seconds later, the Hunter's interest grew further as he read the words, "United States Stellar Marshals."

He poured through the information to assess who they were, what they could do and the tactics they were known to employ. Most importantly, he wanted to know how Starr and her associates thought.

Then, an alert came to his desk, and when he opened the comm, a holographic image of Ahnk-Hume's true face appeared.

Haley jumped, grabbed the ledge, pulled herself up to the surface and stood. It was another chunk of old flooring that stuck out from the wall. She was using these as platforms to make her way between the different floor levels. Haley had gone through a huge room full of large pipes with all sorts of plumbing and pumps. The noise of the pumps was quite obnoxious to Haley, so she covered her ears and ran through the pump station. After that, she went down a couple floors and then back up to a different area.

She began down another corridor when she heard a horrible noise. It sounded like somebody was having an asthma attack and choking on their own mucus. The awful sound actually made Haley feel like she was struggling to breathe, then she heard the sound of tapping. A couple of seconds later, both the tapping and gurgling sounds stopped.

What is that? she thought. The empath reached out with her senses but could feel nothing.

The tapping sounds returned, and she looked ahead to see something that was about the size of a large dog running down the corridor and heading straight for her. It had green scaly skin, a long-spiked tail and nasty sharp-looking teeth. The creature had large claws on all four feet, which made the tapping sound as it moved. The thing had no mind or consciousness, so there was nothing for Haley to sense.

This strange beast charging straight at Haley left her petrified in fear for half a second, then she snapped her head clear and fired off a blast. The creature stumbled a bit from the concussive burst, and some damage was evident on its face and shoulder, but it kept on coming.

"Ahh!" Haley shouted in fear as she fired again. The blast hit the creature, but it still did not go down.

The beast, with a gurgling snarl and its claws out, lunged right for her, but Haley dodged to the side, barely avoiding what could have been a devastating slash. She let loose with another shot, hitting the creature, and it turned to gel.

Taking a minute, Haley tried to catch her breath and steady her nerves. The very sight of that beast was the stuff of nightmares, but after regaining her calm, she returned to searching for an exit.

There were some doors throughout the corridors, and Haley had looked into a few of them. The farmer was surprised to find perfectly normal and working light switches just inside. The rooms looked like abandoned offices or labs, but they didn't lead anywhere else. So, she continued searching for another way to move upward, which she found at the end of the corridor where the ceiling was cut away, and she began to climb.

As she made her way up through the opening, Haley found that she was in a large, poorly-lit vertical shaftway. Seeing a door up just a couple levels, Haley continued from ledge to ledge, heading toward the potential exit. She was grateful when she reached the door as the next ledge upward was out of her reach.

The door was made of a thick and heavy metal, and the handle looked more like a large lever. Haley grabbed hold and pulled, but the handle didn't budge.

"Now what?" she asked herself, not at all interested in backtracking. She looked at the handle and thought for a moment. "I think I'm pulling it the right way," she quietly said.

Haley decided to give it another try, grabbed on, and started to pull. It wasn't moving, but she leaned in, grunted and gave it everything she had. The handle moved slightly, and some rusty dust fell down to the chunk of floor. Another moment of rest, and she tried again. After some more grunting, the handle finally complied, and she managed to unlatch the door.

"Phew," she said while trying to catch her breath. She recovered her wind and pushed the heavy door open to see nothing but darkness beyond. Haley couldn't see or sense anybody around, so she stepped through the door and tried waiting a moment for her eyes to adjust.

No luck. This place was too dark, and the dim light that did come in through the door revealed nothing. She had no idea how big or small this room could be. Feeling defeated, she turned to leave and find another way. As she stepped back out to the vertical area, Haley looked at the potato gun on her arm, and her eyes widened as she got an idea. "Why didn't I think of this in the ductwork earlier?"

She turned and stepped back into the dark room, raised her arm and gathered her energy. The blue glow began to emit from the barrel, and she intended to use it as a flashlight.

While it did provide some light, the glow seemed to just highlight where Haley was standing in a large dark area, and she felt extremely exposed. She dissipated her energy and turned to find another way.

O'Connor threw one of his opponents into the other, followed by a couple of energy blasts, turning them to gel. They were responding to the call from the guards at the elevator but were quickly dispatched when they ran into the Marshal, who had just come down from the corridor above.

Another couple of guards came running around the corner, and O'Connor jumped toward them. The guards were surprised when he kept moving through the air. The Marshall flew straight into them and slammed them both into the wall while a Hunter in an enhanced Joey shell arrived.

While Logan was dealing with the two guards, the Hunter pulled out a small device and hit a button. When he did, a large blast door began sliding out of the wall, closing off the Marshal's exit.

O'Connor turned around to see the blast door seal shut and the Hunter standing in front of it. "You might want to move," the Marshal said.

The Hunter stood there and smiled as if he were taunting O'Connor. "You first," said the Hunter.

"Okay," Logan said as he waved his hand forward. When he did, the Proctor, who had snuck in behind him and was lining up a shot, suddenly went flying forward, past Logan and crashed into the Hunter. O'Connor then conjured his firearm and put a shot through the guard. The next couple of shots hit the Hunter, but he was as resistant to the bullets as the others in these shells.

O'Connor held his hands close to each other in front of him and gathered his energy. A purple light with swirls of green appeared between his palms. The light elongated vertically and then split as he pulled his hands apart, forming into two plasmatic-looking machetes. By the time the Hunter had stood back up, O'Connor was moving like a blur, and the telekinetic blades quickly turned his opponent into gel.

The Marshal dissipated his energy, and the two machetes lost their form and faded away. He walked up to the blast door and sensed a mystical binding was in place. "Figures," he unhappily said. There seemed to be all manner of bindings and wards on the walls in this facility, making it pretty much impossible to energetically sense beyond whatever room in which one stood.

He checked through the clothing left by the Hunter and did find the control device. Logan hit the button and waited a few seconds as nothing happened. He clicked it a few more times. Nothing. So, Logan pulled out his phone and scanned the blast door, but it appeared that the Archons had some new encryptions, and he couldn't bypass the security.

Logan sensed into the mystical barrier and realized that he could adjust his own vibration to counteract the binding spell placed on the blast door. Then he could telekinetically rip the door from its place, but this was a potent binding and would take a while.

O'Connor also knew the Archons had a habit of ripping places apart and retooling them. He had no idea how the structure of this facility had been altered and compromised. The last thing he wanted to do was cause a collapse and bury the people he was trying to save under a pile of rubble. He shook his head, knowing that it would take too long and wasn't worth the risk, so he recorded whatever data his device could glean to analyze and process. Logan was hopeful that Gus' programs would adapt to the encryptions, and he would be able to open the door when he came back.

He then turned to continue his search for Haley and the other townsfolk.

CHAPTER 11
Take Another Look

Gentry was walking down the corridor after eliminating a few more guards, looking for a way to the lower levels, when he felt a vibration in his pocket. He reached in and pulled out his phone, surprised to see he had contact with his ship.

"Gus, Remy, can you guys hear me?" Chuck asked over the com.

"I read you," came Remy's reply, followed by confirmation from Gus.

The Marshal's phone had been scanning and mapping as he went. Gentry immediately marked his current location on the map displayed on his screen.

"Are you underground?" Gus asked.

"Yeah," Chuck responded. "I'm standing in a cement corridor. I can't believe we've got a connection."

"Looks like you've found a kink in the armor. Note that location!" Gus said enthusiastically.

"Already have," Chuck said back. The map data was uploaded to the others, which were just a couple of corridors so far. He also informed them about splitting up to search and the planned rendezvous time. "How are things looking up there?" he asked.

"Looks like everything's calmed down around the warehouse," Remy said. "Still some activity around the Town Hall. Nobody's gone near the arcade."

"Good," Chuck said.

"The vents behind the diner are now spewing crud like a New Jersey smokestack," Remy reported as he could see the plumes start to rise from his position.

"Oh yeah?" Chuck responded. "And how many people are eating there?"

"I haven't seen anyone there at all," Remy answered while conjuring his helmet. He looked through his visor at the smoke rising up to meet the breeze, and his scanners started analyzing the particulate. What Remy could see was displayed on the screen of Chuck's phone as well as Gus' monitor back at the ship.

"Trash incinerator. Must be the exhaust vent for that complex," said Gus. "And I think I've figured out that energy reading coming from the Town Hall."

"What have you got?" Gentry inquired.

"We gave off an energy burst when we ported into this universe. The energy from the Town Hall is the same except, instead of a burst, it's a low-intensity constant."

"Are you saying that they're keeping the door to our universe propped open?" Gentry asked.

"I think so, but it wouldn't be open wide enough to move anything through," Gus answered.

"That's gotta be a huge drain on their power supply," Chuck stated. "Why would they do that?"

"It would be," said Gus. "And the only explanation I can think of is that they don't know how to navigate omnispace. This might be their tether."

"Keep digging," said Gentry, "and I gotta get moving."

"Good luck," the Marshal heard from both his teammates and then resumed his search. The signal faded after moving just a couple of steps.

Remy was observing the activity around the Town Hall. He was familiar with this town in his own universe and had already found some striking differences.

Even though the topography was, for the most part, identical, the town borders were much more constricted. In Remy's universe, Columbia was about twenty-two square miles with a population of more than five thousand. Here, the town was much smaller, with less than two hundred residents.

The roads and buildings were in different places. The Town Hall before Remy looked just like the one in his universe, but the location he was familiar with would be outside the town borders here. Also, the well-known sign that read "YEOMANS HALL" was absent.

The strangest thing to him was the county names of Windham and Tolland were reversed, making Columbia part of Windham.

On top of that was the time period. It was the nineties, and his local counterpart, if he had one in this universe, would be two years old.

The Marshal watched as some people came out of the building and made their way to a couple of box trucks. They climbed into the cabs, started the vehicles and took a right out of the parking lot, heading toward the north.

Even though Chuck and Logan had attempted earlier, Remy held up his phone and tried to get some scans. He couldn't get any readings from inside the building, which wasn't a surprise. The Archons were practiced at shielding their activities from probing sensors. He also couldn't detect anything energetically as there were mystical bindings on the walls. Again, not a surprise. He figured that the doors and windows would likely be physically reinforced as well.

Secluded in the woods behind the Town Hall, Remy reached into a pouch, retrieving what looked like a coin. It was about the size and color of a silver dollar but had the image of a bike stamped onto the surface. He tossed it onto the ground, and the nanobots began collecting mass from the surrounding area. In a couple of minutes, it would gather enough material and configure itself into a dirt bike. The Marshal had done this twice earlier in other locations, having them ready to go at a moment's notice.

He decided to head north and follow the trucks. He also wanted to make sure that they stayed away from the arcade. The Marshals knew that there were still two people in there that had managed to avoid detection from the Archons, and they were certain that one of them was Elizabeth.

Remy couldn't help but think about how strange this entire situation was. Ten-year-old versions of Haley and Elizabeth. From his perspective, they were women in their thirties and amongst his very few friends who could actually keep up with him in parkour. They had gone on their weekly run two days ago.

The others would sometimes join Haley, Elizabeth, and Remy, although they had to "cheat." Gus and Chuck would often use the thrusters in their PJs to boost their movements and Logan, his telekinesis. The others from

Mystified Investigations would sometimes join them too, but they also would use their abilities to run the course.

Haley and Elizabeth, on the other hand, actually kept up using balance and agility. Remy would also activate the binder in his PJs, negating his own abilities and forcing him to rely on his athleticism. Although, he did have to use his thrusters a time or two when he got sloppy and missed a step.

Even though Remy would pick on the others about using their abilities for the run, he didn't really care. He was just happy that they would come along. The more, the merrier because Remy loved a good adventure, and he loved his job. A job he was grateful to have, considering that he was technically too young to qualify for the position.

The Marshal took to the trees and continued past the back of the warehouse. He smiled as he thought about when they would take their runs into the woods. That's where Haley usually would be able to pull away from him. Even though Remy was a little more agile than Haley, her smaller size afforded her more maneuverability amongst the branches and limbs.

He moved around the back of the grocery store. The two box trucks were backed up to the delivery docks behind the building. Remy figured they were loading up more supplies and decided to pass by the arcade.

A few moments later, the Marshal approached the strip mall and held up his phone. The bindings on the walls stopped his energetic senses, but the scanners in his device showed two people still inside. One, about five feet and the other, over six. The Marshals had searched through some records earlier and saw that the business was owned and operated by a man named Neil Portman. Remy had heard Haley and Elizabeth mention the name Neil on occasion and wondered if this could be him.

He wanted to go speak to them, but he also knew that the fewer people that the Marshals had to interact with, the cleaner they could keep things.

Elizabeth took to binding just as easily as she tuned in to the elements. Neil had taken a crystal that he could sense and placed it in a cabinet. It was only a couple of moments before he could no longer feel the crystal's presence. She was quickly removing the binding and putting it back into place with almost no effort. She was doing it so well that Neil, after carefully looking out the back door and then the front windows, dropped the bindings on the arcade walls and had Elizabeth put them back into place.

"Very good," Neil said with a smile. "Now, I want you to think about when Bast was here. Think of how her energy felt, and then focus on your bindings. Reach out with your intentions and adjust the field. You want to allow her energy to come through."

Elizabeth concentrated as she fine-tuned her energy in the protective barriers on the walls. Neil was very focused as well, sensing the energy to confirm that she was successful. He smiled and nodded in satisfaction a moment later. "Excellent," he said. "I'm going to grab a couple bottles of water. I'll be right back."

"Okay," Elizabeth responded, sounding a little distant as Neil went out to the vending machine on the arcade floor.

While waiting, she looked back to the rock. It was still bugging her. She felt it so clearly but just couldn't seem to interact with it. Elizabeth, despite her unbelievable progress, was becoming quite frustrated.

No, she thought to herself as she felt her frustration growing. *It's not the rock. It's knowing Haley's out there and I can't help her.*

Elizabeth's aggravation increased as she tried to focus on the rock as a distraction from her worries, but the frustration of the rock not moving combined with her concerns for Haley just sparked her rage. She concentrated, gritting her teeth. She sensed the energy so strongly that Elizabeth felt like her entire field matched the vibe.

Nothing.

Reaching the boiling point, Elizabeth spun around. With something between a shout and a grunt, she threw a left punch into the back door just as Neil walked back into the room.

She hit it hard and then stood there with her head hanging down. Breathing rapidly from the adrenaline and angry tears in her eyes, Elizabeth was holding her fist against the door, afraid to move it as she expected the painful throbbing to start. It didn't.

After a couple of seconds, she lifted her watery eyes and looked over at her fist against the door. After a sniffle, Elizabeth slowly pulled her hand away to see two dents in the metal from her knuckles. Then she looked at her hand. It didn't hurt at all and showed no sign of the impact. She looked back up to the dents, and her jaw dropped. She called out, "Neil, I'm sorry."

Elizabeth jumped when she heard Neil's voice behind her, "I'm right here. You don't have to shout."

She was making her way back through the corridor. Haley was looking for another way up but, so far, had found nothing. There was scaffolding by some ductwork that she had seen on her earlier transit, but it looked too small for her to fit.

With her options appearing to dwindle, Haley sighed with a shrug and figured, "Why not?" She walked over to the metal ladder mounted on the wall and climbed up to the scaffolding.

As she stepped onto the platform, Haley could clearly see that there was no way she could fit into these small vents, so she sat down and let her legs hang off the side while taking a moment to think.

Haley was paying attention to her surroundings, just like her mom taught her and had been keeping a mental map. She had explored in one direction since she crawled out of the vent, and there were at least two corridors that continued in the other direction. "I guess it's time to check out the other tunnels," she quietly said.

Before coming down from the scaffolding, Haley first reached out with her other senses. She couldn't energetically sense anything beyond the immediate area of the corridor. She could, however, sense others empathically from all directions, but none of it felt close. Haley wondered how many people were in here and if any of them could be her dad.

Then she felt a spike of adrenalin with a surge of fear, and it was getting stronger. And closer!

Haley focused in on that feeling and then began to hear those horrible snarls echoing down the corridor. The empath looked down to the floor and saw a black cat with a pink flea collar running underneath her and three of those creatures chasing it. Her eyes went wide with horror, and she shouted, "No!"

Without even thinking, Haley jumped off the scaffolding as the creatures turned back toward her voice. She let out four blasts as she dropped toward the floor, and three of them hit the creature closest to her, turning it to gel. She landed on the floor as the cat ran into some ductwork.

The other two creatures ran straight for her. Haley hit the one in front of her with a blast, but it kept coming. The creature, claws extended, lunged at her as she quickly jumped straight up.

As the creature's leap carried it beneath Haley, she pounced. Her feet connected with the beast's back, and the burst of energy she released bounced her back upward, turning the creature to gel.

She released a few more shots on her way back down, hitting the final creature once. When she landed, Haley hit the mindless beast with another shot as it lunged for her. She dove to the side, releasing a final blast and gelled the beast.

As she caught her breath, Haley felt a rush of adrenaline, but it was different. It was invigorating! Like the first time she had solved a Rubik's Cube. Then her mind snapped back to the situation. "Kitty!" she suddenly said and turned to the vent where the cat had taken cover.

Haley, still able to feel the nervous cat, walked over to the ductwork and knelt down, bringing her face to the small opening. "Kitty?"

Squeaks was an indoor-outdoor cat who lived in the neighborhood around the corner from the church. She was an excellent mouser and made sure her humans knew it by often bringing home "presents." She let out a soft but high-pitched "Meow" while moving toward Haley.

The farmer couldn't see a thing in the dark ductwork until a pair of amber eyes emerged from the opening. "Meow," Squeaks said and then backed away into the shadows.

"Kitty?" Haley again asked as she pressed her face up to the vent, trying to see the cat. "Kitty?"

Then she felt it. The sense of zeroing in on a small sound and peering into a dark corner. The anticipation of bursting into sudden action. The pride and exhilaration of a successful hunt.

She felt the energy coalesce in her eyes as they adjusted, and she was able to see the cat but in a silvery-purple hue. Haley realized that she could see the inside of the ductwork. She could see!

When she leaned away from the vent, her vision adjusted back to normal. Squeaks, who was now completely calm, stepped out of the vent. Haley didn't think she had seen this cat before, and there was no tag on the collar.

The short-haired cat rubbed against Haley's leg as she trilled, and the empath smiled, petting Squeaks on the head. Then, with her tail in the air, Squeaks turned around, said one last, "Meow," and stepped into the ductwork. Haley could hear the slight sounds of the cat's feet as she trotted away into the ventilation system.

The young farmer couldn't believe it. "I've got night vision!" Haley said to herself with a smile. And she knew exactly what to do with it.

The fluid drained from the vat, and the clear cylinder retracted into the base. The shell opened its eyes and stood up. Ahnk-Hume stretched all four arms out and wiggled his twenty-four fingers. "Ah," he said with a smile as he gave the wings a couple of good flaps. "Much better."

When he took a few steps away, the clear cylinder raised from the base and the vat automatically refilled with fluid for a new shell to begin developing.

Ahnk-Hume knew he had to eat soon, but these new shells did not need to consume nearly as much as the previous kind. All the shells were now being made with this new method.

Ahnk-Hume looked around the lab. He had received a message from Kone that there was something he needed to see, but the Cetatian leader would not specify.

Nokitahm, one of the Archons who ported to this universe with Ahnk-Hume, was approaching with some clothes. He had discarded the Mary shell and was now in one that matched his physiology.

"Nokitahm, do you know what this is about?" Ahnk-Hume asked.

"I do," the other Archon replied. With a bit of a smile, he motioned in the direction they were to head. The two walked through the lab and headed toward an area that Ahnk-Hume had not visited for over a month. They walked past a row of new mindless creatures being grown for security patrols. The Drakel smiled as he thought of how those claws could tear through a person.

A section of the lab used for employing and testing new methods is where they were met by the Cetatian Uniralt. And he was there in person.

Kone was five foot eight, barrel-chested and had thick muscular arms. He, as usual, was nicely dressed. His shirt was gray with a black sports coat over the top and a red tie perfectly in place with the gig line. His pants were also black, and his shoes, which looked very expensive, were polished.

He kept his head shaved, and the color line of his skin was clearly visible. His face was pale, but the skin on top of his head was a grayish-blue. This pigmentation ran down the back of his neck and torso. The rest of his skin was the same pale white as his face.

The color lines for Cetatians were quite varied. Some were a bit of a gradual fade from one to the other, and some were a speckled pattern. Occasionally, people have been recognized as part of a family tree by the patterns in their color line. Some, like Kone's, were a solid line, where one color ended and the other began.

The Uniralt was smiling, and it appeared to be genuine. Kone was not one for becoming friends, nor was he one for empathy. But he was one for appreciation, and Ahnk-Hume had brought him some major advantages.

"I'm sure you're wondering what this is about, so I'll get right to it," he began in his deep voice as he turned toward a large covered vat. "My geneticists have been working with the Hive and managed another breakthrough a couple of weeks back. And now, we've confirmed its viability." He motioned to the technician, and the curtain was pulled to the side.

Ahnk-Hume was pleased with what he saw, and the smile on his face made that quite obvious. There, in the vat, was a duplicate of Ahnk-Hume's real body. The four arms, the wings and the tail. All ten feet and four inches of it! Even the coloration, the spots…a nearly perfect duplicate.

"Wow!" Ahnk-Hume exclaimed. "That is an impressive shell!" he said, becoming invigorated just by the sight.

Kone stood there smiling, his hands clasped behind his back. "This is not a shell," he said.

Ahnk-Hume turned to Kone for an explanation.

"As I have said, we've been working with the Hive. And together, we've found that you can permanently transfer consciousness to a viable body. This is not a shell. It's a true clone. An empty vessel."

Kone continued, "We've taken the liberty of making an upgrade. As you can see, this body exists in the human plane unaided."

Ahnk-Hume's smile grew bigger with everything he was hearing, but the words that came next were pure music to his ears.

"And its most important feature," Kone said as he began tapping his index finger against his temple, "it comes with all the working parts."

Ahnk-Hume was so amazed by what he had just heard that this level of excitement was a new experience for him. His lower hands clasped together, and he began rubbing his upper palms as he said, "Complete with Wi-Fi!"

Kone turned to Ahnk-Hume and asked, "What's that?"

CHAPTER 12
Ups and Downs

"Not even a little bit," Elizabeth said as she looked over her hand and wiggled her fingers. She had fully expected to be hurt by the punch, which is why she swung with her left. The young mystic had a strategic mind and, even when angry, tended to think a bit ahead. Though her emotions would sometimes lead her to make a foolish choice, she usually wasn't completely reckless about how she did it. Elizabeth didn't want to lose the use of her right, but now she was flabbergasted at her hand, seemingly unaffected by the hard punch into the metal door.

Neil brushed a couple fingers across the two dents in the door. He then, with a look of curiosity, turned to Elizabeth and asked, "Can you do it again?"

Unsure of whether or not she could, the Elizabeth shrugged. She turned back toward the door, made a fist with her left hand, held it against the metal surface and bumped her knuckles against the metal a couple of times. And then, Elizabeth drew her fist back.

Neil held his hands out and suddenly said, "Just…don't hurt yourself."

Elizabeth looked up at him and nodded, but she thought, *Wouldn't be the first time.*

Throwing a half-hearted punch, Elizabeth thumped her knuckles on the door. She felt the impact and knew that if she had swung like last time, it would've hurt. Elizabeth turned back to Neil and said, "Whatever it was, it's not there now."

Neil replayed things in his head. When he had walked back in, Elizabeth was obviously angry, and emotions can significantly affect one's energy work, but there was certainly more to the moment than that. What were you thinking about when you hit the door?"

With a sigh, Elizabeth said, "About Haley." And then the frustration made itself evident on her face. "I should be with her."

Neil placed his right hand on her left shoulder and looked into her eyes. "I understand how you feel," he said gently. "I'm worried sick about her too, and I'm kicking myself for letting her go back out there. But the police are there to help her, and from what Bast described, they know what they're doing. So, for now, let's let the professionals do their job. And let's do ours, so if the time comes for us to help Haley, we can."

Elizabeth dropped her eyes to the floor, then lifted them back up to meet Neil's and nodded. "Okay," she said with another sigh.

Neil took his hand off her shoulder, stepped back and gave her a moment. Then he asked, "So what else were you thinking about?"

Elizabeth pulled her mind back to the present, then turned and looked at the rock. "I was trying to make the rock move."

"Try it again," he said with the curiosity becoming evident on his face once more.

She looked back to the rock and, after a couple seconds of thought, smiled. Elizabeth felt the vibration of the rock. Felt its resonance. She focused in deep.

Neil was paying attention to her vibe and felt it harmonize with that of the rock. Then he sensed something. If he wasn't paying close attention, the arcade manager would have never noticed, but a part of Elizabeth's energy field, right at the surface of her skin, seemed to increase in density. He smiled and said, "Try the door now."

The young mystic turned back to the door and gave another half-hearted swing, but when her fist connected, it felt just a little different. "Hmmm…"

She threw another punch, a little bit harder this time. Her fist thudded against the door, and she smiled. Elizabeth drew her arm back farther and, with confidence, drove her knuckles hard into the door.

A faint, small splash of amber light rippled out from where her fist impacted the metal. This punch left a bigger dent.

"Wow!" she said and then drew back for another.

"That's enough," Neil said while holding up his hands, palms out.

The young mystic stopped and reeled in her excitement while the manager inspected the dent. He let out a whistle as he considered the force that was needed. Neil could have put a dent just like this in the door with a punch, but his hand would've been swollen and useless for at least a couple of days. If not in a cast! Elizabeth wasn't physically strong enough to make such a dent, yet she still did, and her hand was just fine.

He turned to Elizabeth with a smile and pointed over to the workbench in the other room. "Bring me my tool bag," he said.

Elizabeth began laughing and said, "Yeah, right." She had tried to move the bag once a few weeks ago, but it was too heavy, and she had to drag it across the floor. And she could see that it was currently up on the workbench.

Neil continued smiling and again said, "Bring me my tool bag."

Her smile faded after a couple of seconds when she realized that he was serious. Elizabeth looked over to the bag and actually seemed intimidated. The young mystic was facing a mental image of the heavy tools landing on her toes. Still seeming a little apprehensive as she walked over to the bench, Elizabeth grabbed the bag handles and tried to lift it. It took her a little effort, but she was able to pick it up.

"She turned back to Neil with a look of astonishment on her face. "I can't believe it!" she exclaimed. Elizabeth waddled over to Neil and quickly set the bag down. "Phew! It's still really heavy, though."

Neil was actually planning to separate the tools into two bags because it was getting so heavy, but the way Elizabeth carried them showed that her strength had significantly increased. He was amazed but also concerned. She was now doing things that he could not, and Neil had to help her through. He was beginning to wonder if he would be sufficient for the task.

While Neil was considering what should be covered next, Elizabeth looked back to the rock and focused in again. She had forgotten her earlier frustration and was tuning in deep. When she fell back into her sweet spot, Neil noticed her energy gathering.

He looked over to see that Elizabeth had her eyes closed, and she seemed very calm. Her energy field was still harmonized with the stone but somehow felt a little different. As he took a couple of steps toward her, Neil could sense something a little more definitive, like he was approaching a wall. He held his hand up, pushed it forward and was physically stopped.

When his hand contacted that portion of her field, a faint splash of amber and indigo light rippled out a few inches along the surface of the spherical barrier around the young mystic.

Elizabeth snapped her head toward Neil when he touched her shield. "What's that?" she asked as she clearly felt the contact.

Neil stood there for a couple of seconds, looking dumbfounded. Then he tapped the air between himself and Elizabeth a couple of more times, with the faint light rippling out from every point of contact.

With a quick laugh, Elizabeth said, "I can feel that. What is it?"

Neil shrugged. "This is new to me." He tapped it a few more times, and then the field dissipated. "Interesting. Think you can bring it back?"

Elizabeth closed her eyes and found that she could do so with no problem. When she did, Neil walked over to his desk, picked up a pen and tossed it to Elizabeth. In a ripple of light, the pen hit the field and fell to the floor.

They both chuckled at the sight, and Neil tossed a few more random objects from his desk. Elizabeth was surprised at how she could clearly sense any contact made with the field.

Then Elizabeth's eyes went wide with wonder as she said, "I've gotta try this in the rain!" She was imagining what the sensation might be like if a gentle spring shower was drumming off the top of her field.

Neil enjoyed feeling the energy of rainfall and, as much as he hated shoveling, a good snow. He then thought of Elizabeth maintaining her field in a nor'easter. A pile of snow above her, on top of her otherwise invisible field. Neil started laughing.

"What's so funny?" she asked. Neil described his mental image to her, and Elizabeth got a big open mouth grin as she said, "I'm totally gonna do that!"

The farmer stepped back through the heavy door into the dark room. When her eyes adjusted, she could see that it was another corridor much like the others, and the area looked as if it was bathed in a silvery-purple light. Haley could clearly see the shapes and textures but no differences in color. She would not be reading any books without a light, but the walls, crates and other objects in the corridor were easily visible for about seventy feet. Beyond that, everything faded back into darkness.

She approached a door in the eastern wall of the corridor and turned the handle, opening it into another abandoned office room. Haley reached out and flipped the switch on the wall, but the lights remained dark. She took a walk around the large office-like room, but it was much the same as the others. There was another door in the corner of the office, so she went to investigate and pushed the door open to find a bathroom.

Haley walked over to the sink, pulled the handle upward and was pleasantly surprised to find that the water flowed. She opened a stall door and saw that there was a bit of toilet paper. "Yes!" she exclaimed, and a few moments later, a much more comfortable Haley exited the room and resumed her exploration of the area.

Continuing to the end where the corridor intersected with another vertical shaft way, there were lift platforms around, but nothing had power, and Haley wouldn't have known how to make them work. There were some sources of light coming from above a few of the ledges and platforms that she could use to start making her way up, and up is where she wanted to go.

Haley jumped and climbed, making her way to the top. There were entrances to other corridors along the ascent, from which the light had come, but after a quick peek through the openings, she continued upward, hoping to find an exit.

Upon reaching the top, Haley found a lone door. She opened it and saw a staircase that went up to another level. "Actual stairs! I think I'm on the right track," she said to herself, feeling hopeful.

She walked up the steps, turned at the landing and continued up to another door at the top. Haley turned the handle, pulled the door open, and the light came spilling in. She blinked as her eyes quickly adjusted to find…

"Another big hallway," she sighed with disappointment.

Haley focused on her empathic senses and determined that nobody was in the immediate area. She stepped into the corridor and tried to figure out which way to go.

Unsure of how far away the people might be, she sensed more to her right than her left. Not wanting any unnecessary encounters, the empath turned to the left and walked down the corridor.

It was much warmer up here, and as she continued, the temperature rose. There were more doors along the way, and Haley stopped to investigate. A couple looked like more unused offices or computer labs. Another was stacked full of supply crates, but none led to an exit. She was also hoping to find a pen and paper or something that she could use to draw a map as this place was huge, and she was starting to lose track of where she had been.

At the end of the corridor was a large cement wall housing a metal door with a lever, just like the previous one. The area was uncomfortably warm. Haley walked up to the wall and put her hand on it, feeling the heat, but couldn't sense anyone on the other side of this wall, so she carefully grabbed the lever and found it wasn't too hot to the touch. She then gripped it tighter and pulled.

This one moved much easier, the latch disengaged, and Haley slowly pushed the door open into a very hot room. She stepped inside and immediately began sweating.

It was a large cement room with a giant object in the middle that Haley thought looked like a big canon, aimed straight up, with some thin, dark smoke rolling out of the top. In the center of the floor, next to the blast furnace, was a circular seam that looked like it could open. The walls were darkened with soot. The air was smoggy, full of particulate and very difficult to breathe.

Haley pulled her bandana up and over her mouth to block out the floating particulate, but it only helped a little. She tried to make her way across but began to choke. Not even halfway through, Haley's eyes were watering, and she could barely breathe, so she turned around and ran back to the door. As soon as she exited the incinerator room, the farmer pulled her scarf down and coughed out some phlegm. She took a few deep breaths, wiped her face and pulled the door shut.

The entire area was almost like a giant hardware store with all manner of pipes, parts and tools shelved in this section. Chuck's com-system was scanning and recording everything as he went, adding to the map displayed on his screen. All info that the Marshal recorded would instantly transfer to the others as soon as he was back in contact.

There was a stairwell with grated steps, and Chuck found more tools and maintenance equipment for the next couple of floors down, but when he made his way across one of the storage rooms, he discovered a cargo elevator.

His com immediately synced in and called the car. When it arrived, the cage door slid open, and Gentry stepped into the lift.

He decided to take it down as far as it would go and work his way back up. When the car came to a stop, the door slid to the side, and Chuck stepped into what looked like a major HVAC station. The large room was full of ductwork, and the loud humming of fans was constant.

The Marshal walked over to a control panel and set his phone on its surface. The com began reading the info as Chuck inspected the area but found nothing other than more ventilation and some plumbing. As he was looking around, a beeping sound came from the small speakers in his collar.

Chuck held up his hand, and when he did, the phone on the control panel broke apart and turned to dust as the nanobots in his sleeve began to move toward his hand and change shape, reforming the phone in his palm.

He looked at the screen to see the HVAC schematics were obtained and had been integrated into his map. The screen zoomed out and overlayed the data, indicating to the Marshal just how big this facility might be.

"Great," he said, unenthused by the new info. While it was nowhere near the largest that he'd seen, it was definitely bigger than he was anticipating. In the lower right corner of the map read the numbers 5:32-65:58. The first number, displayed in green, was the estimation of how long it would take to get back to the rendezvous point from his position, and the second, displayed in yellow, was counting down the time he had remaining.

Haley slid down a ventilation shaft, so Gentry decided to continue searching along the main duct. But as the Marshal was preparing to leave the room, he saw people coming in from a corridor. Chuck stepped behind some ductwork and conjured his helmet. He had his com-system filter out the noise of the machinery, allowing him to hear what the people said as they entered. A Harry in a boilersuit was pushing a dolly with a large box. The dolly had no wheels but instead hovered about six inches above the floor. Behind him walked a Joey and a Hank, both in Proctor's uniforms.

"The tech should be here shortly to install it," Joey said to the others.

"I'm in no rush," Hank said. "I'm on duty until eight."

The three began chatting about the outcome of the World Series, and judging by their enthusiasm, they were definitely Yankees fans. But they mentioned nothing that would be of use to Chuck, other than a fond memory of his favorite team's win.

He could easily take them all down, but then they would just tell the others in the Second Density where he was. The Marshal decided that it wasn't worth giving away his position just to interrupt some HVAC maintenance. While they passionately continued to retell their favorite parts of the game, Chuck slipped into the corridor.

Haley had gone past the staircase and found herself in a room full of loud pumps and pipes. She thought it to be the same one as earlier, but she was up near the top. A catwalk spanned the length of the room from one door to the other, and she covered her ears, running across just as quickly as before. When she exited the other side of the pumping station, Haley discovered that this was as far as she could go because the corridor ended abruptly at a large metal door. There were a few piles of clothes around the floor and a small object with a button. She also saw a few of what looked like those weird pistols on the floor, but they were crushed and broken.

The empath could sense that she was closer to other people, but it mostly seemed to be from below her. But then she started to notice sensations from above. Further away but, now that she was focused, far more intense. It was like a collective sense of hopelessness and fear.

Haley shuddered at the horrific feelings and tried to concentrate on what she could do. She picked up the object and clicked the button a couple of times, then tossed it down on top of a pile of clothes. She sighed and made her way back, through the loud pumping station and to the stairwell, trying to remember everywhere she had been. "I need a map!" Haley said to herself in frustration as she went back down the stairwell.

She entered the dark vertical shaft and began her descent. Haley stopped at the first opening and, shortly after entering the corridor, found another section of ceiling that had been cut away. The empath could sense some people on the next floor, so she cautiously climbed to the upper level while making as little noise as possible.

Haley slowly raised her head up to see that, in the corridor, were three people standing together near the wall across the way, talking. None of them had those nasty vibes, but they were all look-a-likes. A Joey, a Hank and a Harry. Two of them were wearing what looked like police uniforms, and Hank was wearing a boilersuit.

"The Podmen aren't too worried about it. They said the Hunters will take care of them, and the Archons will all port here tomorrow as planned," Joey said to the others. "They're not even going to call in the Commandos."

"But can we really trust them?" asked Hank.

Joey and Harry both snapped their heads toward Hank, a look of fear on their faces, and Haley could feel that their concern was genuine.

"Be careful!" Harry said to Hank. "You don't want anyone to think that you question Kone's plans."

"Of course, I don't," said Hank. "The plan's solid."

In truth, nobody knew what any plan might be outside of doing as told, and since being accused of questioning Cetatian progress was practically as good as being found guilty, none dared discuss it.

"But there are only seven Archons here now, and you've felt their presence," Hank continued. "Imagine fifty thousand of them! Can we really trust these people?"

The others didn't disagree with Hank's mistrust of the Archons as the Cetatians were typically xenophobic. And that phobia was heavily enabled over the years by Kone himself. So, it was a surprise when the Cetatian leader vouched for the aliens from another universe.

"We don't have to trust them," Joey said. "Kone does. And if Kone trusts them…"

"Then he's probably got leverage," Harry finished for him with a grin, and the other two snickered.

The conversation wound down, and the three of them just stood around quiet for a moment. They were all close together, and Haley had a good line of sight.

The farmer got her mischievous grin as she aimed between them for the wall at their head level. She let a blast fly, and the kitten-shaped orb impacted the wall next to their heads. The concussive force immediately gelled Hank and Harry, while Joey was badly damaged.

Haley jumped up to the floor and lined up for another blast to finish him off when she heard that horrific snarling and the tapping of claws on cement. She turned her head to look down the corridor and saw seven of those beasts charging her way. Then she felt the energy coming from the Joey shell.

The farmer turned her head back in time to see Joey throw a mystical bolt of amber energy. It hit her in the chest, and she staggered back into the wall. "Uh," she grunted. She then fired a blast in return, gelling him out.

While the bolt that hit Haley felt very unpleasant, there was barely any lingering pain, but she certainly didn't want to take another one.

She looked up to the creatures closing in and felt the adrenaline. But this time, the fear was mixed with a bit more excitement as she thought, *I know how to handle these guys.*

Haley fired off three quick blasts, all hitting and gelling the first beast. She shot a blast at the second and then jumped backward, landing by the hole in the floor, and waited. When the next mindless creature dove at Haley, she jumped up and over, letting the beast fall down the hole. She came down with a pounce on the third, actually laughing a little as she rebounded back into the air and fired some more blasts.

Haley was having fun.

Jumping and dancing around them, she practically forgot that they were even dangerous. The last three were close together and charging at her when she smiled. Haley wanted to try something.

She let them get close and then jumped up for a pounce. Haley shot down feet first and giggled while rebounding back up from the gelled beast. She gathered her energy as she rose and then came down with another. The energy burst propelled her back upward again as she gathered for a third.

But it just wasn't quite there.

Her eyes suddenly went wide with fear, but she quickly lowered her arm to fire four blasts at the last creature before falling back onto the floor. Two of the shots landed, but Haley suddenly stumbled from dizziness.

She fell over backward as the beast leaped straight forward and then hovered in the air above her. Haley looked up in shock at the weird reptilian creature's underbelly. Its four limbs and tail were uselessly flailing about. The beast suddenly flew backward and hit the wall as a smear of gel. The empath then noticed the sense of worry and concern as she lifted and turned her head to see O'Connor running her way.

CHAPTER 13

Lucky Numbers

"Are you okay," an approaching O'Connor asked Haley as she sat up.

"I don't know…I'm dizzy," she weakly replied.

O'Connor stopped a couple feet away. He tuned his empathic senses to Haley and recognized that feeling well. "You used too much of your energy at once," Logan said as he reached into one of his pockets.

He pulled out a small container and popped the lid open as Haley sat back up. Logan tipped the container into his hand, and something that looked like a small pill tumbled out. "Hold out your hand," he said.

She did so, and Logan dropped the object into her palm. "This is a B-twelve supplement," he said. "Put it under your tong and let it dissolve."

She took the supplement and softly said, "Mm, berries,"

Logan looked down at the map display on his phone screen. The com was still working on the data from the blast door encryption, and the numbers in the corner read 02:44-50:23. The first set was displayed in red. "You should feel better in a moment. Then we gotta get you outta here," O'Connor said.

"Thanks," said Haley, already sounding a little stronger. She noticed the Marshal's emotions had just disappeared from her senses. "Are you an empath?" she abruptly asked.

Logan looked over to her, turned his head to the side a bit, nodded and then continued looking over his map, trying to discern a likely exit.

"Are you making your feelings disappear on purpose?" she asked.

"Yes," he flatly replied while planning their route.

"Why?" she asked.

"So, it'll be easier for you to sense others coming," he said, then turned and faced her directly, "We can't get back the way we came in, but it looks like this place might connect with the fire department."

Logan had passed through the same pumping station as Haley did earlier and, while he was there, managed to get the plumbing schematics for the entire complex. It overlaid with the corridors where he had been, then cross-referenced the data with the building locations above. They already knew this complex connected with the Town Hall as well as the warehouse, but now Logan thought that the fire department was tied into the system as well as the diner.

He held his phone out and showed Haley the screen as she stood to her feet. The partial map of the complex was displayed, and it highlighted his intended route. Haley was amazed at the sight of the phone. It looked like clear glass or plastic with rounded edges and corners, but the flat surface displayed an image as sharp as the best monitors or televisions.

"Wow!" she whispered as she looked over the map image, and then her face dropped with disappointment. "We can't get through that room," Haley said, pointing at the map. Her fingertip accidentally touched the phone's screen, and the room became highlighted. "Cool!" she said, intrigued by the technology, but then focused back on the situation and said, "It's very hot, and the air is too smoky to breathe," Haley went on to explain how she tried to cross the room and almost choked.

Logan stood up straight, propped up his right elbow in his left hand and set his chin between his thumb and index finger. He looked at her bandana and could see that it was well soiled. After a few seconds of thought, he suddenly shook his head and smiled as if something had just occurred to him.

The Marshal held up his phone between himself and Haley like he was looking at her through the device. Haley asked, "What are you doing?"

"Scanning your neural patterns," he replied.

Haley looked at him, awaiting more explanation.

Even though he was sure that he knew the answer, Logan asked, "What's your favorite color?"

"Purple," Haley replied.

Logan gave a quick nod and a smile as the clothing around his neck looked like it started rippling. The motion was very fluid-like as the fabric shifted to a new shape and color. A few seconds later, a deep purple bandana was around O'Connor's neck.

He reached up and grabbed the front of it. When he did, it came untied, and he held it out before Haley.

Awestruck, the farmer reached out and wrapped her fingers around the simple-looking cloth hanging from O'Connor's hand. He let go of it, and she held it up for a closer look. The scarf felt like regular fabric. Haley looked up to the Marshal with an expression of wonder and confusion. "What's this made from?" she asked.

"Are you familiar with nanotech?" He asked.

The young sci-fi fan was definitely familiar with the concept, but that was books and television. She wanted to hear about the real thing. "Kinda," she replied.

"It's a bunch of tiny robots that can work together to form different things. They can also take mass from other objects to build more of themselves," he said.

Haley nodded with a look of excitement. Seeing that she apparently understood, Logan continued. "This will properly filter the air for you and can even act as a rebreather if needed. When you put it on, the bots will spread out through and integrate with your clothing. That way, if you need to pull more mass for the scarf, it'll have points of contact with the ground, okay?"

"Okay," said Haley. Then she asked, "Aren't you worried about gray goo?"

Logan laughed, now knowing that she understood the concept of nanotech quite well. And he wasn't surprised either, as he thought of all the time he and Haley had spent talking about and watching movies. Gray goo was the worst-case scenario of nanobots self-replicating out of control until there was no more available mass to harness. Such a catastrophe could forcibly turn an entire world into a giant blob of tiny bots.

"Gus told me that's why forty-five percent of the programming is nothing but safeguards," Logan said. "You can just lay it over top of the bandana you're wearing now. It'll do the rest."

Haley held the nanotech scarf up to hers, and it started to move of its own accord. It seemed to almost soak into her brown bandana, transforming the material as it went. She felt the rippling run down through her coveralls and into her shoes.

"Whoa!" she whispered at the strange sensations. It was also moving through the sleeves of her shirt. The lines of nanobots crisscross through the fabric, and then it all went dormant and felt like her regular clothes.

"That is so cool!" Haley exclaimed.

"But do you know what would be really cool?" Logan asked with a knowing smile.

"What?" inquired a curious Haley.

"Getting you outta here," he said. "Ready to go?"

With a smile, Haley gave a definitive, "Yes."

"Alright." Logan turned and then said, "By the way…" He reached into his pocket and pulled out a small object. "…I think you dropped this," he said, then lobbed it over his shoulder toward Haley.

The farmgirl reached up and smiled as she caught the potato from the park.

As they approached the vertical corridor, Logan asked, "Can you see in the dark yet?"

"Yeah," Haley replied. "Just a little bit ago, I…" Her eyes went wide. "You guys are from the future!"

"Not exactly," he said as they stepped through to the darker area. When they did, Haley's eyes shifted to perceive a higher part of the spectrum, and Logan activated his helmet. His voice was now also heard from small speakers that formed in Haley's bandana, just beneath her ears. "We're from a parallel universe." He then looked upwards and said, "I'm going to carry you up to the top."

"Okay," Haley replied while also looking up. She felt the energy surrounding her as she lifted into the air. "Whoa!" Haley quietly exclaimed as she was quickly elevated to the upper ledge with Logan moving through the air right beside her. They entered the stairwell, made their way up to the corridor and turned toward the incinerator room.

"So, a parallel universe. Is it kinda like *Sliders*?" Haley asked.

Logan, a little familiar with that show, said, "Actually, yeah. It's a lot like that…" He then looked unsure. "I think…This is the first time we've ever ported to another universe, so this is still new. But Gus can explain it better once we get back to the surface."

Haley smiled, "So those other two are here," she stated.

"Ah, yep," he responded, thinking about Haley's description of the Incinerator room as they approached the metal door. The nanobots started to move, and they extended from his collar, went up his neck and wrapped around his head, forming a pair of safety goggles. The Marshal reached up, pulled them off of his head and handed them to Haley.

She placed them on top of her head, slid them down over her eyes and the goggles automatically adjusted to fit. She noticed Logan's emotions were detectable again as his focus was beyond the wall in front of him, but no one was detected. There was, however, an ongoing clacking sound that Haley did not hear earlier.

O'Connor looked at the counter on his map, and it read 01:56-40:42. Then he pulled the lever and opened the door. The circular panel in the floor was open, and a large vertical bucket scoop system extended up from the cylindrical shaft below.

It had a series of buckets that were full of waste. The buckets traveled up the track and dumped their contents onto a horizontal conveyor up above. The waste then rode the belt to fall off the other end into the blast furnace.

It wasn't nearly as hot as before, and the air was much clearer but still oppressive. When they stepped inside, Haley's bandana immediately moved up over her mouth and nose as Logan donned his helmet. Haley was surprised to find no impediment to her airflow.

Logan shut the door behind them, they turned and started for the other side of the room, and only a couple of steps were taken when the buckets stopped moving, followed by the belt up above just a few seconds later.

The vertical conveyor began to retract into the floor as they neared the center of the room. The horizontal one up above was sliding into the wall.

Haley and Logan hurried to the door at the other side, figuring that the system was preparing for a burn. Thankfully, the door gave them no problem, and they exited the room as jets could be heard preparing to ignite. O'Connor shut the door, dismissed his helmet and then looked around the new area while Haley took off the goggles.

Another corridor, but the floor was paved and had a double yellow line painted down the center. The wall went up twenty feet to where the arch of the ceiling began. Lights lined the length of the tunnel, and surprisingly, a fair amount of them worked, but where he was hoping to see an elevator was a large metal security gate blocking their way.

The Marshal sighed as he held the phone up for a scan but found another encryption that was similar to, but not the same as, the one from earlier. "Looks like they're changing all the locks," he said to Haley.

The com-system began to process this new encryption data as an alert appeared on the screen. Cameras were detected in the area, but his com had already synced with them and set them to a repeating loop, allowing them to pass through the corridors undetected. It was also trying to use the cameras to pivot into the security system but was encountering more encryptions and firewalls.

According to the map extrapolations, they were likely close to the southern end of the complex. O'Connor took another look around to make sure that no one was near and then tossed his phone onto the pavement in front of himself and Haley. Upward, it projected a holographic image of the facility map. The Marshal placed his hands into the image and spread them apart, stretching the display to a larger size. The blast doors were highlighted, and the countdown to rendezvous was at thirty-nine minutes.

"This is working on the encryptions, but that's waiting for something that might not happen," he said, "The only thing we can really do while we wait is to see what's in the rest of this corridor."

Haley looked around at the area, clearly disappointed with the news but a little hopeful as well. This tunnel looks like a road, so cars would have to be able to get in here from somewhere. They began walking when she asked, "Are you from the same universe as the Archons?"

"Yeah, and we have to figure out how to get them out of yours," he replied as he picked up the phone. "Don't know yet who these guys are that are working for them," he added as they began walking.

Haley's eyes went wide, suddenly remembering the Cetatians' conversation from earlier. "I heard one of those people say that seven are here now, and the rest are coming tomorrow," she informed the Marshal.

Logan asked, "The rest?"

"Yeah," she continued, "I think he said fifty thousand."

That was consistent with the intelligence agencies' estimation of the Archon population after the war. O'Connor said, "Porting all of them would take an enormous amount of power. How could they…" It seemed as if a light bulb switched on over his head. "Tomorrow's Samhain!" the Marshal stated as if that explained everything.

"Sour what?" Haley asked, looking confused.

"Samhain," he said again. "Sow, rhymes with wow…and win. Samhain."

Haley looked very lost at the poorly attempted explanation, so Logan tried again. "It's an older name for Halloween, and it's also one of the two times of the year when the veil between worlds is at its thinnest, which means it would probably take a lot less power to pull off this stunt."

The phone buzzed, and O'Connor pulled it from his pocket as they walked. The Marshal smirked when he looked at the screen and said, "Speaking of power, kinda good news." He looked up from the screen to Haley and said, "It's been trying to hack the security through the cameras. It hasn't gotten into the system yet, but the com did manage to unlock some of the power data. Looks like we've got the electrical schematics for part of this place."

He handed the phone to Haley, and she looked at the screen. She could see the electrical overlay itself into the map, and the com began to make further extrapolations, refining the depiction of what the full complex might be and adding details to established areas. She saw the countdown at thirty-seven minutes.

There was a Peterbilt truck with a trailer parked on the right side of the tunnel, and Haley held up the phone. She looked at the abandoned vehicle through the glass-like screen and watched the display change to depict the scanning process. It somehow determined that the truck would likely function and that the fuel tank was half-full, but there was nothing unusual detected. Then the screen suddenly changed back to the map. Haley said, "Oh," and started to chuckle when she saw a very large room highlighted with new information.

"What's up?" Logan asked.

"If they need a lot of power to move here, what happens if we pull the plug?" Haley asked with a mischievous smirk as she handed the phone back to Logan.

The Marshal looked at the map to see that, although a bit of a way down, the power generator for the complex was almost directly below them. Which also happened to be the only direction left that they could go.

The tunnel abruptly ended in a perfectly smooth wall of earth and stones. A grid of metal bars, just like the ones below the warehouse, lined the wall, and a big section of the road's end was cut away, revealing a vertical corridor.

This section was not cut as clean as the other corridors. There were chunks and slabs of asphalt piled along the eastern wall, and the edges of the floor around the shaft were broken and crumbling.

They looked down through the opening to see scaffolding and planks along the sides. There were also a few platforms with lifts for cargo and metal ladders that were mounted to the concrete walls, connecting some of the landings. Haley looked at a ladder that came up through a square hole in one of the higher platforms and then noticed that this particular landing had pulled away from the wall a bit. She looked at the angle braces underneath, which were rusted to the point of near uselessness.

With a scoff of frustration, Haley asked, "Don't these guys need stairs too?"

Logan shrugged and said, "You would think."

"So, is it the future in your universe?" Haley suddenly asked.

"It's the year two-thousand-twenty-two back home," he said.

"And there's another me that's from your universe?" she asked.

"Actually, we think she might be from yours," Logan replied and instantly regret, realizing the conversation to which he had just opened the door.

"You mean…the other me might be…really me?! Is she here too?!" Haley asked.

"No…probably not. Uh…I mean, she's not here, and she's not you…" He stopped stammering, took a breath and then started over. "Just as there are multiple universes, there are multiple timelines that make up a universe. Think of the last time you went left when you could've gone right. The idea is that the timeline would split, forming a second one where you did turn right instead."

"And it would make another…every time I chose to do something?" the farmer asked.

"Pretty much," Logan said. "Well, I think that's how the theory goes…the multiverse is weird. But the odds of you two being the same, Haley, are slim to none. And Slim's stepping out the door as we speak."

"But it's possible that we're the same, isn't it?" Haley suggested.

"I guess…but if we did any little thing different than how it went for her, including this conversation, then it's a different timeline, and you're not the same Haley," Logan said.

"Oh…" Haley said, considering what this all means. She visually imagined herself splitting into two and walking in different directions down a corridor. A single soul that was two individual spirits who used to be one and the same. And then again and again at every choice to be made. She said, "Every move would make another me. And they could all become different, making them not me. But they all used to be. What am I?

"You…" he paused, thinking of how to answer, "…are whichever of those that you choose to be."

"Huh…" Haley said as she tried to think of her life as a choose your own adventure novel. But in this case, she couldn't turn back any pages. After a moment of thought, Haley suddenly blurted, "Don't tell me what I did."

"What do you mean?" Logan asked.

"If I know how I did things, I'll probably do them differently. And if we meet again, I want us to have the same memories…or at least close to."

Logan chuckled to himself as he thought about how many times Haley and Elizabeth had refused to talk about whatever it was in which the Marshals might someday be involved. And they stated this exact reason. Logan looked at her with an expression of admiration and said, "Haley told me she was a really smart kid…" he then looked off into the distance, as if he was suddenly saddened and softly said, "I wonder what happened."

"What?!" Haley said in shock.

Logan couldn't hide his laughter in the slightest, and Haley, realizing the prank, joined him. They quickly got their laughter under control as this was not a place to let down their guard.

O'Connor was thinking over what they should do, but Haley was quickly becoming overwhelmed by the thoughts of being so many possible people throughout potential timelines. She wondered what her choices could be. Then mist appeared in her eyes as she wondered if, in some realities, her mother had not been taken. "What is it all?" She suddenly asked. "What's life? What's it supposed to be?"

He could feel her loss and sense how overwhelmed she'd become. Logan looked in her eyes and, after a sigh, he gave her a slight smile then said, "It's the experiences we share."

It was an over-simplistic answer, but simple was what Haley needed to hear after her mental gymnastics. And it was an answer that just made sense to the empath. She was pulled back further from those contemplations when they sensed people getting closer from below.

They both focused their attention down the shaft and could hear voices. It sounded like at least two people, and then they could hear the mechanical whine of a lift moving up a track. The talking got louder as the lift ascended, and then a third voice could be heard.

The people came into view, and there were four altogether. Three of them were in large shells. A Hank, a Harry and a Frank. The fourth, who spoke with a Spanish accent, was in a regular-sized Joey shell. "…and Sahmbo said that he doesn't think those guys came here alone, so we keep our eyes open for the other two."

Hank said, "I ran a data analysis on our port systems and the Archon's, but there were no unauthorized transfers." He then threw his palms out as he asked, "How did they get here?" then he pointed his thumb back into his chest and said, "I want to find out!"

"So does Sahmbo," Joey replied. "He brought that up, too. If they can port without linking to an established gate or beacon, then we need to get our hands on that tech."

"Maybe they used sorcery similar to what our wizards did with the people from town," Harry offered. Haley thought it very strange to hear her father's voice with a thick New England accent.

"Not likely," Joey replied. "All four of them have abilities, but none of them practiced mysticism or magick. Also, they…what's so funny?" he asked a smirking Harry.

"It's just you talking with that voice," he said with a slight chuckle.

Joey flashed a smirk for just an instant and said, "Maybe so, but stay focused. These people are dangerous prey." He walked over to a dolly, and when he grabbed the handle, the cart lifted up about half a foot and hovered. "Just because we can't get hurt in these shells doesn't mean we don't take this seriously. Playtime is over. Remember who we are. We're professionals. We're Hunters…act like it. No more clowning around. Now, you guys go on. I'm gonna put this dolly down with the crates. I'll catch up in a few." He then pushed the hover dolly onto the lift, and it began to descend. Hank, Harry and Frank walked onto another lift and continued upward.

Ducking between the big rig and the wall, Logan whispered to Haley, "There's only one way they can go that I can think of."

"Firehouse elevator," Haley whispered back with a smile.

They waited behind the truck for the Hunters to pass by, hoping that they would open the security gate at the other end of the tunnel. As the three Cetatians were passing the trailer, Frank said, "I'm gonna step behind the truck…"

Haley silently gasped as Logan muttered, "You gotta be kidding me!"

"…I can't believe we gotta do this in these shells," Frank finished.

"It's biology," Hank said. "If it eats, it excretes."

"All I'm saying," Frank responded, "is that when I get back to my real body, my pants better not be wet."

Hank and Harry started to laugh and, despite the unfortunate circumstance, the two empaths had to stifle their own chuckles as well.

Then Logan turned to Haley and, with a smirk, whispered, "I'll take care of this." He stood up and moved toward the back of the trailer as Frank was about to come around the tailgate.

Frank turned to step between the trailer and the wall when his face was suddenly met by O'Connor's left fist, knocking the Hunter halfway across the width of the tunnel.

"Bathrooms closed," he said as he ran out from behind the trailer. The Marshal rushed in on the other two Hunters a began exchanging blows.

Haley went around the front of the truck and crouched, trying to see while remaining covered, but then she felt just a slight sense of determination coming from behind her. She turned around to see Joey stepping off a lift platform onto the pavement.

Joey locked eyes with Haley, and he immediately began to charge as the farmer stood up and fired off some blasts. The Hunter put his hands up in front of him to protect his face and torso. The concussive bursts knocked him back, but he seemed just as resilient as the larger shells.

Haley heard Frank shout, "Stupid primate!"

Logan shouted back, "Kiss my high-functioning Neanderthal…"

"Hey!" Haley reflexively interrupted as Joey reached for a coiled object hanging from his belt.

O'Connor clenched his fist as he curled his arm and a slab of pavement lifted into the air. He went through a throwing motion as he shouted, "…asphalt!" The chunk of amesite sped forward and gelled Frank.

He noticed the emotional state of the other two. Hank was very aggravated, but Harry seemed somewhat amused. Logan capitalized by taunting, "At least he didn't wet his pants," while he rushed forward. Hank became a little sloppy in his strikes as he began to make moves out of frustration, while Harry was very sloppy from trying not to laugh.

Joey pulled the coil from his belt. The Hunter unraveled the item, revealing it to be a long metallic whip. It was covered with tiny bumps which electrified, making the entire surface of the whip crackle with blue-white arcs.

Haley's eyes went wide as she shook her head and said, "Uh-uh!" She then sent a barrage of blasts at the Hunter. He moved his arm, and the whip quickly and gracefully arched through the air. The demonstration of skill was both beautiful and intimidating as he easily snapped away her orbs, the concussive bursts too far away to affect him.

The farmer took note of what was around the Hunter and then fired four shots. The first shot was aimed at Joey's chest. The second at his neck.

Joey easily snapped them from the air to see the third and fourth shots coming in simultaneously. The third was aimed low and would fall short while the fourth was coming at his head!

The Hunter snapped the high shot from the air as the low shot shuddered the pavement near his feet. His eyes went wide when the amesite on which he stood crumbled and slid down. The Hunter smacked his face on the crumbling edge of the shaft as he fell to one of the landings further below.

Haley ran to the edge, jumped onto one of the upper landings and then down to another one where she had a good shot at Joey, who was standing back to his feet. Haley began blasting, but he was just as fast and began snapping them from the air with his whip.

With his left hand, Joey pulled out a pistol, aimed up at Haley and began to shoot. "Whoa!" Haley exclaimed as she backed up to the wall and crouched.

Joey ran over to the ladder on the adjacent wall and began to climb. Haley saw him coming up, so she backed up a bit, and the Hunter had to climb higher to get a shot. He came up more, then Haley moved back a bit. And waited.

As soon as his eyes came up into view, the farmer backed up again. And waited. He came up the ladder further, and Haley decided that he was high enough.

She burst into a sprint toward the end of her landing and jumped to the platform above the ladder. She shouted, "Mashed potatoes!" and then pounced. Her feet hit the surface, and she rebounded upward as the already compromised platform broke away from the wall.

Joey's eyes went wide as the decking above him came tumbling down. He tried to jump away from the wall but didn't move quick enough to get out from under the collapsing structure. He and it fell to the floor, quickly followed by Haley, who landed on her feet.

She immediately aimed her potato gun at the Hunter but found that he was gel. An object had slipped halfway from the pants pocket, so Haley stooped down for a closer look. When she reached for it, a second lump in the pocket was seen, and she stood up holding two of these items. A couple of two-inch, oblong-shaped…stones, perhaps?

Flat on one side and rounded on the other. Greenish-gray in color, they both had the same odd cone shape on one end and a small indent right by it, but looked and felt like it was made from polished stone.

She looked up at where the platform was and realized how far she had dropped. It was at least twenty feet, and she didn't even think about it while it was happening! It gave her the strange sensation of being both exhilarated and terrified.

Logan landed right beside her, and she looked up to the Marshal with a smile and said, "I tricked him good."

Looking over the twisted decking, he said, "I guess so." When he noticed the whip, Haley felt something inside him shift. Then the damaged whip had a surge, and the electrical arching flashed across the surface one last time.

Haley sensed a sudden spike in anxiety accompanied by a sense of loss. It felt like someone had just ripped out her heart. She looked at the Marshal, and he seemed to be having a little trouble breathing. Then the feelings disappeared. His breathing became deeper and more deliberate, and the farmer began to worry.

"Are you okay?" she asked, not sure what was happening.

The Marshal placed a hand on the wall to steady himself and then seemed to struggle a bit to speak the words, "Just…trying to figure something out." His breathing now seemed deep and deliberate.

Haley dropped the stones into her front pocket and walked up to him. His eyes were closed, he seemed to be concentrating, and his breathing had become a little steadier. The empath couldn't sense his emotions, which unnerved her further.

"Hey?" Haley gently asked as she reached out to tap him on the arm.

Logan opened his eyes to see her reaching. "No!" he said in what sounded like a shouted whisper, but it was too late. Haley's fingers touched her fellow empath's forearm.

And the dam broke.

She suddenly fell into a stormy, turbulent sea of swirling emotions. All so vivid. All so intense. All of them crashing together and chaotically mixing. It was overwhelming to the point where Haley felt lightheaded and dizzy. She couldn't breathe. She was falling. Tumbling.

Haley's stomach turned and was queasy with a feeling of dread while her breathing came back but involuntarily sharp. Suddenly overtaken by another intense sense of loss, thoughts and doubts began swirling together in her mind, and she spiraled down into wounds older and deeper.

She began to feel a great heaviness come over her. Empty and alone, the sense of isolation and disconnect seemed to drive the very air from her lungs as she again struggled to draw breath. Haley felt worthless, inadequate and disconnected. A solitary spec in an infinite, nihilistic void. She was convinced that this deep depression was all that she would know for the remainder of her days.

Haley didn't want to be and wished that she never was.

Then…something seemed different. Perhaps she adapted, but Haley began to realize that there was more than just emptiness. She again could start to sense other emotions. And then all of them. The entirety of the emotional spectrum was still present and now seemed more manageable than before. And the endless void of lonely nothingness was smaller than it first seemed. In fact, it was very small. Haley could instinctually tell that it used to be much, much bigger, but it was filling in.

He was healing!

And under the crushing depths of those suffocating sorrows, Haley found something she never expected.

Hope.

Her presence of mind snapped back, and she was standing there with her hand on Logan's arm. It was like an eternity occurred within an instant. Tears were streaming down her face, and her nose was stuffed. Haley realized she had been hyperventilating but was already calming back down. She was woozy, but after a few more breaths, she became clearer and steadier.

Haley looked up at her fellow empath's face and saw a heavy mist in his eyes.

"I'm sorry," he said in a subdued tone while looking back into hers. "I really did try to keep all that away from you."

Haley gave him a sad smile, then leaned in and hugged him tightly. Logan hugged her back, leaned down and, with a quick pat on the back, gently said, "C'mon. We need to keep moving."

CHAPTER 14
This Generation

They knew others were likely coming, so Haley and Logan made their way down the vertical corridor in the same manner as their earlier ascent. They found a doorway on the northern wall halfway down, but the striking difference here was that it was a regular-looking set of double doors.

They could both sense people on the other side, so Logan looked through the square glass window and immediately backed away.

Haley felt the energy surround her as she was lifted from the floor, and they quickly flew the rest of the way to the bottom, where there was another corridor entrance on the same wall.

"What was in there?" Haley asked.

"About thirty people that I could see…and two of 'em were Archons," Logan told her. "It looked like a mess hall. Everybody was eating."

They cautiously made their way into the corridor and saw that this area, although cobbled like the rest of the complex, was better maintained, and all of the lights worked. The other corridors had arched ceilings, but this one was flat.

There were tarped crates stacked along the eastern wall and some smaller containers against the western side. O'Connor took a good look around and then carefully opened a crate to see the blast pistols neatly packed.

"Guns," he said and took another look around before he began telekinetically crushing them.

Haley was surprised with herself. Despite the intense emotional turbulence over the last few moments, she actually felt a degree of calm on the inside.

Logan sensed her calm but was still very concerned. She had already been through more than enough, and now she got caught under an avalanche of his worst emotional baggage.

Haley heard a small voice say, "Meow." She turned around to see a gray cat with darker gray stripes between the tarped crates.

Lulu stood up and stretched, then made her way out toward Haley.

"Hi, kitty!" the farmgirl happily said.

"Meow," Lulu responded.

Logan turned around and smiled when he saw Haley and her new friend. Then he noticed a significant shift.

Haley felt Lulu's love of climbing trees. The claws digging into the bark. A good purchase from which to move herself to new heights and commanding views. The empath felt the energy gather and coalesce in her fingers and toes. She looked at her hands in awe as her fingernails began to glow purple, then the light extended out past her nails in the shape of ethereal claws.

Suddenly and in unison, they jumped up, and Lulu clung to the tarp while Haley clung to the cement wall. "Wow!" she exclaimed while Logan watched in amazement.

Haley giggled as she climbed around the wall like a cat on burlap. She pulled her hand away from the wall, but there was no hole from where her claw had entered.

She got curious, so she placed her fingers against the cement wall with the intention of remaining connected. Then she pulled her hand back, and the wall held her in place, but as soon as she wanted it to come free, it did.

Next, she attached her fingers to the wall and pulled, wondering if there was a breaking point. There was…for the cement. And when she pulled hard enough, the bit of concrete around her claw crumbled and broke. She held up her finger to see little chunks of cement still stuck in her ethereal nail. As soon as she decided to release, the tiny pebbles fell out.

"Something interesting about that wall?" O'Connor asked. Haley turned and looked back down toward Logan, who had finished destroying the pistols, standing on the floor, and Lulu was rubbing against his shin.

"Yeah," she said excitedly. Then she got a look of shock on her face when she realized how loud she had said it, "I can climb it!" she finished in a hushed tone. The farmer then went up to the top, placed her fingers on the ceiling and hung there as she swung her legs. "Ha ha!" she laughed. Then, she swung her feet up and stuck them to the ceiling as well.

"So, is this how you've been learning to use your energy?" Logan asked as Haley hopped back down to the floor.

"Uh-huh," she happily said, squatting down to pet Lulu.

"That's awesome!"

"Meow," Lulu said and brushed against Haley's leg before trotting away.

The generator was further below them and just a bit toward the north, so they began to walk through the corridor. They didn't have to go very far before they found a door to a stairwell on the eastern wall.

There were two other doors on the way, but they followed the stairs down to the bottom, where they entered another passageway. This corridor was only about five hundred feet long and had a large opened overhead door at each end. The ceiling was cut away right before the northern door.

Turning right would probably lead to the generator room, but Logan quietly said, "Let's see what's in there first," pointing to the overhead door on the left, "If we make a run at the generator, it's going to draw attention, and I don't want any nasty surprises coming in behind us."

"Okay," Haley whispered as she followed along.

They entered and saw a huge room with shelving units holding various generator parts and supplies. There was also equipment and repair stations along the eastern and western walls. But along the back wall was an odd-looking monolith.

It was fifteen feet tall and twenty feet wide, with a depth of about three feet. The monolith appeared to be made from polished stone and had intricate aquatic-themed carvings along the surface. An archway, about twelve feet high and seventeen feet wide, went through the center.

"What is that?" Haley asked.

"A portgate…and a beautiful one!" Logan answered as he began scanning.

"Does it go to your universe?" she inquired.

"It's not going anywhere right now," he said as he read the scans. "It's functional, but a mechanism has to be turned inside to activate it. And, of course, these guys love their bindings, so telekinesis is out." He then pointed at a slot to the left side of the archway and said, "I think some kind of key goes there."

Haley looked at the small opening and recognized the size and shape. She reached in her front pocket and fumbled past the goggles and gloves. Pulling out the two stones she had taken from Joey, Haley held them up to show Logan.

Either of the two polished stones looked like they would fit perfectly within the suspected key slot. He looked up from her hand with a smile of surprise as he asked, "Where'd you get those?"

"From the guy with the whi…" She immediately paused, not certain if she should have said that.

"So, the guy with the whip turned out to be useful after all," he said with a genuine smile, putting Haley right back at ease.

Logan took one of the stones and placed it in the slot. It immediately pulled itself inward and settled smoothly into place as part of a dolphin's head. Every seam in the monolith began to glow with a pale white light for about three seconds. Then it faded away.

"Did you break it?" Haley asked.

"Not yet," said Logan as he took new scans. "It's active, but the com is still trying to sync in." He found an encryption much like the blast door and security gate. The Marshal set his com to start working and was surprised when it immediately generated two codes to try. Both codes displayed on his screen were depicted in yellow and blinking. The first code blinked faster and then turned a solid green as the second code turned a solid red and faded.

"We're in!" he said as the new information became available. "Bummer, we can't go anywhere because it's on a closed network. There aren't any other active ports on the system to link with right now, at least none that I can see. But if we find some, we might be able to turn 'em on."

"Aren't you worried about others coming through if you leave it on?" Haley asked.

"Actually, no," the Marshal replied and with an impish grin, he finished, "Because I just changed the password." Haley chuckled mischievously.

Logan turned and looked toward the room's exit. It was time to make a choice. He looked back at Haley, who was getting excited to shut them down, but he didn't like the idea of doing this while she was there. This was certainly going to raise some alarms, and he didn't want Haley in harm's way, but there was nowhere else they could go at the moment, and the generator was right here. This might be their one shot to prevent a much bigger problem.

O'Connor looked at the electrical data, which also displayed info on the generator in use. He then tossed the phone to the floor as another holographic image projected upward, showing Haley some of what they might expect when they get there.

The generator itself was a cylindrical object. Encased in a metal housing, Haley thought it looked like a wider version of the new water heater that her father installed a couple of months ago. There was a decking on top of the unit with control panels and a coolant reservoir tank. Six pipes were evenly spaced around the generator in sets of two, one for intake and the other for return. They came out the top of the decking and ran down the sides, circulating the fluid through the system to maintain a proper operating temperature.

"This thing is actually huge and takes up the entire center of the room," Logan began while highlighting the sets of pipes. "There are three coolant lines. If I break them at these fittings," he then pointed to the ninety-degree elbows on top of the generator decking, "the system will detect a drop in pressure, and the valves will divert the flow into this tank. The generator needs all three to run at peak efficiency but can function alright with just one."

"And when they're all broken, it'll turn off?"

"Yeah, it'll almost instantly get way too hot, and the whole thing will go into emergency shut down." Logan then looked at the coolant reservoir tank, to which he pointed with his finger as he said, "I'm probably gonna want to stay away from that, though."

Haley tilted her head in curiosity as she asked, "Why?"

"Because this isn't antifreeze that you put in a car," he said. "This stuff has a ridiculous boiling point, and it's *nasty* when hot. It'll melt the flesh off of bone."

The empath shuddered at the thought.

"They probably got security in there, so when we go in, I'm gonna take them out, fly up to the top and shut this thing down," Logan said. "And once it stops, I'm gonna fly and punch a hole right through the unit to make sure they can't fix it too quickly," he finished with a grin.

"Can't you just do that first?" Haley asked.

"No," he replied. "That would turn Columbia into a crater, and then you'd be mad at me."

"Oh…Don't do that," she responded with a calm, flat expression. But then she wondered, "What am I supposed to do?"

He said, "Hopefully, just wait by the door while I take care of it."

Haley was disappointed but also knew that would probably be best.

They got to the overhead door at the other end and could sense others nearby. Cautiously entering the room, they saw that it opened up much wider inside. There was a freight lift on the other end of the room for generator parts and a few control panels throughout the area.

They were barely in the door when voices could be heard. Ducking down behind a panel, the empaths listened to a short conversation between two people.

Logan slowly stood and got a look at the two Cetatians. One was in a Hank shell and wearing a Proctor's uniform. The other was also in a Hank shell and was wearing a boilersuit.

The Marshal had seen many of the people in the mess hall dressed the same way. As he thought about them, he suddenly realized how odd it was that so many would be eating when there was a known security breach. And it also reminded him that they weren't very far away.

He ducked back down, and they listened for a moment, but the conversation ended quickly, and the only thing they learned was that the Proctor truly adored his wife's tuna casserole.

They backed out and then flew up to the opening in the ceiling. The empaths could sense people up top, and Logan slowly raised his head above the floor for a look.

The northern end of this corridor ended in the same place as the one below them, but on this floor, there were two guards, a Harry and a Joey, standing in front of a large metal sliding door with a rectangular glass window, about eye level for the Marshal.

Despite his caution, as soon as Logan poked his head up, one of the men saw him. The guard on the right started to move, but then both of their heads slammed hard into the wall. As they turned to gel, Logan waved his hand, and their clothes lifted and moved in his direction.

He crushed their weapons and said, "They're probably telling everybody where we are right now, so it's go-time!" He ran over and held his phone up to the door, finding familiar Archon encryptions that the com had dealt with in his past. "Oh good," he said in relief. He looked through the window, then prompted the door open.

It slid to the right, and Logan ran in, firearm in hand. There were more guards already charging the door before it opened, blast pistols at the ready.

Logan crushed the pistols right in their hands and began slinging bullets at the approaching shells. Some of them managed to return fire in the form of mystical bolts, but the Marshal blocked them easily as he dropped most of the guards with headshots. A couple of them were in the newer and more durable shells, so he followed the bullets up with some well-placed energy blasts.

The Marshal flew up to the top, and as Haley watched, she began to feel those nasty vibes from behind. While Logan engaged with opponents on the decking of the generator, Haley turned around to see at least twenty people coming down the corridor. Mostly shells she'd seen before, but three of them were different. Two were about six feet tall with inhuman facial features, and their proportions didn't look right. And one was seven and a half feet tall with four arms, a tail and wings!

Her eyes went wide as she hopped backward, down to the floor of the generator room, and the winged lizard-like being stepped into the doorway and looked down at Haley. She felt his sickening energy, and the growing smile on Ahnk-Hume's face sent horrible chills down her spine. Haley was utterly speechless, and he seemed to become invigorated by her fear.

The Drakel rubbed both his lower and upper palms together. With a sinister chuckle, he said, "Hello, Kitten." He then stretched his wings out and opened his arms as he crouched, ready to dive at her.

"Goodbye, Douchebag!" they heard as Logan came flying back down and slammed Ahnk-Hume to the side with an ethereal sledgehammer. The Marshal landed in front of Haley to see the many people who were standing behind the Archon in the corridor. He sharply inhaled as his eyes went wide, and he told Haley to, "Run!"

Haley turned and broke into a sprint toward the generator as Logan sent a mental command to his com. It hijacked anything in the room that would function as a speaker, and a blood-pumping tune from Kick Axe began to play.

Logan unleashed a massive blast through the door into the corridor, knocking most of the surprised crowd over and even gelling a few of them, including the other two Archons.

"Wretched hillbilly," Ahnk-Hume sneered as he threw a mystical bolt. It looked like a shadow, a dark hole in the air with an angry red glow. It smacked O'Connor as he turned toward the Drakel, staggering him just a bit.

He flung a blast back at the Archon, who dodged but was then shoved telekinetically into the wall as the Marshal began shooting at guards coming in from the door.

Haley didn't know what else to do, so she went straight for the scaffolding. As she ran, Haley felt the mystical bolt that hit Logan, and while it caused her no pain, she somehow knew how it felt to the Marshal. Similar to, but much harsher than the bolt she had taken earlier. Haley reached the scaffolding and started her ascent as the vocals to "Nothin's Gonna Stand in Our Way" began.

Logan took down about seven more shells before the Drakel stood back up, but instead of going after the Marshal, Ahnk-Hume took to the air, flying for Haley! Then, the Archon felt the vibe around him as Logan took an energetic grasp. Ahnk-Hume tried to counter the telekinesis with his own energy, but O'Connor's grip was too strong, and he slammed the Archon back to the floor in a splash of red light and darkness.

The Drakel stood up, and Logan's pupils glowed with green light as he glared at Ahnk-Hume. The two charged at each other, and more shells began rushing into the room as they clashed.

Haley jumped from one plank and landed on the catwalk, then began running up the sloped surface as it wound around the large cylinder. A Proctor coming down pulled out a pistol, and as he raised his arms to take aim, Haley felt a surge of energy in her eyes.

The Cetatian was startled by the fierce blue light emitting from Haley's pupils, and the empath could feel his intimidation. No time to question it, she blasted while the guard was hesitant.

Continuing upward, Haley leaped from catwalk to ladder to scaffolding and back. She zigzagged amongst the various staging planks, noting their locations while trying to keep her distance from the guards.

Stopping at the edge of a scaffolding, Haley sent some blasts down at the approaching men. She hit three and gelled one. The guards shot back with their blast pistols, but Haley was getting used to dodging and evading their shots. She returned fire and gelled most of them.

When she turned to move upward, Haley caught a shot in the back of her right shoulder. "Uh!" she grunted, learning that this was not like the mystical bolt from earlier. It felt similar to a painful shock and left her shoulder sore.

Haley turned back around and fired as the guard got off another shot. She dodged the Cetatian's blast as her own shot landed, then continued for the top.

Logan felt the hit to Haley's shoulder and immediately looked up in her direction. A move on which Ahnk-Hume capitalized.

The Archon landed a blow on the side of the Marshal's face and quickly followed with a barrage of punches from all four arms. Logan managed to regain his bearings and began blocking and countering as a couple of Hunters joined the scuffle. It puzzled Ahnk-Hume that O'Connor, despite the vast growth of his telekinetic abilities over the last few years, would still fall right back into the habit of engaging physically.

Haley looked to the wooden scaffolding above her head and leaned out to see past the visual barrier. Almost to the top! Then a guard leaned over the railing from above her, and she quickly pulled back in before the man could shoot.

The guard hopped over the railing and landed on the catwalk below, but Haley wasn't there. A shower of kittens suddenly rained down upon him from Haley, who was clinging to the underside of the scaffolding.

Climbing back out and over the railing, Haley quickly reached the top. She saw the three coolant fittings and a man in a one-piece jumper by a control panel, holding a pistol.

He opened fire, but the technician was not practiced, and Haley dodged his shots without trouble. She quickly blasted him and was turning her attention to the pipe elbow when Ahnk-Hume landed on the surface before her.

Haley felt the decking shudder as the Archon touched down, and he towered over her with a twisted smile. Haley could feel how much he wanted to tear her apart and his gleeful anticipation of doing so.

"I have been waiting for this," he said as his smile widened. Then he wondered if a particular creature existed in this universe. Ahnk-Hume began speaking words from another language that Haley had never heard before. There were heavy hissing sounds in his voice, and the farmer felt the chilling energies in the air.

As it happens, the creatures on Ahnk-Hume's mind did exist in this reality, and they obeyed his summoning. The space on either side of the Drakel looked like it began to warp and twist. The two vortexes opened up to about five feet wide, and a large canine-like creature jumped out from each and stood beside Ahnk-Hume. "I'm going to like this universe," he said.

The two creatures radiated negative energy. They stood about four and a half feet high and had very little hair, grayish-brown skin, and eyes that were black.

Haley started to shudder from fear but then snapped herself to it and raised her potato gun. When she did, the hellhounds moved out to flank her, growling as they stepped. She charged toward the right hound while blasting at the left. Three of those shots hit the creature as she closed on the other, waiting until the last second to jump.

The hellhound swiped its claws under the quick farmer's feet as she leaped into the air, coming back down with a pounce. The hound whimpered from the impact as Haley rebounded back up, leveling her arm cannon with Ahnk-Hume as she rose. But a mystical bolt was already incoming, and it hit her square in the chest, knocking her back down to the decking.

"Oof!" Haley blurted as she landed on her left side. That hurt, but she still quickly raised her arm toward the hound next to her. Haley blasted, and the concussive force knocked the beast back.

Then, both hellhounds were suddenly flung off the sides as Logan came flying up behind the Drakel. Ahnk-Hume turned around to see the Marshal dive down, tackling the Archon, and they rolled on the floor trading punches in a full-blown grapple-scrap.

They were getting back to their feet as Logan clocked the Drakel with an energetic punch, knocking Ahnk-Hume onto his back about five feet away. O'Connor then crouched while motioning with his hands to, "Giddup!" as green light flared in his eyes.

Haley felt the surge of energy in her own eyes as they emitted a blue glow in unison with her fellow empath. She thought it looked like some kind of absurd pro-wrestling match but quickly focused her attention on the coolant pipes. She sent blast after blast into one while trying to mind both Ahnk-Hume, who Logan was keeping busy, and anyone who may come up the staging.

It took about fifteen shots, but the elbow finally broke while she was stepping back, seeing some of the coolant starting to splash out. Fortunately, the sensors were working, and the valves had already diverted the flow of this pipe set, preventing a pressurized spray.

When she turned for the next one, a hellhound made its way back to the top. Haley sent a couple of blasts, both hit and the demonic creature faded back to its realm. Haley ran to the second coolant fitting, blasting the entire way. The pipe snapped right below the elbow, and the coolant was diverted. She glanced over to the tank and turned toward the third fitting when she suddenly snapped her head back. There was coolant leaking from the reservoir.

Then, the other hellhound returned, snarling and drooling as it prepared to charge.

Haley remembered where the scaffoldings were placed, so she made a break for the edge of the decking as the hellhound burst into a sprint. The creature watched her dive over the side, and it followed her path, jumping off and finding no platform on which to land.

Clinging to the side of the generator, Haley blasted at the falling creature and landed most of her shots as the beast fell to the ground, resulting in an impact that banished the canine.

She hopped back onto the decking to find no one there. Haley could hear the commotion down the other side where Logan was fighting with Ahnk-Hume and could hear someone else coming up the scaffolding. She saw Ahnk-Hume's hands grab the side of the decking, and his head started to come up into view when he was quickly yanked back down as a couple of guards made it to the top.

Haley didn't give the first one a chance, pouring it on and gelling him as soon as he set foot on the deck. The concussive bursts knocked the other guard back down to a lower platform.

She unloaded on the last fitting as Logan and Ahnk-Hume's fight returned to the top of the generator. Haley turned back to the scaffolding as the guard came back up, accompanied by another, and she knocked them both back down.

Turning back to the pipe, Haley saw Logan throw a telekinetically enhanced forward kick into Ahnk-Hume's stomach, which sent him arching out into the room and plummeting to the floor below.

Haley blasted once and then again, finishing the job while Logan gelled the returning guards. As the final coolant line diverted to the reservoir, the operating temperature rose too high, and the emergency shutdown process was initiated. Just then, Logan's phone buzzed, and he checked to find that the com had generated two codes to try with the security gate.

"Oh…*now* it figures things out," he said sarcastically.

That's when they both felt a boiling rage. The empaths turned toward the nasty vibes to see Ahnk-Hume flying in fast! He spun, whipping his tail around to slam Logan.

It launched the Marshal off the platform and across the room, face-first into a thick glass panel on the western wall. An unpleasant squeak could be heard as he slid down six inches, fell away and plummeted. In a faint splash of green and purple light, O'Connor thudded to the floor, motionless.

CHAPTER 15
Trashed

Ahnk-Hume turned toward Haley with a sinister grin, though his shell was showing signs of wear. The Drakel had a split lip, yellow bruising and welts could be seen on his face and arms, as well as some slashes on his legs and wings, but he did not seem concerned. "At last," he said with a chuckle.

Haley lifted her right arm to fire, but Ahnk-Hume quickly grabbed it with his lower left hand, pushing it out to the side while he grabbed her by the throat with his upper right.

The Drakel hoisted her into the air and slammed her back down to the decking. Blue and purple light splashed out from Haley as she grunted from the impact and was instantly hoisted back up. He threw her across the decking, and she landed roughly on her right side.

Haley was dazed and tried to orient herself. As soon as she could process what she saw in front of her, her eyes snapped open wide. She was right next to the leaking reservoir tank. Before she could move, Ahnk-Hume was on top of her again, picking her up and throwing her back across the decking in the other direction.

She landed with a thud but kept her presence of mind. Despite the pain, Haley jumped right back to her feet and spun around as she heard a word being spoken. Three shards of red light were flung from Ahnk-Hume's hand and whipped by the farmer. One of them nicked her upper left arm, slicing it open.

The nanobots in Haley's clothing were instantly in motion, rushing to the area and forming a second bandana around the wound. The makeshift bandage cinched itself snug, keeping pressure on the fresh wound as Haley fired a shot back.

The blast came zipping in, and Ahnk-Hume folded his wings back as he easily side-stepped the orb, which would have only grazed his lower right forearm. But he wasn't Haley's target.

The blast hit the full and leaking coolant tank, bursting it open as the contents gushed out onto the legs of Ahnk-Hume. The Drakel fell over from the sudden rush of fluid, and his legs and tail were stripped down to where some of the bone was visible.

Ahnk-Hume tried to get back up, but the lower limbs of his shell were too damaged for him to stand. Pushing himself upright using all his arms, the Drakel was seething in disbelief as he looked at Haley and spat, "You might think you've succeeded, but you have not."

The empath felt an anger rising as he continued to speak, "I will find you shortly, and when I do, I'll make sure that you stay alive long enough…" the anger continued to rise as well as the volume of Ahnk-Hume's voice, "…to experience pain and torture that you never would have thought possible!" He slammed his lower two fists on the decking as he finished. His last few words sounded more like a growl and were dripping with bitterness.

Haley, although very sore, could no longer contain her laughter.

Ahnk-Hume's blood boiled as he shouted, "You dare laugh?! Why!?"

Haley maintained a slight smile as she tilted her head a bit and said, "Because there's an angry Marshal right behind you."

The Archon turned his head just in time to see Logan in mid-swing with a sledgehammer. It connected hard and launched Ahnk-Hume into a familiar pane of glass, cracking it with the impact. The Archon energy vanished as the body turned into gel and dribbled down. Shards of glass started to fall from their place.

"That poor glass panel," Haley said in mock sadness.

Logan, still looking at the broken covering, said, "Both he and the panel had it coming."

Suddenly, Haley felt a great amount of energy gathering in the Marshal as he said, "Be right back." He then flew out of the room and turned around toward the generator. In a blur, the Marshal shot forward into the large cylinder punching straight through to the other side, where he turned to make a second pass and then a third, all in just under a second. This assured that repairs could not be complete before Samhain would pass and the Archons would miss their window.

Haley was then lifted off the decking into the air alongside Logan, and they returned to the floor in time to see another group of guards and some Hunters coming in from the corridor.

The Proctors' uniforms were littered around the generator room, so it was an odd sight now that they had taken whatever clothes they could grab and got dressed in a hurry. One guy had an orange unbuttoned dress shirt and pink sweatpants. Most of them weren't even wearing shoes.

Their exit blocked, the empaths turned and flew to the door at the other end of the room. Upon entry, Logan shut the door, quickly looking around to see cleaning supplies and some industrial-sized laundry machines. There were carts of boilersuits, towels and rags.

Logan waved his hand, moving a washing machine in front of the door, but he knew that would only buy them several extra seconds.

"There's some kind of chute over here," Haley said.

Logan looked to see what did look like a laundry chute, but it would be a very tight fit. He looked up to see a vent cover and quickly checked the schematics to see if it might be a viable exit. While looking at the phone screen, Logan raised his hand, clenched his fist and yanked down as the cover broke from the vent and fell to the floor, revealing a shaft large enough for the Marshal to fit.

A Hunter in an enhanced shell shoved the heavy machine to the side. He and some Proctors entered the room and immediately saw the vent cover on the floor.

"They flew up into the vents," a guard shouted.

The sergeant from the squad of Proctors stated, "We await the Hunter's orders."

"Three of you, clear the room with me. The rest of you, go cover the vents," the Hunter said as most of the Proctors hurried out to potential intercept points. The remaining three immediately started digging through laundry carts, looking in the machines, opening closets and checking shower stalls. The room wasn't all that large, so they were finished in under two minutes. The Hunter then assigned two of the Proctors to remain posted at the door.

He was upside down. Holding very still, the Marshal had made it down just far enough to not be seen by the Proctor, who looked in the chute. He would have breathed a sigh of relief when he heard the Cetatian say, "He's not fitting through there," but breathing was a chore due to the very tight fit.

As soon as he thought that they were gone, he used his telekinesis to push himself, slowly to avoid unnecessary noise, further down the chute. He reached the opening at the bottom and took a full breath as soon as his shoulders were free.

The end of the chute was hanging out from the ceiling of a very large tunnel that possibly traversed the entire complex. The floor, about thirty-five feet below, was pitched at forty-five degrees from both sides to a ribbed conveyor track that ran the center of the tunnel. The area was covered with trash.

Haley was on the ceiling waiting for the Marshal to emerge from the chute and was quite thankful when he did as she could feel the tightness of his breathing.

After Logan caught his breath, Haley asked, "Can you believe the way those guys were dressed?"

Both of them still were still hanging upside down as Logan said, "You're the one dressed like Chucky's big sister."

Haley had never seen *Child's Play* but was familiar with the character and beamed with pride at the reference as she giggled and said, "Thanks!"

He shook his head with a snicker at the farmgirl's response, and they flew down to the floor. The Marshal's com-system was already scanning the area and sending any monitoring devices into repeating loops but still could not overcome the security system's firewalls.

They looked up the intermittently lit tunnel toward the north. The conveyor led to a barrier of large, thick bars from floor to ceiling and set in the center was a trash grinder. The bars prevented larger chunks of trash from passing this point, where there was another conveyor that took the processed waste to a hopper by a bucket lift. When activated, the hatch in the ceiling would open, allowing the lift system to extend up to the incinerator room.

Logan's phone buzzed, and he looked to see that the com had determined a viable exit. There was a ventilation shaft, further north in the tunnel and large enough for them to fit, that would bring them back up near the warehouse elevator on the other side of the blast door. He smiled as he looked at Haley and said, "Good news."

The Marshal showed her the map, and the farmer's face lit up. The counter was at 04:20-05:09, and the ETA was now displayed in green. She said, "We might make it on time!"

"Let's hope so," he said, sounding optimistic.

They flew down to the bars, and with a wave of his hand, Logan bent a couple of them apart. On the other side of the bucket lift was a conveyor coming from the north, where there was another grinder just a bit further up the tunnel, also set with straining bars.

They began walking toward the barrier when Logan noticed a slight gathering of energy from Haley. Then it was gone. Then again and again, alongside a growing frustration. "What's up?" he asked.

"When your eyes glowed," she replied," I think mine did too."

"Probably from the empathic entanglement," he said, "but you seem irritated."

"I'm trying to make my eyes glow, and it isn't working," Haley explained. "It happened twice. I know what it feels like, so why isn't it working?"

Logan shrugged. "I guess it's one of those things. Kinda like whistling," he thought out loud more than explained, "Suddenly, you figure it out and wonder why you couldn't before."

As they approached the barrier, Logan waved his hand, intending to bend the bars. But then, he felt the disruption as Haley suddenly started to notice the weight of her rig. "Something doesn't feel right," she said.

Even though the Marshal looked very calm, Haley felt the nervousness in his stomach. He turned to her, sighed and said, "They must have gotten their hands on a disruption emitter. It broadcasts frequencies that stop people from using their energy."

Logan felt Haley's stomach sinking with the news. She started to look terrified and asked, "You mean...our powers are gone?!"

O'Connor looked at her and nodded. Even though he was horrible at interpreting facial expressions, he still did not need to be an empath to see how much this terrified the young farmgirl. "But that means they can't use 'em either," he said in an attempt to comfort her somewhat. "Anyone who uses their energy or mysticism or magick is out of luck. It's all the same part of the electromagnetic spectrum."

This didn't settle Haley's stomach much as she was less interested, at the moment, in how it works and more interested in how they could get out. Haley was right to feel very vulnerable without access to her energy field.

"Unfortunately, I don't have any gear that can cut through these bars, but I'm trying to find us another way out right now," Logan said, attempting to reassure Haley. But Haley could tell that her fellow empath was very concerned as he thought about activating the bucket lift.

They could ride it up to the incinerator room, but random activation of that system would certainly draw unwanted attention.

Haley noticed that he hadn't blocked himself from her empathic senses since his flashback. She then thought about how his emotions seemed to click more into a focus at the generator when he played the music. And that led her to think about her mother's favorite song, which she started softly humming in an effort to keep calm.

Logan immediately recognized the tune and, after a moment, started humming along. It seemed to be helping her a bit, and Logan focused his own empathic senses outward, as well as double-checked for anything on the com's scanners to make certain that no one was nearby as Haley's volume was starting to steadily increase.

As they got to the chorus, he finally gave in and sent a mental command to his com, activating the speakers in both his collar and Haley's bandana as Don't Stop Believing began to play.

With watery eyes and a bit of a nervous smile, Haley continued to sing along until the recording finished, helping to lift the spirits. It was foolish. It was downright reckless. But more than that, it was needed.

As they finished the song, Haley looked at the trash-covered floor with another nervous chuckle. Logan looked over at her and suddenly got an idea.

The Marshal sent a new command to his com-system. It was searching for a way that they could leave, but now, it was looking for a way that Haley could leave. His face lit up when the com immediately came back with a route.

Haley felt the surge in optimism and asked, "Did you find something?"

"Yes," he replied with a smile. Then he turned his back toward her, squatted down and said, "Piggyback. We're going up!"

The farmer hopped on his back and held on, wondering how he was going to do this without his telekinetic abilities, but they started to rise as the Marshal engaged the thrusters in his PJs.

At various points along his arms, legs, torso and the bottom of his feet, the nanobots formed small thrusters granting lift to the wearer. The thrusters weren't discernable from the rest of the clothing by sight, but the air around them was distorting like heat rising up from a car radiator.

They got up to the ceiling and found an air vent in which Haley could fit. "There's no way you're gonna fit through there," said a disappointed Haley.

"I know," Logan said as they lowered back to the floor. "But you can."

Haley was instantly nervous when she thought of going without the Marshal, but her fellow empath gave her a reassuring smile and said, "Here's the plan." He tossed the phone on top of a cardboard box, and the map projected up. The planned route for Haley was highlighted, and it led right to up to the pump station by the blast door. The counter read 02:13-02:45 with the ETA displayed in yellow, close enough to still rendezvouses with Chuck.

"But I can't go alone," Haley said. "And I can't climb up the vents without my powers."

"About that…" the Marshal said as he walked over to the wall. "Just give me a moment." He turned around, leaned against the cement, and the nanobots went to work gathering mass and reconfiguring it to Logan's purposes. The clothing rippled as he conjured his weapons. Bulletproof vest, guns, knives, even a shotgun in a scabbard on his back, clips of ammo all along his belt and a bandana in case he had to go back to the incinerator room.

He held up his phone, and the bots began to move, splitting the device into two. The Marshal felt the pistol shot that hit Haley in the shoulder earlier. That bolt would have seriously hurt most people, and without her energy, it would have done so to Haley. He would not let her go without protection.

Logan put the secondary phone in his pocket and then held up the primary. He didn't need to speak but did so to make it easier for Haley to follow. "Grant Haley Starr access to basic PJ user interface."

When O'Connor finished speaking, his clothes and phone started to ripple again as the bots collected around his wrist and formed a thick, metallic bracelet. It unclasped on one side and had hinges on the other. He removed it and took Haley's hand as he said, "Now, you can fly," and he clicked it shut around her wrist. "It'll respond to your mental commands, just like the scarf." Logan then held out his hands and said, "Give it a shot."

As soon as Haley allowed it, the bracelet changed shape, moved up her arm to her sleeve and began to fully integrate into her clothes. They rippled through, and a few seconds later, the entirety of her clothes was made up of nanobots. "Wow! It made my pack feel lighter."

"The PJs move with you, helping support the load," Logan explained. "It's like having your strength back. Anything you want to see on the phone screen can also be seen in the helmet's visor."

Logan said it, Haley thought it, and the helmet immediately came up, displaying the map before her eyes on the inside of the face-shield. "That's awesome!" Logan heard her say through the helmet speakers. Even beyond the face-shield, the inside of the helmet displayed what was around her, allowing the farmer full use of her peripheral vision.

"Yeah, but now it's time to learn to fly," the Marshal said. Haley sent a mental command, the com responded, and the thrusters came to life. She floundered around in the air for a few seconds but got the hang of it quickly as it was working based on her thoughts.

"It's that time," Logan said. "He should still be nearby when you get there, but you gotta go now."

Haley went from having a bit of fun to being scared. The thought of going by herself again and without her powers was daunting, but at least she had a plan and some equipment. She looked up at Logan, who felt her fear, and asked, "What about you?"

"Maybe I'll play a few pranks…mess around with their equipment, who knows? Maybe I'll go raid the cafeteria. I could use a coffee." He finished with a smirk. "But it's time to get you out."

Haley practically leaped forward, wrapping him in a tight hug. Logan hugged her back and then playfully asked, "Don't you have somewhere to be?"

Haley, with a little mist in her eyes, smiled, then engaged the thrusters in her PJs and lifted to the ventilation shaft in the ceiling. She looked back down to O'Connor, gave him a wave and a sad smile, then disappeared into the shaft.

Logan looked at the screen on his secondary phone, and Haley's signal vanished.

She flew into the dark shaft, and the helmet automatically came back up with night vision in the visor. The turns that needed to be made were highlighted overtop the actual view, and she had no problem understanding which way to go next. The thrusters silently carried her up the shafts as she thought about everything that had happened since she slipped into this twisted place. Haley always wanted to go on an adventure, and now that she was on one, all she wanted to do was go home and hug her dad. Haley still didn't know where he was, but at least she didn't have to worry about more of these Archon people showing up.

She finally exited the ductwork in the loud pumping station. The com's audio system filtered out the sounds of the pumps' motors, and she dismissed the helmet after she left the room.

Haley was finally there. Butterflies were in her stomach as she pulled out the phone and applied the codes—of which there were now four—that were ready to try. And two for the security gate.

The four codes began blinking in yellow, then the first and third blinked faster, turned red and faded. A couple of seconds later, the second code blinked faster, then turned a solid green while the fourth code blinked to red and faded.

A clank reverberated from the walls, the door started to retract, and the ETA displayed in yellow switched to green. The warehouse elevator was less than a minute away!

CHAPTER 16
Let's Settle This Outside!

The way before her was revealed. The warehouse elevator was in the corridor above, and there was an opening in the ceiling just ahead. Haley sensed people as she slowly lifted to see the next floor.

They didn't see her, but she could see the two Proctors standing in front of the elevator. The detective's daughter started to take a good look at the surroundings for some possible advantage, but then they suddenly became agitated and started to talk.

Haley was too far away to make out the words, but she could feel them become much more alert as one of them turned and ran the other way through the corridor. Now there was one.

Taking a deep breath, Haley looked at her phone screen to see that the com-system was already connected to the elevator controls and awaiting her command. The car was on this level, and the door would open as soon as she decided. The counter, now displayed in red, was at 01:58 and counting upward.

She hovered back up for another look to see that the lone guard was standing in front of the elevator door, pistol in hand and watching the direction that his partner had gone. Haley lifted into the corridor and silently flew toward the guard.

The butterflies were circling in her stomach as the farmgirl, yard by yard, got closer. Then she raised her arm and aimed for the guard's head.

The elevator door suddenly opened, and the guard turned his head to see why. As soon as he did, a potato hit his temple, knocking the stunned man down. Haley flew into the elevator car, and the door started to close.

The guard, still lying on the concrete, fired into the lift as Haley dashed to the left behind the closing door. She quickly raised her right arm, putting the potato gun between herself and an incoming bolt. It hit the gun, but Haley remained unharmed.

Then the door was shut, and the elevator car was ascending. She was almost out! She was nervous, anxious with anticipation, and Haley jumped a little when the door on the shaft wall behind her started to open. She turned around to see a familiar dark room with light spilling into the corner across from her at a ramp and in another corner through a stairwell.

The helmet came up, making the mostly dark room visible. She could also now see something on the ceiling that looked just like the cylindrical object that was on the warehouse floor. No time for sightseeing, Haley ran toward the stairwell but had only gone a few feet when a couple of people came hurrying down the ramp.

Haley spun, raised her arm and…nothing. The potato gun wouldn't work, and her eyes went wide as the two men charged straight for her. She turned to run, heading straight for the stairs. The men closed the gap as Haley was halfway up the steps, and the first one grabbed her ankle. Engaging her thrusters, she pulled right out of the surprised man's grasp and out of the stairwell.

Once outside, she felt it. Whatever was disrupting Haley's conscious connection to her energy field was gone, and she spun around, a blue glow in the barrel of her busted potato gun. The phone in her pocket buzzed as she lined up her shot.

Their eyes went wide as Haley's blasts zipped toward them. The two men, regular workers in regular shells, were quickly taken down, but she could hear more people coming from the basement.

Haley went for the woods. Remembering the cave from earlier, she looked and quickly spotted the tree that was above it. She touched down by the oak, saw the rocky opening, and crawled in.

The ground dropped a couple of feet down just inside the entrance, and she dismissed her helmet as her eyes immediately adjusted, revealing the interior of the cave. There was enough room for her to stand. The walls were rocks and roots, stretching down from the tree above, which also formed the cave's dome-shaped ceiling.

She stood and started to turn, taking in the room. Haley thought it looked like something out of a fairytale…and then she saw the large cat sleeping in the corner. The slumbering feline began to stir as soon as the empath laid eyes on her. The bobcat rolled over and opened her eyes to see a shocked Haley standing there against the opposing wall.

Watseka stood up and stretched, never breaking eye contact, then began to walk across the cave toward Haley.

Every step seemed to have a certainty to it. Haley could feel confidence just radiating from the powerful feline as her energy began to coalesce. The inside of her potato gun began to glow, and as Watseka came closer, Haley's energy continued to build. She could feel the intensity begin to reach new heights as the glow from her barrel brightened and blue light began to wisp along the outer surface of the potato gun. "Whoa…" she whispered.

A slamming sound followed by a grunt was heard, causing both Haley and Watseka to turn. They looked out the cave entrance and between the trees to see Chuck taking on four Hunters.

Watseka and Haley looked back at each other, then Haley turned, crawled out of the cave, stood to her feet and aimed.

Chuck took down one of his opponents when he and two of the remaining Hunters noticed the surge of energy. They looked up to see Haley release the charged blast, an orb that sped forward and was larger than the others. Instead of having that kittenish shape like her regular blasts, this one resembled the head of a bobcat.

It slammed one of the Hunters, gelling him and severely damaging the one that was next to him, with the stronger concussive burst. Gentry rushed in at the other Hunter and finished him quickly as Haley was charging another shot.

Remy landed on a tree branch and aimed his rifle. He had one of the Hunters in his sights, but suddenly a large orb of blue and purple light gelled his target. "Even back then?!" he asked in disbelief. "Oh, it's on!" he finished with a confident smirk as he took aim at the final Hunter.

Haley aimed at the last Hunter, but then he jerked weirdly and dropped in a heap of gel from the sniper round. "Hey?!" she whined in disappointment.

Chuck immediately ran for Haley. "You okay?"

"Yeah, but Logan's still way down deep," she replied.

The Marshal only slowed down on his approach and guided her by the shoulder to turn as he said, "Let's go!" and they both flew up to the trees.

"We need to get to the ship," he said as they made their way around the back of the grocery store and toward the park. Remy remained in place, covering their exit.

"Can we stop at the arcade?" Haley asked. Then realizing how childish that sounded, she quickly clarified, "My friends are hiding there."

"No. They're safe for now, but we don't need to draw attention to them," the Marshal said. "Remy's been keepin' watch."

"What are you gonna do about Logan?" she asked.

"We'll get him. And everyone else too," the Marshal assured her.

As they were flying, Haley saw Snow walking along the ground. The cat looked up at her, sat down and said, "Meow." Haley went low, coming down to the ground a little bit before the white feline.

Chuck followed her down and asked, "What are you doing?" But then he felt the energy change.

Looking into Snow's eyes, Haley felt the feline's calm, and her energy gathered in her left arm, coalescing at her wound. The nanobots moved to the side, exposing the injury as she looked to see what was happening.

Right in front of her eyes, the gash in her arm began knitting together as the pain faded away. Snow brushed against her leg, and a wave of warm energy and peace washed through the empath, joining with her own field and sealing the rest of her wound instantly. The soreness from the mystical bolts and blast pistols vanished, and even the slight scrape on her arm was healed.

"Woah!" Haley whispered as she looked over her arm.

Other than some dried blood, there was no sign that she had even been injured. Haley, with a smile, picked up Snow and snuggled him. She then looked up to see a leaf blowing by and suddenly felt it as it smacked to a stop against her energy field, a ripple of blue and purple light resulting from the contact. The surprised farmer saw another one floating on the breeze. Haley watched as the light rippled out from where this next leaf touched her protective sphere.

"Woah!" she whispered yet again.

Snow purred as he gave her one last snuggle, then he hopped down to the ground and wandered off.

The ramp lowered as Haley watched in awe. She could clearly see the inside through the opened ramp, yet the outside of the cloaked aircraft was invisible to the naked eye. "Wow!" exclaimed an excited Haley as curiosity quickly got the best of her. She hopped up and clung to the underside of the cloaked ship, crawling around on apparently nothing as she giggled.

Chuck suppressed his laughter but couldn't hide his smile as he said, "Alright, Spider-Kid. Come back down."

Haley jumped back down with a smile as she playfully said, "That's not my nickname."

"Then what is it?" asked Chuck, wondering if it was the same one that he knew.

"Bad Kitty." She said with a mischievous smirk.

It was. Walking up the ramp, Chuck asked, "How'd you get that name?"

"When I was really little, I used to knock glasses off the table and laugh," Haley explained. "My mom said I was just like a bad kitty, and my dad still calls me that on the walkie-talkie."

She followed Chuck up the ramp and into the ship. "Welcome to the Wavelength," the Marshal said as they walked through the cargo hold, in which was parked a pickup truck and a Jeep. As they walked through the bay and into the ship, Chuck suddenly asked, "Remy, what's going on out there?"

"There's some activity around the Town Hall. Other than a couple guards, there's actually nothing happening around the warehouse right now, and nobody's gone near the arcade." Remy reported. "But the thing that's bugging me is the firehouse," he continued. "I've only seen two people there all day, but it's the most heavily warded place around here."

Following Chuck through the ship, Haley breathed a sigh of relief to hear that Elizabeth and Neil had been left alone. "I'm on my way back to you right now," Remy told them as they entered the front of the aircraft.

Walking through the door, Haley found herself on the bridge of the craft. The large windshield wrapped around the front and extended back most of the length of the bridge. There was a counter-like surface, in which the controls were set toward the front with two seats for a pilot and co-pilot, that followed along the windshield and continued to the bridge's back wall.

About ten feet further back was another seat, set in the center, for the ship's captain. Two more chairs were in the back corners of the bridge, where the floor was elevated a couple feet and sloped downward around either side of the captain's chair.

Some monitors and other equipment were seen along the surface of the horseshoe-shaped console.

"Haley," Chuck said with a smile, "meet Marshal Gus Decker, Captain of the Wavelength," gesturing to the man before her. He was over six feet tall, of medium build, and had a mustache and a slight greenish tint to his skin.

"Hi, Haley," Gus said in his thick Texas accent. The young empath knew the warmth in his smile was genuine. She felt immediately at ease around the man. "I'll bet you've got quite a story to tell."

"Yeah, and it has a lot of Archons," she replied.

"And we need to hear it," Chuck added, sitting in the chair to the right of the captain's as Remy walked on to the bridge.

"By the way," Gus said as he motioned to the entryway, "This is Marshal Jeremy Sinclair."

Haley turned to see a younger man of about five foot eight, wearing cargo pants, a tan T-shirt and a haircut just like her dad's. "Hi," she said with a smile that matched the Marshal's grin. "Are you a Marine?"

"Yes, ma'am!" Remy said happily as he grabbed the back of the co-pilot's chair. It disengaged from the floor, and he rolled it over to the others. Gus sat down in his seat and motioned to the chair, offering for Haley to sit.

A couple of the monitors were displaying videos of places from the complex. Haley recognized the fight at the generator and asked, "How'd you get that?

"This was recorded from the PJs. It all uploaded as soon as you came out of the warehouse," Gus told her. "But now we need to hear about what you saw."

Haley sat in the chair and began to tell them everything she could remember of the earlier events. From her father being teleported to meeting Bast and things, she overheard people say. She mentioned the Podmen and Hunters, handed the portgate stone over to Chuck and told them that there were only seven of the Archons here, but fifty thousand were coming tomorrow. "Until we shut down their generator!" she said excitedly, but then noticed that the Marshals didn't look as hopeful as she'd expected.

Gus looked to Haley and said, "As soon as you got clear from the interference, Logan's com reconnected with ours, and we got the info on the generator. But now, it also has the information from Chuck's com and…" He pointed to the phone, Haley looked at the screen, and her stomach dropped. Gentry had obtained the electrical schematics for another portion of the facility, which showed another active generator.

"Oh, no…" she said with a heavy heart. To make matters worse, these schematics only covered about two-thirds of the complex. This made Haley and the Marshals think that there might be one more generator.

"We're handlin' it," Chuck said. "Remy and I are going back in and shutting down their entire operation. And we're gonna need to bring Logan his PJs."

Haley raised her arm, and the nanobots formed the com-band on her wrist. "Is it alright if I keep using the scarf?" Haley asked.

Gus stood up. "Actually, I'm gonna upgrade that for ya," he said with a smile. "And run a splindie."

"What's a splindie?" she asked.

"Split and individualize," Gus elaborated as he held up his phone, and it began to ripple. The phone split into two, and he handed one to Haley. "This is now its own individual com-system, and it's assigned to you. Your very own set of PJs! And I've added some options." Gus said. "It can turn into things, like the clothes you're wearing. A variety of hats, scarfs, gloves, shoes, jackets, headphones, safety or sunglasses, pouch, headband…"

He suddenly noticed Chuck giving him a particular look, reminding Gus of his tendency to overexplain when he gets excited. "…you get the idea. And you can program more clothes into it." He then pointed at the phone as he said, "And you can make that phone look like any model you see available, so it won't look out of place."

"Even those cool new flip phones?!" Haley asked excitedly.

"Sure," Gus replied as he was looking at her potato gun. "May I take a look," he politely asked as his eyes landed on the misaligned air cartridge. "I think I can fix that."

"Yes, please!" Haley said as she took off the ring and handed it over to Gus. The technically-inclined Marshal held up the potato gun and immediately saw the engraved badge number. Haley sensed the solemn respect from Gus. The Marshal didn't know Heather Starr, but he knew Haley and how influential the detective had been in who the farmgirl could or would become. Gus, along with the other Marshals, held their deceased colleague from another universe in very high regard. He and Chuck went to the back corner of the bridge, where some equipment formed from the counter.

"Think fast!" Haley heard Remy shout. She turned her head in time to see a tennis ball flying her way. Haley laughed as she caught it and tossed it right back to the fun-loving Remy. The ball went back and forth for a couple of moments while Chuck and Gus had a conversation about with whom they may be dealing.

"I've taken a look at the history of this universe, and it's mostly identical to ours," Gus said as he scanned Haley's rig.

"The Archons influenced our world's events," Chuck said. "If it's the same here, then who's messing with them?"

"Looks like there's an Illuminati in this universe as well, but instead of answering to Archons, they apparently answer to a people known as Cetatians. They seem to be using the same playbook, which is why our histories are so similar." Gus' eyes lit up as he thought about some information that he's found. "Remember the Challenger?" he suddenly asked.

Chuck thought for a moment and asked, "Was that one of the shuttles that were decommissioned in twenty-eleven?"

"Yep, but in this universe, it exploded during a launch back in eighty-six," Gus told Chuck. "Looks like it was sabotage by the Cetatians, and the incident brought many space programs around the world to a near stand-still." He then shrugged and said, "But the Titanic never sank here."

"What else do you have on these guys?" Chuck asked.

"They're an aquatic humanoid species and native to this Earth," Gus answered as he tried to remove the stuck cartridge from Haley's gun. "They inhabit the Second Density here as the Archons do on our world, but unlike them, the Cetatians can exist naturally in the First Density as well."

Gus shifted his energy, altering his right hand to be a little out of phase with this plane's density. He reached into the gun, hand passing through the solid object, as he gathered a bit more of his energy and overlapped it with that of the cartridge. The pneumatic container harmonized with the vibration of Gus' hand, making it tangible to the Texan, allowing him to wrap his fingers around the stuck object and pull it out through the side.

"That's cheating," Chuck said with mock seriousness as Gus returned his comment with a lazy, if not slightly smug, smile.

Schematics for Haley's rig was on one of the monitors, and Gus selected a micro compressor to replace the air cartridge. A clear box, about three feet tall and wide, sat on the counter as the nanobots inside came together, building themselves into a new miniature compressor.

"So, this is Harry's first design," Chuck stated while looking at the screen.

"Yeah, and he's a genius," Gus said with admiration as he pointed at the flexible tubing. "The hose wall is all vacuum lines. The air cartridges drove the clips and allowed the trigger to turn the clock springs. He used simple methods to make something complex. He was as precise as a watchmaker."

Haley giggled as Remy bounced the ball off the floor at an angle, making it shoot up toward the wall and bounce toward Haley's open hands. She easily caught it and sent it back with a single bounce off the floor.

She could feel the enthusiasm radiating from the Marshal. Haley thought that if she asked him, Remy would say that life is motion.

"Hi, Kitty!" she exclaimed as an orange and white cat walked up to her. Both Chuck and Gus looked over their shoulders at Haley and smiled as they watched her greet yet another new old friend.

"Meow," the cat said.

"That's Scott," Remy told her.

Chuck and Gus turned back toward the desk and the nano-printer, which held a new compressor. "So, Bast managed to talk with them through the bindings," Gus commented. "Guess I shouldn't be surprised. Nobody can slip between the worlds quite like she can." He inserted the micro compressor into place, and it powered up.

"Yeah," Chuck agreed. "She's always been a real Houdini." He then switched subjects, "I'm still trying to wrap this thing up quick and clean," He began. "But before we go, we're gonna have to leave an incident report with someone we can trust."

"I already looked him up," Gus replied. "From what I can find, He seems to be just as trustworthy as the one we know, and it looks like he already has a clue about the Cetatians."

"Not surprised, really," Chuck said. "You have some autonomy on this one. If you think we need to make the call sooner and you can't get ahold of me, you make it," he firmly stated.

Gus nodded as Haley and Remy went back to tossing the ball, and Scott hopped onto the desk. Gus rubbed him under the chin as he said, "Just stay off the keyboard."

"Why do you even have a keyboard?" Chuck asked. A question he seems to reassert every couple of months.

"Why do you still carry a notepad and pen?" Gus asked with a smirk. He then picked up the potato gun and carried it over to Haley. "Okay, Darlin', need to give you a heads up!"

Haley turned to see Gus holding her repaired rig.

"You're definitely gonna have more kickback, but you won't need a cartridge again. There's a micro-compressor in its place that runs on the ambient energy."

"Thank you very much," said a grateful Haley as she slipped her arms through the straps and pulled them snug.

Chuck then said, "Remy, get ready. Gus, I want you to monitor the arcade."

"What do I do?" Haley asked.

"You wait here until we get back," Gentry said firmly.

"But I have to go too," Haley insisted, "my dad is down there. And you need to find Logan. I can tell where he is, especially after the whip."

"The what?!" Chuck asked as all three of them suddenly seemed very concerned. Haley had forgotten to mention that part earlier, but as soon she said the word whip, she picked up a very uncomfortable feeling in all three of their stomachs combined with a sense of loss.

"He couldn't breathe, and I was worried," Haley explained. "When I touched his arm, I…" she took a deep breath and blew it out with a sigh while lowering her head, "I felt what he felt."

Gus pulled the records from Logan's PJs, and the info came up on the screen with a readout of O'Connors' vitals from that point in time.

Chuck looked at the screen. "You empathically entangled…during a flashback?!" he asked and turned back toward Haley, the worry written all over his face. "Are…are you okay?"

"Yeah," Haley said. She looked down to the floor, wondering how to explain this, then looked back up and said, "I…I actually feel better."

"What?" asked a shocked Remy.

"I feel better," Haley said with more conviction.

The three Marshals were at a total loss.

"I don't know what happened," Haley said, "but I know how he felt. And I know how I felt when my mother was tak…" Her lips quivered, and her eyes began to water. "…when Mom died."

Haley sat in the chair and took a deep breath. "The councilors keep telling me that I have to move on. That sounds like forgetting…so it doesn't hurt anymore."

With a sniffle, she wiped her eyes. "But I know something now…" Her eyes dropped to her right arm as she thought about the badge number engraved on her potato gun. "…she's always with me." Haley looked up at the Marshals, and her voice began to break with the next words. "So, we don't move on…we keep going…"

After another sniffle, her lips quivered between a smile and a grimace as she said, "…and we get to take them with us."

No one in the Wavelength had a dry eye. Chuck ran a thumb across the bottom of his, removing a couple of tears. Gus' orbs were also misted over as Remy did a bad job at trying to hide his face. Even Scott's cheeks were soaked.

Haley snapped her head back toward the cat to see that he was indeed crying. Everyone else followed her gaze, and they all realized that Bast had been part of their company.

The goddess felt what Haley had said on the deepest levels. She thought back to her oldest friends. Akhenaten could talk about the color of sand and make it sound fascinating. Meresankh had a way to brighten anyone's day with the warmth of her smile. These friends, and others near and dear, helped shape and mold Bast into the person that she had become, yet not a mortal alive today knew they ever existed.

One by one, Bast had to say goodbye to them all. She could only watch so many friends pass before the weight of those sorrows became too much. And so, she and the other immortals began to associate less and less with the regular humans until they had faded into myth.

But hearing Haley's words reminded Bast that they were part of who she was. And she was part of this world which means *they* were still part of this world.

Scott walked across the floor to where Haley was seated and hopped up into her lap. "Thank God you're okay," Bast said with more tears streaming down Scott's wet cheeks. The cat snuggled into Haley, and the farmer hunched over, wrapping her arms around the cat and burying her face in

Scott's fur. They empathically bonded and continued to cry, sharing the bitter-sweet moment of both sorrow and comfort.

Chuck and Remy were forming their plan as they got ready to go. "Despite so much interference, it looks like the signal still carries through the entire complex," Chuck said as he projected the map from his phone. "I think it's near here," he said, pointing to an HVAC control station, "but everything, including the electrical system, is compartmentalized. The only systems that look continuous are the plumbing and the HVAC. We shut down the emitter first," Chuck said. "Then we get Logan and shut down the other generator…or two."

"I Looked over the footage of Haley's escape," Gus said, "there was conduit running through the inside of every air shaft she was in. And when you remove the emitter," Gus added, "try to replace it with one of our repeaters. Maybe we'll finally be able to communicate down there."

Scott, still in Haley's lap, stood up as Bast began to speak, "I'm going to go to the Arcade and tell them that Haley is safe, then I need to rest again."

"And let them know to stay put," Chuck added. "If things get too hot…" he motioned toward Gus.

"I'll let them know," Bast said. "Give Scott a scratch on the head for me, blessings on your quest and thank you for helping to protect our world." With that, they felt Bast's energy disappear.

"Alright," Chuck began. "Let's…"

The energy shifted again as Bast unexpectedly returned and said, "They're searching the town, and they're almost to the arcade!"

Immediately, Chuck looked to Remy, his expression grim, and said, "Do it."

Remy turned to run as Chuck made very clear, "Not like last time."

"I'll keep it reasonable," Remy assured Gentry.

"Just don't…I don't want the place to look like Peter Griffin fought a chicken, okay?"

"Relax," Remy said with an easy smile. He then gestured toward the farmgirl as he said, "I'm not gonna break Haley's hometown." He turned and ran.

"Who's Peter Griffin?" Haley asked.

"Never mind," Chuck answered as he turned to Gus. "I know we're trying to interact with as few people as possible, but we might not have that luxury anymore. Once clear, get those two out of the arcade and bring 'em here. I'm gonna go shut down that emitter and find Logan." Gus nodded.

"I'll go with you," Haley offered.

"Not a chance," Gentry said without skipping a beat.

"How are you gonna find him? I can sense him and tell you which way he is." She closed her eyes and focused, then looked at Chuck with great concern. "He's angry right now."

Logan used language Haley would not approve of as he sifted through the trash beneath his feet, searching for the lighter he had just dropped.

"Not happening," Chuck firmly said once again and turned to leave.

"Fifty thousand," Haley said, and Chuck stopped moving. "They're all moving here tomorrow. We're running out of time! You need to find him fast."

Chuck turned back toward Haley as she continued. "I know I'm just a kid, but you know I can do stuff, and this is my world. I need to stand up for it." She took a deep breath, "I won't back down." she said with determination written all over her face. "And I'm the only one who can fit in the vents," she added, sounding a little more like a question than a statement.

Chuck made a bit of a grunting sound. Haley felt great conflict within the Marshal as he handed her Logan's com-band and said, "I can't believe I'm doing this."

CHAPTER 17
Don't Make Me Angry

Remy got to the strip mall in time to see the Proctors approaching the building. He made his way to the top of the gas station canopy unseen and went down to his stomach, then lifted his head just enough to get a good look. He pretended to sneeze, and when the Proctors and Hunter below looked in his direction, he dropped his head like he hoped he wasn't seen.

They all started coming his way, and the Marshal got to his feet, ran and jumped off the canopy toward the road. The men opened fire, but Remy was quick and moved erratically, making him very difficult to hit. Only the Hunter managed to nick his shoulder, not even a nuisance, before the Marshal made it to the trees across the street.

Remy could still be seen running through the woods as the squeal of tires was heard from both directions. He moved deeper into the woods and south, which drew the growing crowd down toward the diner.

Logan dropped a lot of Proctors and even managed a couple of Hunters, but he was out of ammo. Without his abilities and PJs augmenting his strength, the gelatinizing Hunter in front of him had worn the Marshal down.

Some of the Hunters were as skilled as Logan, and most were better. They were also in enhanced shells, and Logan knew he owed this latest victory, if he could call it that, to luck just as much as his prowess. But as he turned, another Hunter in a Joey shell approached. He had his pistol up as he said, "It's set to full power. Hold your hands out to the sides."

Logan picked up a prideful feeling as he slowly held his hands out, palms open. *Maybe I can get him yapping*, he thought.

As he blew out a sigh, O'Connor said, "Look. I've already used more Plan Bs today than I care to admit. Please don't make me use another one." Then he sheepishly added, "I only know the one alphabet," as if that would appeal to his kinder senses.

"Oh, yeah?" the Hunter began with a chuckle. "Let me tell you something about your alphabet, Primate…"

The Hunter was interrupted by a pistol cracking Logan over the back of his head, knocking him out. He fell to the trash-covered floor as the Hunter with the Spanish accent was standing behind him. In person. "You received their profiles. What did it say?"

"Not to verbally engage," the Hunter answered, obviously embarrassed. "It's one of their tactics."

"You've come a long way, Samuel," said the Hunter. "Don't let pride undo all the self-control that you've worked so hard to achieve."

The Spanish Hunter then placed a disk on Logan's back. Four metallic tendrils extended out from the sides of the disk and wrapped around the Marshal, cinching themselves snug. The disk then levitated, hoisting the Marshal into the air. His head lolled off to the side, and his feet were dangling a few inches off the ground.

"I will swallow my pride," he said with determination, and the Hunter with the Spanish accent believed him. He knew that just saying those words was difficult for the younger Samuel.

This Hunter had been a mentor to Samuel over the last couple of years and watched him grow as a person. "I believe in you, Samuel. Now get him to holding right away. Even without powers," the Hunter said, pointing at the many piles of clothes mixed in with the trash. "They're still very dangerous."

At first, Chuck thought getting back in would be a bigger chore. There was bound to be a great deal of security in the warehouse, but Remy had captured a lot of attention and probably thinned out some of the resistance that Chuck and Gus would have encountered.

Nobody was near the strip mall as Haley and the Marshals went by. Chuck was still just half a heartbeat from telling Gus to take Haley and stay with them at the arcade, but she was right. They had to shut this down before the Archons ported. The emitter was most likely in the ventilation station, and the air duct that Haley originally entered allowed her easy access.

"As soon as we go inside, we won't be able to use our mojo," Chuck reminded Haley. "We're gonna find the disrupter and shut it off. Then we get communication with Logan. After that, you go back out the vents and let us handle the rest."

"Okay," Haley said.

They landed in the woods behind the grocery store. Chuck held up his phone and said, "Take a look at this." Haley observed as a thin rectangular slot opened across the bottom of his com-system's handset. What looked like a thin sheet of clear plastic, about the size of a credit card, slid out from the bottom. The Marshal held it up and said, "This is a repeater. Your com can make them too." Haley nodded, and Chuck continued. "Put one near the top of the ductwork and another when you get to the bottom, so you'll still be able to talk to Gus and Remy."

"No problem," Haley said.

"Once you get to the station," Gentry continued, "stick another one to the inside of the ducts. Your com will be able to scan the area and let us know if the emitter is there, but if it is, there's probably going to be heavy security so stay in the vents," he said, his expression quite serious.

"I'll stay in the vents," Haley confirmed.

"Good," he said and then continued going over the plan. "I'm gonna have to use the elevator to make my way back in, which must have some heavy security by now. I'll be out of contact as soon as I go in, but Gus will be on the line with you. And when Gus tells you that it's clear, you go back out and leave with him." Haley nodded, and as he finished.

They flew around to the back of the warehouse and found two guards with a Hunter posted at the stairwell as three men were working to seal off access.

The Marshals both conjured a rifle from their PJs and took aim. As the engine of a dirt bike could be heard screaming by the front of the warehouse, followed by some speeding vehicles, the Marshals squeezed off six quick pops. Then Chuck went for the stairs as Haley flew down and hopped into the vent.

She placed a repeater near the top of the shaft as Chuck placed one at the top of the stairs. Haley activated her helmet, and the bots that made up her clothing separated and extended out, pulling her pigtails in and underneath the outer layer of clothes. The bots also formed a long-sleeved undershirt and some gloves, keeping her covered head to toe.

Haley lowered down the air shaft to where it bent forty-five degrees, and she followed it to the bottom, where she placed another repeater and looked around as she asked, "Can you still hear me?"

"Loud and clear," Gus replied as he entered the stairs. Chuck was halfway across the cellar, dropping a couple more hostiles. He approached the elevator and attached another repeater to the wall as Gus fired at more people coming down the ramp.

This is where she first came into the facility and turned left. Now, she would be going right toward the HVAC station and this time. She was here with a plan. Haley felt like a secret agent but resisted the urge to hum the *Mission: Impossible* theme, knowing that the others would be able to hear her do it. Making her way through the ducts, Haley imagined "MISSION" being typed onto a paper and the words "DISABLE THE EMITTER" being stamped below.

Haley pulled her focus back from the imaginative dramatization and attached a couple more repeaters as she used her thrusters to float silently to her destination without incident but could sense people in the room before she got there. Upon arrival, she looked through the slotted vent cover as she attached another repeater.

There were four Proctors and a Hunter, as well as three other people in boilersuits working on various tasks. Haley's helmet filtered out the whooshing sound in the air ducts, allowing her to hear them speak. The Hunter was on a wall-mounted intercom and then abruptly turned to address the room, "Looks like they're coming! Be ready!"

The workers grabbed their tools as weapons.

"I can see eight people," she informed the others while her com scanned the room. "One of them is big. And they know you're coming." She whispered as she spoke, which was unnecessary as her voice could not be heard outside of the helmet. Haley's com detected the disruption emitter and the info displayed in her HUD. "It's here!" she said in an excited whisper.

"Acknowledged," Chuck said with guns pointed toward the elevator door as it opened. He fired, taking down the two Proctors in the lift while Gus watched the room. Using the com, Chuck made the lift move up as far as it would go and, with a smirk of satisfaction, said, "It's enough."

The Hunter and three guards knew that the lift was coming down, and they were ready with pistols pointed at the door, waiting. When the doors slid open, they were expecting to see a couple of Marshals, but instead was an empty cargo lift that had stopped just a bit higher than it should have been.

One of the Proctors leaned into the shaft and took an energy bolt to the top of the head from Gus' pistol. Gus was leaning into the shaft from the door up above as he shot a few more rounds, finishing off the surprised guard.

The other two guards leaned in with pistols up, sending a barrage of return fire. Gus backed away from the shaft door to avoid the shots, and the guards poured it on harder, providing cover for the Hunter, who began to climb the inside of the shaft.

The Hunter was about halfway up when the lift suddenly started to move. The upper door closed as Chuck slipped out from under the lift platform and into the corridor, throwing smoke pellets in both directions. The door slid shut behind him, and as expected, there were more guards and a couple of Hunters, but the place quickly filled with smoke, and Chuck had his helmet up with the visor set to infrared.

With one gun in blast mode and the other set to conventional, Chuck targeted one of the Hunters first, firing two blasts to the chest, followed immediately by a bullet from the other gun. The two blasts weakened the resilient skin of the shell, allowing the bullet to penetrate and do critical damage to the internal organs, turning him to gel.

The Marshal quickly spun and did the same to the other Hunter, leaving only a handful of confused Proctors. He dropped them all within a second and then used his thrusters, hurrying for the HVAC room.

"Chuck is on his way to you," Gus said to Haley. "I'll let you know as soon as it's safe to come up."

"Okay," she said, still whispering. Haley didn't have to wait more than a minute as Chuck flew through the corridors, gelling a couple of surprised guards along the way. Haley could sense that intense focus quickly getting closer as everybody in the room tensed up and turned toward the elevator.

The lift door opened, and one of the guards fired immediately, striking the back wall of the empty shaft.

Realizing the ruse, the Hunter was spinning around before the Proctor's bolt hit, but the Marshal was already there. Haley watched from the vent as Chuck conjured what looked like brass knuckles from his PJs. In he leaped, striking the enhanced Hunter across the face as electrical shocks discharged from the knuckles on impact. The Hunter fell over backward as Chuck opened fire, quickly gelling the workers and pressuring the Proctors while making his way toward the emitter.

"He's here," Haley told Gus.

"Don't come back out yet," he responded, "it's still too hot up here."

Chuck landed a shot on two of the Proctors, then quickly dashed to the side behind a cluster of ductworks, firing as he went while the guards fired back. The technicians, not trained in combat, were taken out quickly.

The Hunter was already getting back up as Gentry moved around the ducting and fired a couple more shots, hitting a third guard and gelling the second. He moved back around the cluster to deal with the bigger threat.

Chuck twisted to the side while leaning back, getting his face out of the way just before the pistol bolt whizzed by his nose. As he moved, Gentry fired two blasts from the gun in his left hand, then he followed it with a bullet from his right.

As quick as it happened, the three remaining Proctors were flanking around the ductwork, and Chuck spun back around in time to drop his gun and grab a guard's wrist, wrenching his arm back. Gentry slammed the Proctor in the face with his other gun, and when he did, the guard's blast pistol discharged, hitting the ductwork above.

As Chuck finished off the Proctor, a support strap gave way, and the ducting separated at the joint, causing the newly opened end to tilt downward from Haley's weight, dumping her to the floor.

Remy tore down the road and leaned into the left turn. He shifted his weight, leaning back to the right as the road curved along the bottom of the hill. The cars on his tail fell behind as the bike hugged the corner. The Marshal leaned left again while rolling on the throttle, the road straightened out, and he zipped by Haley's farm.

He was already approaching the next corner as the cars behind him came onto the straightaway. Remy leaned left and looked up ahead to a hairpin corner. He rolled on the throttle again, pulling out of sight from his pursuers.

Remy came to a stop at the edge of the woods of the next corner and let the bike drop next to a tree. He then ran a couple of steps into the woods, looked over his shoulder and waited a couple more seconds.

Three cars chased the bike. The passengers all heard Sahmbo's voice come onto the radio, "Where did he show up?"

When Remy saw the first car come around the corner, he started running. Into the woods he went, expecting the others to stop their cars, get out and chase him. Two of the cars stopped suddenly and began turning around as the lead vehicle came to a stop and parked by Remy's bike.

Four men got out of the car and began to chase Remy. "Two of those cars chasing me just turned around to go back. You okay?"

"Yeah," Gus replied. "Dealing with some heat behind the warehouse, but nothing outrageous."

Running through the woods, Remy asked, "Well, I just became much less interesting to them."

"Haley's in play," Chuck just unhappily announced. "Somebody, get eyes on the Arcade."

The Hunter and Proctors were running as fast as their shells would allow when Remy abruptly spun around with a yellow glow coming from his blue eyes.

The Hunter fired a shot, and the Marshal side-stepped the bolt. Then, Remy put his foot down.

The ground trembled in the immediate area, enough for all of his attackers to stumble. He held up his fist, releasing a blast of energy. It looked like a yellow distortion in the air as it quickly rippled ahead and slammed into the Hunter. The seismic energy vibrated the cellular structure of the shell, dropping the Hunter right back down. The next blast finished him as the Proctors opened fire.

Remy casually dodged their shots while returning fire, quickly dropping the three guards. He fired his thrusters, went straight up and took off for the Arcade.

Gus dropped the last couple of Proctors and turned toward the north. As he started to move, the Marshal heard the footsteps of the next Proctor to come out from the warehouse. Gus spun around with his firearm to see the

Proctor suddenly knocked to the ground by the bobcat tearing into him. The guard destabilized, and Watseka recoiled from the gelatinizing mass. She turned around and went back to her den as Gus turned for the Arcade.

Haley landed on her feet with a look of shock on her concealed face as another Proctor rushed into the room. One of the Proctors aimed his pistol while Haley raised her arm, but Gentry shot the guard before he could fire. She quickly shifted her aim to one of the remaining guards and felt that firm kickback as she launched a potato into his hand. The flying spud hit the Proctor's fingers, and the pistol discharged, the bolt hitting a wall as the guard dropped it, and Chuck capitalized on the opportunity.

The farmer launched another potato for the final guard as three more men entered the room. The guard was staggered by the force of the missile, and the Marshal finished him as well.

The newcomers, two Proctors and a Hunter, came in fast. Haley was closest to the emitter, and she went for it while Chuck engaged with the hostiles.

Haley ran up to the control panel mounted to the side of the intake unit, hoping to see some kind of obvious off button. Her HUD showed that her com had been trying to sync into the unit, but until then, it needed some kind of key fob to interact. She didn't even know what a fob was.

She turned around to see Chuck had already taken down the Proctors and was tangling with the Hunter, but more people started coming in. One of them, another Hunter, was in a Harry shell and seeing this over and over was again getting to Haley.

Chuck was moving furiously. His hands were a blur to the eye as he overwhelmed a couple more guards and then took on the latest Hunter. Haley saw two guards coming for her with pistols up. They fired, and she jumped up with her thrusters out of the way. The bolts hit the emitter unit, but nothing critical.

Haley landed on top of the unit as the guards charged forward and fired. She jumped again but took a hit knocking her to the floor. The PJs did provide protection, and it felt similar to the shot from before, but if it weren't for the nanotech, Haley could have been seriously hurt.

On the floor was a big pipe wrench that one of the workers had intended to use as a weapon. Grabbing the tool, she threw it at the closest guard, her strength augmented by the PJs, and hit him in the solar plexus.

Haley engaged the thrusters to right herself as the wrench hit, knocking the wind out of the guard and temporarily disrupting his control of the shell. She dashed to the side as the other Proctor fired his pistol. Haley launched a potato in return but missed as she dove behind some more ductwork.

She popped out and launched another spud, catching him on the chin. The Proctor lost balance and fell over as Haley ran back to the emitter.

Chuck slammed electrified knuckles through the gelatinizing Hunter's face and then fired shots at another wave of opponents, wondering how much longer before the com-system would sync with the emitter console.

Haley aimed her arm at the guard as she ran by and tried to launch a potato, discovering that she was out. "Uh-oh!" she gasped as she passed by and got back to the machine. "Think, think, think!" Haley said aloud.

The frustrated Proctor had regained control of his shell and stood up, grabbing the wrench from the floor. He yelled as he charged at Haley and swung down with a mighty overhand blow. Haley dodged to the side, and he hit the emitter.

Chuck made his face shield flip up because he wanted his enemies to see the fierce blue light in his eyes as he slammed his fist to the floor, unleashing a circle of ethereal flames that expanded out ten feet and dissipated. Most of his opponents had already taken on damage, and the wave of fire finished them off. There were two Hunters and a Proctor remaining. One Hunter broke away to get Haley while the other two tried to take down Gentry.

With her powers back, she quickly took down the two guards and then looked up to see a Hunter wearing her father's face. Haley's blood boiled, and she started blasting.

The false Harry held his left arm up to take most of the impact as he fired a pistol with his right. The first shot hit Haley but didn't seem all that harsh, as she pushed her energy out into a protective sphere, blocking the other shots. She could feel their points of impact, but it did not discomfort her at all. However, she could also feel that every shot was a drain on her energy.

Using her thrusters, she jumped to the side and took cover behind the ductwork again. Haley looked up toward the ceiling, figured, "Fair is fair," and shot above the Hunter's head at the ductwork support straps.

The straps broke and the ductwork mangled from the farmer's blast, but it didn't tumble down. It did, however, make the Hunter reflexively look up and back away. The farmer didn't miss her opportunity and sent four blasts straight to his chest. He staggered back onto the emitter console as Haley charged up a shot. The Hunter got his balance back just in time to see a large ethereal bobcat face slam into him.

A scowling Haley sent more blasts into the already gelatinizing Hunter. "Stop using his face!" she screamed in rage. "Stop! Stop! Stop!"

"Hey!" Chuck said, snapping Haley back to her senses. Her breathing was labored as she seethed toward the dissolving gel puddle. Then she calmed, and her eyes went wide as she realized the results of her actions. The console was a mangled wreck and inoperable.

Knowing that more were on the way, Chuck said to Haley, "Let's go." He then said, "The emitter's down, but the repeater won't work. We gotta move."

"Acknowledged," came the reply from Gus and Remy.

The signal was lost as they ran out of the HVAC room and toward the northern end of the complex. A few Proctors were encountered and quickly gelled, but most were coming from the other direction.

It took a few moments, but there was another HVAC center up ahead, and Chuck was hoping that there might be an emitter console but was disappointed upon arrival. He did, however, get the rest of the facility's electrical schematics, which confirmed the third generator. They went back to the corridors and down deeper, successfully avoiding any more hostiles.

Remy flew through the air, straight for the arcade. He came over the tree line to see a group converging on the strip mall. "The Arcade's hot! They're all in front of the building, and I'm dropping in on top of 'em." He said, watching the men get out of the vehicles that broke away from the chase.

"I'm gonna come around back," Gus replied, "and try to get them out."

"Acknowledged," Remy said. "Here I go!"

It wasn't even an effort for her now. Elizabeth made the flame flicker around any way she chose and could move the air in the room as easy as breathing. She seemed to have reached a tipping point of sorts as Neil noticed that she was now maintaining that denser field of energy at all times.

"I'm not trying to," Elizabeth said, surprised that her increased strength and durability seemed to now be a default state.

"That's probably a good thing," Neil said.

The young mystic's eyes dropped to a deck of cards on Neil's desk. She remembered the magician and how good he was. Her eyes lit up, "Hey, the magician last year at my birthday party, was he using actual magick?"

With a smile, Neil answered, "No, he was using stage magic. Sleight of hand and misdirection."

"Oh," Elizabeth said, seeming a little disappointed.

"Why do you look like that's a bad thing?" Neil asked.

She shrugged, "I don't know…I guess it was just cool to think that he was doing the real thing."

"I see," replied Neil and then thought for a couple of seconds. "You know, I could tell you exactly how his tricks are done…but I can't pull off a single one of them."

Elizabeth was surprised to think that this man who could manipulate energy couldn't accomplish a card trick.

"He trained for years to do what he does. Precise movement at perfect times, coupled with understanding the crowd and directing their focus. Properly presenting an illusion is an incredibly difficult skill."

She listened, her mind almost already going to where Neil was leading.

"Just because nothing mystical was involved in his work doesn't make it any less amazing. Energy can be very exciting and cool and fun, but don't lose sight of the…" he held up his hands and made quote signs with his fingers, "…'mundane world,' because it has just as many wonders to offer as the mystical." He went and leaned against his desk as he added with a smile, "And that's also where we live, so…kind of important."

With a laugh at Neil's last comment, Elizabeth walked over to the couch and turned around to sit. As soon as she started to bend her legs, the building suddenly trembled as she fell into the cushions.

Neil managed to not fall over, but they heard a commotion continuing out front as his cell phone started ringing. Surprised, he grabbed his phone and opened it. "Hello?"

"This is Marshal Gus Decker. I'm coming to the back of your unit to get you guys outta there. Right now."

A knock was heard at the back door as he said the words. Elizabeth looked to Neil, and with a wave of his hand, he said, "C'mon, it's the Marshals," and went to the door.

Neil, hoping that this wasn't a trick, opened the door to see a man with a slightly greenish tint to his skin. "Hi, I'm Gus, and we gotta go," he said, holding up his identification. He turned around and pointed up the hill. "Remy's gonna keep them busy up front while we go this way."

Neil and Elizabeth started to follow the Marshal, but as soon as they stepped onto the hill, all three of them felt the change in energy. Then four spots of bright light appeared, and when they faded, two Archons, a Proctor, and a wizard were standing in their place.

"Hello, cowboy," one of the Archons said as the wizard softly chanted.

Gus quickly responded with a bullet through the reptilian's eye as Elizabeth felt an energy field envelop and cling to her. "What was that?" the young mystic asked. But then the wizard spoke a word, and in more flashes of light, the attackers were gone.

And so was Elizabeth.

Logan opened his eyes. The back of his head throbbed as he sat up and looked around. Four walls of cement and one of bars. He slowly stood to his feet, looking around at the simple eight-by-ten cell. He had a metal band on each wrist, locked shut but not chained to anything.

O'Connor could sense his field again. The emitter must have been shut down, but the bands on his wrists were still preventing him from projecting his field. He looked out the bars to see more cells on the other side of the room. Logan walked up to them to get a better look and found that there were four cells on each side and an exit at one end of the room, where a Proctor stood watch.

"Remain away from the bars," he stated firmly.

Logan opened his mouth but then shut it and complied, figuring that if they wanted to leave him be for the moment, it was actually to his advantage. He went to the back of the cell, sat on the floor and focused on the bands. He felt the energy emitting from them. Felt the subtle vibrations. After a few moments, his own vibration started to adjust and harmonize, coming to a frequency with which he could work.

He gained an energetic grasp, and the bands finally snapped off of his wrists. He then opened his eyes, looked up to the bars and smirked.

Haley knew she messed up bad and felt Chuck's anger for the situation. The empath dismissed her helmet and shook her head back and forth as the pigtails released from her clothing. She sat on a crate and took a deep breath, looking at the floor while wondering how to make it right.

After checking around the area once more, Chuck walked over, sat next to Haley and looked her in the eye, his expression stern. "So…bit of a temper?"

"I'm sorry," Haley said softly and then looked back down to the floor.

The Marshal let out a long sigh and said, "Look, I get it. If half these snapper-heads around here had my dad's face, I'd probably lose it too. In fact, I have…a lot."

Haley looked up at the seemingly unshakeable Gentry, surprised to hear this. Chuck's emotions were very strong and could fill a room, but he seemed like he had them constantly in check.

"I used to run on anger. Thought it made me stronger…and it could, but it can also make me very stupid," he explained. "I've made some bad choices because of my temper, and one time, it almost got people killed. But it was a mistake that I learned from."

Haley said, "My dad told me that, in the military, they would sometimes make the bad guys mad on purpose, so they would make mistakes."

"Yes, and now you understand why it can work," Chuck replied. "Take it from an old hot-head. Emotions can be like wind in the sails," he said with a sweeping motion of the arm, "but a clear mind has to steer the ship," he continued while pointing a finger to the side of his head. "Use 'em, don't let them use you."

Haley nodded, contemplating everything the Marshal had just said. Chuck let her think it over for a moment, then he got a smirk and said with more of a lighthearted tone, "So, where are we going?"

"Huh?" she asked, not sure what he meant.

"You're the navigator," Chuck said. "Which way is he?"

"Oh…" she closed her eyes and focused. "He's over toward the other side," Haley said, "and a little bit down. He seems calm…oh, his feelings are jumbling again…and they stopped. Everybody does that sometimes, but he does that a lot, doesn't he? Is that also from…the whip thing?"

With a slight laugh, Chuck said, "No, I think that's just normal for him."

"After today, I don't know what normal is," Haley said, looking up at Chuck with a shrug and a sheepish grin.

"Do you really want to know what normal is?" Chuck asked with a smile.

"Yeah," nodded an intrigued Haley.

"Great!" he replied with a big grin. "Once you figure it out, let me know."

Haley playfully punched his shoulder as she said, "Smarty!" Then, before she could blink, Haley was pulled into a headlock and received a noogie.

CHAPTER 18
Power Surge

There would be way too many opponents to go back up and across the complex, and it wouldn't be long before they came searching through Haley and Chuck's current location. So, they went down deeper, hoping to avoid search parties, but it was bringing them closer to one of the generators, which would again mean more security.

"How can we get to the other side?" Haley asked.

"Still working on that," Chuck answered while looking at his map.

"Maybe we'll find another one of those portgates," Haley said hopefully. "Do you think that they would have one near the other generators?" she asked.

Chuck considered that for a moment. Most portgates had an opening about the size of a regular door, but the one he saw in Logan's recording was much bigger to allow freight. There would likely be one near each generator for service equipment. "Probably," he said, "but they've gotta have both generators under heavy guard. Unfortunately, we still can't go anywhere near the upper levels…let's go see if we can learn anything new," he finished.

They made their way near to the bottom levels of the complex, and the pipes were becoming more prominent as they neared the water treatment room. The air, which smelled of chlorine, was more humid in the southern corner of the complex as they searched through, but the two found nothing of use. They did, however, hear a congested snarl.

"These things," Chuck grumbled as they turned toward the sounds.

Three of the mindless creatures came running through the room as Haley and Chuck gathered their energy. They both released a charged shot, ending the confrontation as quickly as it started. Haley immediately turned her senses outward as Chuck scanned the area with his com. Neither could detect anything.

"At least those things can't tell anybody where we are," Chuck commented.

Haley asked, "Where are all those people hiding? Are they really in another dimension?"

"Density, but yeah. You have the right idea." Chuck answered.

"What's the difference between density and dimension?" inquired Haley.

Chuck sighed as he shook his head with a grin. "You couldn't have asked this when Gus was around?"

"Didn't know to ask," Haley said with a shrug.

"Just give me a second to get the spark plugs firing," Chuck said as he smacked the side of his head in an exaggerated manner, making Haley laugh. He then said, "When you think of another dimension, you've got the right concept, just the wrong term. It's a different density of energy. Same world, different realm. Dimensions are a type of spatial measurement. There're only three."

"So, it's 'the creature from another density,' not dimension," Haley stated more than asked.

"You got it," Chuck said. "We refer to this one as the First Density and theirs as the Second Density."

"Why is ours called the first?" the curious farmer wondered out loud.

Chuck explained, "Because ours is the densest that we currently know of."

Haley then said, "I was wondering…was it just the light or is…" The empath sensed people nearby. "Somebody's coming," she whispered right before the hairs on the back of both their necks stood up. "Archons!"

They activated their helmets and flew up to hide. Haley went to a corner while Chuck used a larger pipe toward the center of the room. Then two people, a Proctor and a seven-foot-tall Archon, came into the area.

"Even if they did get out, you know he'll come back looking for his buddy. We'll get him," the Proctor said.

The Archon said, "The Marshal is probably awake by now. We should find out how they ported here without a gate."

Haley could sense agitation in the Archon as well as discomfort from the Proctor, probably from the reptilian's vibe. She could also feel Chuck's stomach sink and his blood boil upon learning of O'Connor's capture, but he remained still, listening for any more information.

"Most people are thinking magick," the Proctor commented.

"Unlikely," replied the Archon.

As they continued through the room, the Proctor and Archon approached an area where they would be able to see Haley.

"I'm gonna jump down and draw their attention," Chuck told Haley through the speakers. Try to stay out of sight. Once the Archon sees you, all the Archons know where you are."

"Okay," Haley responded.

Chuck lifted up above the large pipe and silently flew across the room, unseen by the two on the floor. He lowered to the ground about twenty feet behind them, dismissed his helmet and held his hands out to the side. "Hey, guys." The Proctor pulled his pistol with impressive speed as he and the Archon spun around at the sound of Chuck's voice, "We need to talk."

The Proctor tilted his head a bit. "So, you are still in here. Trouble finding your friend?"

The reptilian smiled as he said, "I can practically taste your anger."

"Oh, yeah?" Chuck said as he began to step backward. "Meet me for dinner, and I'll use it to make you a couple o' knuckle sandwiches."

Haley suppressed a laugh. Chuck was angry, but the empath could tell that he had it all very much in check.

"Oh, yes," the Archon said with a creepy smile as he and the Proctor matched the Marshal's steps. "We will be meeting."

"Bring it on, you sick, sadistic son of a…"

"Hey!" the empath interrupted through his earpiece.

"…bearded dragon," Chuck finished.

Chuck had gotten them to move enough so Haley would remain out of sight. He also realized that continuing the verbal exchange would just allow more time for reinforcements rather than yield any useful information, so he made the next move.

He dashed forward as the Proctor opened fire, and the Archon threw a mystical blast. Chuck accepted the blows in exchange for coming in close, a blade in each hand, jabbing the knife in his left hand under the jaw of the surprised Proctor. The Archon, however, was quick enough to grab Chuck's wrist with both his hands.

The Marshal shot a blue and orange orb of energy out of his right fist, forcing the reptilian to let go while being knocked back. The guard was gel, leaving it one on one.

Haley observed from above, and, considering their previous conversation, she paid attention to Chuck's anger.

It was powerful, yet Chuck moved with precision and calm. *How is he suppressing it?* The empath thought. She watched as his hands moved like a blur, quickly maneuvering the Archon into a prone position. She noticed Chuck's anger flare as he landed the blows, and then it was immediately back in check.

"He's not suppressing his anger," Haley thought to herself, "he's putting it aside until he chooses to use it." She admired the willpower and self-control that the Marshal displayed.

As soon as Chuck finished off his opponent, Haley noticed all that anger suddenly shifted into invigoration, much like her fear did earlier after the battle with the mindless beasts. She considered her frustrations when playing a game. Haley would sometimes lose her temper and throw a fit.

After that, when she finally overcame the obstacle that plagued her existence, she would flop down on the couch, blow out a dissatisfied sigh and say, "Finally," grateful that it was over. But in contrast, whenever Haley controlled her temper, victory over the obstacle turned all that aggravation into celebration, complete with jumping, cheering, and a sense of satisfaction. "What exactly is anger?" the young empath wondered to herself. "Is it the same thing as fear?"

"Let's go before the rest show up," Chuck said. Haley flew down, thinking that if she asked him, Chuck would say life is an accomplishment.

She landed next to the Marshal, and they headed for the closest corridor, which went to a maintenance hub for one of the generators. Upon entry, a portgate was seen along the eastern wall. It was a bit larger than the other one that Haley saw and much uglier. It, too, resembled stone but had no polish and was a dark gray, almost black. There were stone-like spikes all along the edge, and there was a vortex in the middle of the archway, expanding out wider to fill the gap.

"They're comin' through!" Chuck said, and they continued for the other end of the room and out to the next corridor. The Marshal's com-system tried to sync in with the active gate and found familiar Archon encryptions, which it had no problem overriding. But twenty men had come through the vortex before Gus' program took over the gate. Fifteen of them were Proctors, three of them were Hunters, and two others. There seemed to be a shortage of pistols as not all the guards had firearms, but the Hunters were now wearing their usual gear.

A one-piece tactical jumper, the Hunter's suit was black with a zipper up the front and had a body harness integrated into the material. Small metallic discs, about the size of a nickel, were evenly spaced every few inches along the harness.

The other two, a Frank and a Joey, wore blue-green robes that looked more ceremonial than practical, with rope-like belts from which a couple of pouches hung.

"They've taken over the gate," said a Hunter.

Frank reached into one of his pouches and removed a small folded cloth. He lit it on fire and threw it to the floor in front of the portgate as he chanted. The flames from the cloth grew taller and turned blue as they flared with intensity and rolled outward like liquid into the shape of a giant serpent.

The flames faded, revealing a solid manifestation in the form of a basmu. A snake-like body about twenty feet long and covered with blue scales, it had horns coming out the back of its long, triangular-shaped head, two forelimbs and large, leathery wings.

"Let no one enter the gate," Frank told his construct.

Haley and Chuck ran straight through the short corridor, bringing them to the generator room, where there were a few more Proctors and some technicians. They both started blasting, and Haley immediately flew for the top.

"Where ya going?" Chuck asked.

"You don't want me to shut it off?" Haley asked in return.

Chuck had intended for them to quickly pass through and find somewhere else to hide, but Haley was already on the top decking, and no more opponents would be coming from the portgate. Any reinforcements would have to travel around the complex. He didn't know where they would be traveling from, and he also had some guards coming in from the other end of the room, but if he could clear this crowd, they could take the portgate to the other end of the facility.

"If you can do it fast," he told Haley while slinging energy and bullets.

A Hunter in a Harry shell had a small cylindrical device in his hand. As soon as he entered the room, he pointed it toward the ceiling, and it launched a metal disc. The disc flew up and stuck itself flat to the ceiling as the Hunter touched the cylindrical object to one of the metal discs on his harness. The magnetic grappler engaged, and the Hunter was pulled upward toward the generator decking.

Haley exchanged blasts with the guards on top, taking a pistol bolt for her efforts before turning them and a couple of technicians to gel. As she did, Haley took another blast from the Hunter that had just arrived. Between her energy field and the PJs, she had a decent measure of protection from the blasts, but she thought it odd that the more painful shots usually came from a Proctor and not the dangerous Hunters.

She dodged to the side, avoiding the Hunter's next shots while returning fire, but the false Harry also successfully dodged as the two men in robes levitated to the decking.

Chuck dropped some of the Proctors to see the large serpent through the doorways. "Great," the Marshal grumbled as he turned to deal with the Hunters. One threw an energy orb, and Chuck jumped to the side. As soon as he began his movement, the other Hunter threw a blade, catching Chuck in the lower right abdomen.

He stumbled upon landing from his jump, a grimace of pain on his face while he dropped to one knee as another mystical bolt hit him in the chest, knocking him over. When his back hit the floor, his left arm was up, and Chuck was pulling the trigger. The Hunter's shells may have been resistant to bullets, but they reflexively dodged to the sides as the Marshal pulled the knife out with his other hand.

Chuck grunted in pain as he engaged his thrusters to get back up. The Marshal then pushed out a protective spere as more bolts and another blade came his way.

Haley saw the two levitating men in robes and felt the energy radiating from them. Then, the Hunter spoke. "Surrender yourself. There is no need for us to harm you."

From what Haley could sense, the Hunter meant what he said, but the two men in robes seemed eager for conflict. She chose to oblige the wizards by engaging her thrusters while jumping into the air and charging a shot. Haley meant to unleash it on the Hunter, but Joey spoke a strange word as he held out his hand and Haley, for an instant, could see nothing but a flash of light as her entire body convulsed with electricity. The wizard's lightning bolt knocked her back to the decking, dazed and trying to regain her bearings.

"I tell you again…surrender yourself," the Hunter insisted as Frank started chanting.

Still a little shaky, Haley stood back to her feet when Frank finished his chant, causing a field of energy to envelop and cling to her.

"Your decision?" inquired the Hunter.

Haley tumbled backward over the edge, and the Hunter rushed across the decking after her. He looked down the side, but she was nowhere to be seen.

Clinging to the underside of a scaffolding plank, Haley was using the opportunity to heal but was becoming more conscious about how much energy she used, knowing she needed to build it back up. Frank spoke a word, and Haley was surrounded by a brilliant flash of white light. When it faded, she was standing in the center of the decking, surrounded by Joey, Harry and Frank.

She dropped her head and sighed. "Aw, spuds!"

Chuck raised his guns and dropped his field, opening fire in blast mode as he gathered his energy for a charged shot. His wound would regenerate on its own in just a couple of minutes, but using energy, he could seal it in an instant. Not knowing who else might be showing up, he decided to deal with the discomfort for a moment or two and save his juice for offense.

When the Hunters tried to jump aside from the gunfire, Chuck released the charged blast and landed a direct hit. The Hunter on his right hit the floor as the other threw a blade.

The Marshal sidestepped the throw as his clothing began to ripple down his right arm, the nanobots forming a metallic baseball bat with holes spanning the surface. Chuck ran his energy into the bat, and ethereal flames burst out from the perforations. He dodged another blade and knocked the next one aside with the bat while moving in as the other Hunter was getting back to his feet.

Haley took a step backward but realized that no matter which way she stepped, it was toward one of these men. She was holding her hands out to the sides as she said through her helmet speakers, "No, no…stay away from me!" Her fear was genuine, but her actions were deliberate. Haley wanted them to think that she was out of tricks, and she also thought that they might be right. Haley had no idea if this would work.

The men closed in on her. She was hoping that all three would come right up to her, but Frank stayed back as Joey and Harry approached. The Hunter took her wrist to detain her as she figured now was a good time to see what would happen if she pounced while standing still.

The burst of energy released from her feet, knocking the Hunter and wizard to the side as she rode the concussive wave upward, releasing four blasts at the surprised Frank. Two shots landed before the magick user erected a protective field. She pounced again, slamming her feet to the floor as the decking shuddered and another wave of blue light rippled out, knocking Harry and Joey back further. Haley ran to the edge and dove.

Frank spoke a word, and in a burst of light, Haley was standing in the middle of the generator decking, met by another lightning bolt.

Chuck finished off the Hunter to his right with a swing from the fiery bat, a concussive burst releasing on impact and snapping the neck. He pivoted to his other opponent, who was getting back off of the floor. The Marshal brought up the Glock with his left hand and fired a bullet. Even though the shell's skin was sturdy to conventional firearms, its eyes were not.

He looked toward the door and could still see the weird-looking snake creature in the maintenance hub. He also saw a Proctor hurry in from the other side, who was winded due to running through the complex and shocked by the presence of the strange creature. The guard gave the basmu a wide margin and continued running for the generator room, but Chuck conjured his rifle and dropped the newcomer before he could get to the door. Then he was about to check on Haley, but before he could ask, she said a single word over the com.

She was curled up in the fetal position, out of energy, out of potatoes and out of ideas. "Help!" she squeaked. It probably wasn't even a second when she felt an intense rage plow right through Frank. Harry instantly snapped his arms up and fired as Joey's jaw hung open. Haley hoped she had enough in her and charged a blast while they were distracted. She narrowed her eyes as she looked at the Hunter wearing her dad's face. Her blood boiled as she was about to release the charged shot.

"Think now, be mad later," she reminded herself and suddenly aimed for the more unpredictable threat.

She indulged her anger when releasing the blast and instantly put it back to the side. Haley fired the thrusters as the ethereal bobcat burst on Joey's back. She flew forward into Harry while he was shooting at Chuck, shoving the surprised Hunter off the edge. Haley immediately spun back around to deal with the wizard.

Chuck took Frank by surprise when he flew through and grabbed him by the throat. It happened so fast that the Hunter couldn't get a good shot. The Marshal rocketed across the room, slammed the wizard into the wall near the ceiling and pummeled his face. Frank was so disoriented that he couldn't do a thing, so Joey did.

The wizard released a bolt of lightning as Haley started blasting. Her morale was coming back, and her energy seemed to be following suit. The bursts knocked Hank over the edge, and Haley gave chase.

Chuck was hit by the lightning and started plummeting to the floor. Frank looked to see Hank on the scaffolding and taking fire from Haley, so he spoke a word, and Haley was flashed back to the center of the decking, then he began chanting.

Haley charged her energy as she ran back to the edge after Joey, hoping she could finish the worn wizard before he caused any more trouble. But then, the Hunter zipped up on his magnetic grappler, right in front of her. Startled, Haley released the already charged blast, turning the false Harry to gel as she sensed another field cling to her.

She was about to look over the edge again for Joey but then felt the energy and emotion behind her. Haley spun around and threw out a protective sphere as lightning arched against her field.

Chuck felt the field of energy envelop and cling to him as Frank finished chanting. He dodged a mystical bolt and returned the favor with a couple of fiery orbs as he flew upward toward the wizard. Frank did not want to let the Marshal back within reach, but he waited until the last second to speak a word and then, in a flash of light, Haley and Chuck switched places.

Haley realized what had just happened when Frank grabbed her wrists, keeping her arm cannon pointed away. "Interesting choice of a wand," the wizard dryly commented.

They were up near the ceiling, it was a long way down, and Frank looked worse for wear from Chuck's brutal assault, but his grip was solid, and Haley couldn't break it. So instead, she pulled him in tight while firing her thrusters and rotating them ninety degrees, which put Haley on top and the wizard's back to the floor. And she pounced.

In a streak of blue, they rocketed to the floor, Frank taking the full impact, both physical and energetic, gelling him as Haley easily rebounded and fired her thrusters. She was exhilarated and couldn't believe it worked.

As soon as Chuck appeared on the decking, he was dropped to his right side by a lightning bolt, and Joey followed it with a mystical blast. Chuck's face was turned away from the wizard, and he saw a streak of blue shoot down to the floor as he winced in pain from a couple more mystical blasts, but he stayed limp, hoping that Joey would think him unconscious.

The wizard drew a finely crafted dagger and began chanting as he approached. His blade began to glow with a dim red light while Joey grabbed Chuck's shoulder and pulled, rolling him onto his back. Then the wizard saw the gun in Chuck's left hand as the Marshal pulled the trigger.

The shots staggered the surprised man back as Gentry gathered his energy, then released a potent blast, finishing off the wizard.

Haley flew up to the decking, her potato gun wisping with light, but there were no opponents left. So, she unleashed the charged shot at a coolant connector, followed by a burst of four shots while Chuck went to work on another one. Haley broke her connector, triggering the valve to shut and diverting the coolant pressure to the reservoir tank as she turned toward the last one.

Gathered her energy, Haley released an ethereal bobcat at the final connector. She expected it to take a few shots like the others, but the connector was faulty. When her shot hit, instead of breaking at the joint, the fitting shattered under vibrational stress, shooting a piece of shrapnel into Haley's right leg.

"Ah!" Haley screamed in shock as she fell over. "It hurts, it hurts!"

Chuck was there in an instant. The bots in her PJs were keeping pressure around the sharp shard of metal stuck in her leg like a knife. The Marshal scooped her up, flew to the floor and looked through the open doorway toward the gate to see Frank's pet whatever-it-was still present.

Even though she was in great pain, the sight of the basmu still captured Haley's attention. "Is that a dragon?" she asked in a shaky voice.

"I don't know what that thing is," Gentry said as he quickly flew out the other side to find a janitorial station like the one from the other generator. Unlike the one from earlier, this room had another exit.

Chuck carried her through to find a vertical corridor with a large insulated metal door directly across from them. There was a door on the eastern wall for a cargo elevator. Next to it was a wall-mounted panel with three levers and other ledges up the sides of the shaft-way.

"I think people are coming," Haley sniffled, and Chuck flew up to a dark ledge in a corner that had enough room for both of them. Chuck conjured his helmet so that if anyone did show up, only Haley could hear him as he gently set her down.

She was sitting on the platform with her back leaning against the wall, trying not to cry. Chuck asked, "Do you think you can heal it?"

"Mm-hmm," Haley said while nodding and sniffling.

Chuck gently but firmly got a good grip on the metal. "Ready?"

After a couple of quick breaths, Haley said, "Now!" and Chuck pulled.

The Marshal heard her grunt through his speakers, followed by, "Ah…" as the wound began knitting together. The bleeding immediately stopped, and the sharp pain quickly dulled, bringing much-needed relief.

"Now I'm woozy," she said, sounding very tired.

"Then rest for a couple of minutes," said Chuck. "I'll make sure no one comes near you."

Haley felt the intensity of the man and had no doubt that if anybody showed up right now, the Marshal would unleash such a fury. They'd feel it back in their real bodies. She dismissed her helmet to wipe her eyes and nose, then conjured it back and leaned against the wall. The farmgirl drifted off to sleep feeling completely safe.

CHAPTER 19

Sadistic Sorcery

As soon as Haley dozed off, the door slid back open, and a squad of five Proctors entered the corridor from the generator area. They weren't all yet through the entry before the metal door on the opposing wall opened, and two Archons stepped through.

"We're still searching," the group's sergeant told the Archons as Gentry observed from the ledge above.

"There's no sign of them that way," the reptilian said as his partner pointed toward the door from which they had come.

Three of the Proctors immediately looked toward the cargo elevator, and one of them stepped in its direction.

"They didn't go that way," one Archon told them. "Because I shut it down after we stepped out," said the other.

The sergeant then sighed, "They must have gotten by that *thing* and taken the portgate." He looked to his men, "Let's go check the area once more to be sure. Two of you, go double-check the other direction."

"No need…" said one of the Archons. "…because we will be retracing our steps as well," the other finished.

"Alright," the sergeant said as he turned around, holding his finger in the air and spinning it in a circle when he said, "Let's go!" The sergeant stepped back out, and the rest of the Proctors followed. The Archons stood there silently for a moment after they left, then finally turned to open the metal door and leave the area.

Chuck was relieved to hear their assumption and also breathed a little easier as he felt the energy field from the wizard's spell fade away. He looked at Haley propped against the wall and still wearing her helmet, sleeping. Gentry remembered when he first met Haley and Elizabeth, the United States Stellar Marshals was a classified entity at that time, as too was the existence of extra-terrestrials. This woman, who they had just met, tried to go with them. Of course, they adamantly refused, yet still, they somehow ended up with a ride-along during their first off-world assignment.

The Marshal looked at the sleeping empath, "Guess she started that little habit sooner than I thought," he quietly said to himself with a laugh.

Both Haley and Elizabeth, having been taught together by their fathers, were good fighters when Gentry first met them. Elizabeth even once slipped something about being trained by a ninja, but Chuck could not get the mystic to elaborate.

They trained more under the Marshal and brought their skills to new heights. With a little coaxing, Haley finally agreed to a training schedule and, when she took it seriously, could make Gus and Logan work a little in their sparring matches. If she had an actual interest, Haley could probably develop her skills to the same level.

Elizabeth had a true passion for martial arts and relished the training. She was fluid in her movement and furthered her skills to where she could actually press Remy. The two of them were so nimble that seeing them spar was sometimes like watching a game of Twister in fast-forward.

Looking at Haley, Chuck smiled as he thought that the farmer might not be the best in the gym, but she was the only one who could consistently beat him at Tetris.

It had only been about five minutes, but Haley began to stir. As she did, Chuck reached into one of his pockets and pulled out a small container. Haley slowly leaned forward and dismissed her helmet as she stretched and yawned.

"How ya feelin'?" Chuck asked.

"A little fuzzy," she said weakly. "Do you have any of those…what did he call it?"

"B-twelve?" asked Chuck as he held one up before her.

"Yeah," Haley said with a tired smile. "Thanks." She took the supplement and let it dissolve under her tongue. After a moment, she was feeling a little better, so she stood up, stretched and shook out her pigtails.

"How's the leg?" Chuck inquired.

"Good. It doesn't even hurt!" Haley said as she looked down at where the shrapnel had been to find that the gash in her coveralls had been resealed by the nanobots.

"You did good over there," Chuck commended. "I really liked that 'suplex of justice' you did on the wizard.

Haley laughed and said, "Actually…I think I'll call that the Falling Starr."

"I like it," the Marshal said with a grin, "but now we need to find Logan and get you out. Then we'll go find your dad and shut down the rest of their operation."

"Okay," Haley replied. "He's still way over there," she said, pointing toward the southern end of the complex.

Gentry then filled her in on what he overheard while she was sleeping. "It seemed to me that the Archons didn't want the others to go that way. So, stay alert," he cautioned as they flew down to the metal door.

Haley said, "I don't think anybody's on the other side."

Chuck nodded and reached up to open the door, and just as he touched the handle…

"Was it just the light, or is Gus green?" Haley randomly asked.

With a slight laugh, Gentry said, "Yeah, he's green." He opened the door with caution. The next room was a giant walk-in cooler, the rows of shelves filled with food.

Haley was going to inquire further about Gus but lost her train of thought as she walked along a row of shelves to see packs of steaks and burgers. The next was loaded with milk and juice. She went to the one after that and picked up a box of pre-cooked bacon, shrugged, opened the box and started to have a snack. She ate one piece and then another. Before she realized it, Haley had chewed through the entire box and felt like she could eat more.

Chuck walked up to her with a stack of cold cuts and cheese as he said, "Healing wounds can work up quite an appetite." They ate while looking around, and Haley grabbed an iced tea off one of the shelves. After eating, they went to the other end and opened the door to the next room.

Upon entry, Haley and Chuck found themselves in another storage room. Shelves loaded with boxes of food and canned items. They continued through to see cases and jugs of water as well as bottles of soda and various dry goods.

Haley wondered, "Do the Archons eat all of this?"

"No," Chuck answered. "They're exclusively carnivorous, but the shells might require some of it, and I'm pretty sure that the Cetatians eat the same stuff that we do."

"The Cetati…The fish people?!" Haley asked in surprise. Chuck turned to look at her. "I thought they were made up. That crazy English guy on the radio talks about them."

"I don't know if he's crazy, but I do know that he's right," Chuck said. "We have a version of him in our universe too. Everybody laughed at him for talking about lizard people…they ain't laughing now."

"Well, the Archons are really creepy, but the Ceta…Cetaitians almost seem like normal people," Haley commented as she found some bags of potatoes.

"Gus said they're natural to this world, so they might not be all that different from Humans," Chuck mentioned as Haley reloaded her pack with the spuds.

When they came to the other end of the room, Haley felt something through the wall. "Somebody's…really sad. It's awful…" she said with a look of despair.

Chuck was on guard as he slowly opened the door to the next room.

They stepped through and saw that the eastern and western walls were lined with cages, three rows high, five feet wide, six feet tall and ten feet deep. It was like a kennel for large animals, and they were empty, except for one from which the sorrow radiated.

As they walked deeper into the room, in the second to last cage on the bottom row of the eastern wall was a haggard-looking Bengal tiger. The great cat slowly lifted his head and looked at the two people approaching the bars. Haley gasped, and Chuck winced when they saw the gashes on the feline's back. Some of the fur was matted with dried blood, and the wounds were scabbed. The tiger slowly stood and wobbled a little as he stumbled toward the bars.

Haley locked eyes with the tormented animal and inhaled sharply. Her lips quivered as she groaned, and tears streamed down her cheeks. "No!" she said in a cracked voice and immediately ran back toward the storage room.

"Hey," Chuck said as he turned to follow.

She ran straight through the room and into the cooler, where she grabbed a stack of steaks and some burgers. Tears still streaming, she turned to go back as she said to Chuck, "He's starving to death."

Haley quickly returned to the abused tiger, ripped the plastic off of the packages and placed a steak through the bars. The great cat sniffed at the meat and then gingerly began to chew on a steak as Chuck returned to the room with four jugs of water.

In the back of the tiger's cage was a water bowl under a spigot that released a drop every few seconds. Chuck went into the other cages, grabbed some empty bowls and brought them back out. He filled and slid them under the bars of the feline's cage while the tiger ate.

Haley unwrapped the rest of the packaged meat, stooped down, placed it inside some more bowls and slid them into the cage. Still sobbing as she stood back up, the empath said, "We're gonna come back and get you out," though she had no idea how.

Haley turned and grabbed Chuck in a hug and buried her face in his shirt as she sobbed some more. He hugged her back as she calmed a little, and then they started for the other door to continue their search. As they were walking, Haley looked back over her shoulder to see the tiger sit up and return her gaze with a long slow blink.

Haley stopped and turned around, heading back toward the cage. Gentry watched as she walked to the bars and looked deep into the tiger's blue eyes. Again, the empath inhaled sharply, feeling his former life.

From the jungles of India in another universe, lounging on a tree limb or running through the bush, Aastik lived in the moment. Wild and free, Haley felt the confidence and exhilaration with which he used to move. She felt the life he had been taken from.

Tears fell once again while her energy began to gather. And it continued to gather as she tapped into something a little more primal. Wisps of mostly blue and some purple light began appearing and rolling across the entirety of her body. Then it began to arch down to the floor like an electrical discharge as her eyes glowed a fierce blue, and thin lines of purple crackled through her tears. Haley looked like a human Jacob's ladder.

She wanted to make this right. She wanted to make them pay. She wanted to round up every last Archon, present them to the world and show everybody just who these horrific people truly are! Haley wanted justice.

Just then, three guards walked in from the storage area, and their jaws dropped. They did not expect to actually find anybody and were quite surprised to see not only a Bengal tiger but a farmgirl crackling with energy.

Haley looked up and raised her arm as Chuck aimed his gun. The Marshal had seen Haley do this before, but now he witnessed her do it for the first time.

She released her energy into a wide sustained beam of blue. It looked like liquid light and had streams of purple throughout. The purple swirled within the wider plasmatic beam, forming ghost-like images of various types of cats as they rocketed forward into the guards.

They were instantly gelled where they stood, the sustained blast ended, and Haley lowered her arm, taking a few deep breaths. She looked up and over to Chuck.

"We gotta go," he said.

Haley looked back toward Aastik and said, "We'll get you out. I promise." The tiger went back to his steaks, and as they headed toward the next room, the farmer contemplated the energy she had just released. As little as an hour ago, she would have thought it really cool. And she still did, but now Haley thought of it in a bit of a different light. She hoped that she would be wise enough to use it properly.

The Marshal put his hand up to the door and looked at Haley, who shook her head and then Chuck pushed it open.

Haley couldn't believe what she had seen. "Why would they do something like this?" She asked as they stepped through the doorway.

On the other side was a surreal sight as it appeared that they were stepping into a jungle. The room was huge, but they couldn't be sure with all the bushes, trees, and hills obstructing much of the view.

With a sigh, Chuck said, "Because these people are sick. They thrive on the misery of others."

Haley reached up and grabbed a leaf, "It's plastic!" she said and then started touching the other props. The trees, the bushes and vines, everything was fake. "You said they like misery," she mentioned, "that guy by the pipes said he could taste your anger. What are they doing?"

Chuck said, "They actually feed on negative emotions. Your fear, anger, sorrow and pain…they literally use the energy of these emotions to boost their own powers. They can even sustain themselves with it physically…we're food in their eyes."

"I don't understand," Haley said. "If they can feel others' feelings, how can they stand to do that to people?"

"They don't feel 'em like we do," Chuck explained. "They sense another's emotions mystically, not empathically."

"What do you think they were gonna do with the tiger?" she wondered.

"They were…probably going to use him in here," he said. Haley felt the disgust radiating from Gentry as he thought about one of the Archon's favorite forms of entertainment. "They like to capture an apex predator and torture it to the point of desperation. Then they capture some people and put them in a large enclosure like this," he swung his arm out and around, indicating the fake jungle. "Once the people get an idea of the area, they release the crazed critter and watch the show…and feed off the misery that's released."

The revulsion was obvious on Haley's face. "That's horrible! I can't believe…" she stopped walking abruptly as her eyes widened and said in a hushed voice, "I think somebody's in here." The empath could feel both fear and eager anticipation coming from the southern end of the room. She pointed as she said, "And one's very scared."

Chuck readied his Glock, and they started through the artificial jungle. Haley could feel them getting closer to the sensation when she and Chuck started to notice other vibes as well. "You feel that?" the Marshal asked Haley.

"Yeah," she whispered with a shudder as she readied her potato gun. "Archons."

They quietly made their way forward as the sensations became stronger. Through the plastic foliage, the source of the energy was seen. The two Archons who Chuck saw earlier were there and on the other side of them was a girl about Haley's age on the ground in the fetal position, crying.

Haley could not yet see anything from where she stood but felt Chuck's stomach drop like someone just pulled the rug out from under him. And then his blood began to boil. He looked at Haley as his helmet came up, and he gestured for her to do the same. She conjured her helmet, and Chuck's voice came through the speakers.

"Stay very still," he said. "I'm going to handle this right now."

The empath could not believe the overpowering intensity and rage boiling inside the Marshal, yet every movement he made was carefully measured and deliberate. Chuck dismissed his gun, pulled out two blades and then used the thrusters to move silently toward the unsuspecting Archons. He gathered no energy because he did not want to give them anything more to sense. The Marshal was livid, but the Archons were so focused on the girl's fear that he was able to come right up behind them.

"Now your hands are untied. Feel free to carry out your threat," one of them said in a cheerfully condescending tone. "What demon should we summon when the others get here?" the second Archon mused. "There are many with wonderful talents that you…" Both Archon's shells abruptly stopped moving, paralyzed by precisely placed knives. They were pulled closer together as the Marshal leaned forward, placing his head between them and dismissing his helmet. He whispered into their ears, "If I ever…"

Chuck cut off his mic as he continued speaking with threats and promises that he would never even let Haley's adult counterpart hear.

And he meant every word of it.

She would never know what it was that Chuck said, but the empath knew for certain that it utterly unnerved them. Then, with a twist of both blades, the Archons turned to gel.

The frightened young mystic looked up at the Marshal, not sure what to think about the sudden change of events. She sat up, and Haley came out from the bushes, dismissed her helmet, and her jaw dropped. The empath was excited, relieved and shaken all at once as Chuck reached his hand out to help the girl up and said, "Hello, Bet…Elizabeth." After a pause, he said, "I'm Chuck."

She took his hand, and he helped her to her feet, then Haley barreled in and grabbed her in a tight hug, shouting, "Beth!"

Elizabeth returned the hug with equal enthusiasm. "Haley!" she said, sounding relieved.

Chuck immediately started scanning the area and looking around for any other hostiles. The girls were crying while sharing an embrace, but unfortunately, the Marshal could not let them have the moment. "Ladies, we need to move before more of 'em get here," he said sternly, and they quickly made their way back toward the entrance.

"Are you okay?" Haley asked Elizabeth.

"Yeah, except my head hurts from when they knocked me out," Elizabeth replied. When she said that, Haley felt Chuck's anger flare much like it did with the wizards. "What about you?" Elizabeth asked in return.

"I'm okay now, but it was scary for a while," Haley answered. "Now, we're gonna find Logan, and then they'll stop 'em!"

"No," Chuck suddenly said. "Enough is enough. Now, we're getting you two out of here, and I'll come back and finish the job once you're *both* safe."

"But Logan's still…" Haley started to say while pointing toward the southern end of the complex, but she got a look of shock on her face and swung her arm around to the North.

"He just ported?!" Chuck asked.

"Yeah!" the empath said as she started to move.

Elizabeth grabbed her by the arm, and Haley turned to look at her friend.

"Carefully," the young mystic reminded. "We don't want to give ourselves away."

Haley nodded, understanding that she was about to let excitement get the better of her. Then she and Elizabeth followed Chuck's lead through the kennel room, where the full-bellied tiger was sleeping deeply.

Elizabeth looked to the great cat, an expression of shock and anger on her face. "What is…"

"We're gonna get him out too," Haley said with a tear in her eye as they passed through to the storage room. "He was starving, but we fed him." She felt Elizabeth seething from the sight of the abused tiger, and the mystic's eyes began to glow with an amber light as they entered the cooler.

Haley's eyes widened with surprise and excitement as she exclaimed, "Whoa! How'd you do that? Did you learn it from Neal? What else can you do?! Where's Neil?!"

"Haley," Chuck said, getting both girls' attention. She looked up, and he motioned to the door, "Sense anyone on the other side?"

"No," she replied, "But Logan's getting closer.

Chuck thought it very odd. The place should be swarmed with Archons and Proctors by now. While the Marshal was certainly glad that it wasn't, he didn't have much faith in the apparent good luck. With a quick glance upward, he thought, *Where's that lightning bolt gonna come from?*

He then turned to the young mystic and said, "Haley had a good question. What else can you do?"

I can make balls of energy and move fire and air with my mind." she answered, her excitement starting to build.

"Cool!" exclaimed Haley.

Elizabeth turned to Haley and was about to start telling her everything, but Chuck spoke up before she could start. "You two can catch up once you're outta here."

Both girls nodded, then they stepped out of the cooler and into the vertical corridor, looking around for any unpleasant surprises. "He's almost here," Haley stated.

"Good," Chuck replied as he scanned the elevator with his com-system. He then looked as if a light bulb had just lit up, and he asked Elizabeth, "Can you just move fire, or can you also make it?"

"Just move it," Elizabeth answered.

Chuck reached into his pocket and produced an orange lighter. He held it out to the girl, who accepted it with a nod of appreciation.

The entry to the corridor opened, and Logan saw them as he stepped through, a look of relief on his face. "Thank God, you guys are…" his eyes fell upon Elizabeth, and his jaw dropped. "Uh…hi," he said, shocked to see her here as well. Haley felt the spike of anxiety as he was now worried about them both.

"Elizabeth," said Chuck, "meet Logan."

"Hi," she said back.

Chuck and Logan clasped their right hands and gave each other a pat on the shoulder with their lefts, and as soon as they let go, Haley snapped her arms around her fellow empath like a mousetrap and squeezed.

"See what I've been dealing with?" Chuck quipped as he read the information on his screen, but Logan sensed his nerves. Neither of them liked the two girls being in this dangerous territory.

Haley let go and held up her left arm as the bots rippled from her sleeve and formed Logan's com-band around her wrist.

Logan looked at the band, then looked up to her eyes as he pointed at her wrist and said, "Hang on to that until we get topside."

Haley nodded as she lowered her arm and the bots retreated back into the clothing.

"What was that?" asked a curious Elizabeth.

"Nerd stuff," Haley said with a smirk. She was about to start telling her friend about the nanobots, but Chuck spoke next.

"The elevator has power but isn't active…just needs a switch to be manually turned on and…" He looked around to see the wall panel with the three levers. He pointed and said, "Pull that lever."

Logan turned his head to see the panel, "Which lever?"

Chuck jabbed his finger in the air again as he looked at the correct switch, and he said, "That one," then looked back at the elevator data.

Haley sensed a weird spike of anxiety and embarrassment as O'Connor turned back to the three levers, a confused expression on his face. Elizabeth had no idea why he seemed so lost, but she tried clarifying. "The left one."

Logan pulled the lever as his nerves settled right back down. The lift system came to life as Chuck said, "The elevator's on its way." He then looked back to Logan as he pointed toward a door a few stories up. "Once the girls are out, I think that corridor is our best bet to get to the last generator," he said as the lift arrived.

CHAPTER 20
The Hunted

"Sense anybody?" Chuck asked the empaths.

Haley shook her head as Logan said, "No."

The cargo elevator doors slid to the side, and Chuck cautiously leaned through the opening to make sure that no nasty surprises were in store. He stepped inside and motioned for everyone to follow.

The doors slid shut, and the lift began its ascent when Chuck projected an image of the map. "This is where we get out, and I'm hoping we can make our way around to here," he said, moving his finger along the holographic image and highlighting the intended route.

"I was there earlier, and we can get a signal out to communicate with Gus and Remy." Gentry continued. "The Archons will be expecting us to try for the warehouse elevator, so I'm thinking that if we get back to the HVAC station, the girls can get out through the vents."

He looked at Haley and Elizabeth directly. "Once you two are with Gus up top, Logan and I will find your folks and shut down the last generator."

"Okay," the girls said in unison as the lift stopped.

Haley and Elizabeth stood behind the Marshals. Chuck raised his Glock, and Logan gathered energy into his hands as the doors slid to the side, but no one was there.

"Have you seen anyone besides us since you ported?" Chuck asked Logan while they stepped into the corridor.

"Other than a weird snake thing…no," O'Connor replied.

"Is it still there? Inquired Chuck.

"Yeah. As soon as I stepped through the gate, the thing smacked me across the room," Logan answered. "It didn't come after me though, just stayed in front of the gate."

"Snake thing?" Elizabeth asked.

"Yeah," said Haley, excited to tell her friend. "It was huge! It had wings and a couple of legs, and it was blue!"

"Really?!" asked the intrigued mystic.

"Yeah," Haley then continued to tell her friend about the Archons and the Cetatians.

"I can't believe it," Elizabeth stated in shock, "fish people."

"Where's Neil? Haley asked.

"I don't know," the mystic replied. "They came to the arcade, and a guy that looked green showed up and tried to help us."

"That's Gus," said Haley.

"Neil was with him when I got caught," Elizabeth continued. "I don't know where he is now."

As they came to an opening in the corridor above, they found a portgate similar to the one by the first generator. It had the same color and carvings but was much smaller. The stone-like structure stood about ten feet tall and was eight feet wide. The archway inside was about the same size as a set of double doors, and a control panel was mounted to the left side.

Haley pointed to the empty spot where a dolphin's head should be as she turned to look at Chuck. She was about to ask if he still had the stone but saw it was already in the Marshal's hand.

Stepping to the side as Chuck set the stone in place, Haley pulled out her phone and flipped it open as she showed Elizabeth. "Watch this," she said with excitement. "He's gonna take over the gate, and then they can use it to teleport to these two," she said, pointing out the other portgates on her map.

"Whoa!" Elizabeth whispered as she looked at the display on Haley's phone.

"I've said that a lot today," Haley replied. She had the screen display the interaction with the gate to find that the com-system had already taken control.

"Have you gone through one of these?" Elizabeth asked.

"No," Haley replied.

"We're going up," Chuck told them and looked at Elizabeth, "Logan will give you a lift upstairs."

"What, is he gonna carry me?" she started to ask but then felt the energy coalesce around her as she lifted into the air. "Oh."

Haley fired up her thrusters and lifted alongside the bewildered mystic. Taking her hand, the two shared a quick laugh as they ascended to the next floor. They touched down lightly on the surface and surveyed the new corridor. There were arched support beams along the wall every twenty-five feet and numerous crates scattered throughout the tunnel in the southern part of the corridor. To the north, there were a few crates here and there for about thirty feet, then the corridor, beyond that, was empty as far as they could see.

Chuck pointed toward the north, "This way."

There were two office doors, one on both sides, about forty-five feet ahead. Logan checked one, then Chuck checked the other, but there was nothing other than some tables and empty filing cabinets.

The group encountered no opposition as they continued through the corridor. "I don't like it," Chuck said. "They've got something cooking. Probably an ambush."

"I'm sure," Logan responded. He glanced back at the girls and then looked over to Chuck, "How are you holding up?"

"I'm good," Gentry said.

"Your nerves are frazzled," Logan pointed out.

"Yours aren't?" Chuck asked back.

"Mine are always frazzled, Logan said, "but usually not this much.

Chuck shook his head, "How many more kid-versions of our nearest and dearest friends are we gonna meet today?" he asked as he uncapped a water cantina.

Logan looked toward his friend and, with a sigh, earnestly said, "I hope that's all two of 'em." He then looked forward and, as Chuck took a sip, added, "Because I *really don't* want to change Remy's diapers."

Chuck spit the water from his nose as Haley and Elizabeth looked on with curiosity. "Sorry," Logan said, trying not to laugh.

"They're kinda weird, aren't they," Elizabeth stated more than asked.

Haley responded with a long slow, "Yeah." She then smiled and said, "That's probably why they're fun."

"I'm glad that Chuck guy saved me, but he seems a little cranky," Elizabeth said to her friend.

"I guess so," Haley replied. "Especially right after I got hurt."

"You're hurt?!" Elizabeth asked, suddenly looking worried.

"No, I healed it…" her eyes went wide with excitement. "Oh yeah, I can heal cuts really quick now!" she told the mystic.

"Cool!" she said back with an enthusiastic smile.

"But right after that, we found the tiger, then we found you," Haley said, her eyes turned to the side as she recalled the events. "Now he just wants us away from the bad guys," she said as Elizabeth nodded.

Chuck was catching Logan up on what they've learned so far, "…so, not only do we have to find the people, but make sure we shut down their port-connection between universes before they figure out how to navigate omnispace."

"Got any ideas on freeing Bast?" O'Connor asked.

"Actually," Chuck stated while nodding, "yeah, I do. Remy said that the firehouse is the most heavily warded place, yet hardly anybody's been over there."

Logan said. "Probably some wizards in there."

"Yeah, and if we free Bast, then they're all really…"

"Hey!" Haley interrupted.

Chuck turned around, held up his hands with a resigned look and said, "Alright…alright." He turned forward and asked Logan, "What do you think?"

"I think she's going to be disappointed with her future vocabulary," O'Connor replied.

"No, not that," said Gentry.

Logan looked toward Chuck, seeming confused. Then his eyes widened for an instant as his mind came back on track. "The firehouse does make sense," he said. "If we can, let's do two teams. One for the generator and the other to free Bast." Chuck nodded, considering the idea as Logan said, "And we still need to figure out where Harry and the other townsfolk are."

Their speakers suddenly came to life with the sound of Gus' voice. "Can you hear me?"

"Loud and clear," Chuck responded.

"Chuck," Gus said, sounding grim, "they got Elizabeth. Remy and Neil went in after her."

"Yeah, about that…" Chuck replied in an unexpectedly casual voice.

"You got her?!" Gus asked hopefully.

Gentry looked at Elizabeth and held his phone up to scan her as he said, "Yes, I do! And I need you to authorize another splindie."

Elizabeth looked back at him, confused. A moment and a brief explanation later, she had her own com-system and converted the phone to flip-style, same as Haley's.

"Okay," Chuck said to Gus. "Here's the plan if you can contact Remy. You guys are going to the firehouse. Hopefully, we'll be able to free Bast from there. But first, we're gonna send Haley and Eliz…"

The two empaths spoke at the exact same time.

"People are coming," said Haley.

"We might have company," said Logan.

They both turned their heads to the north, and Logan motioned for the girls to get behind the Marshals.

"Gonna have to get back to you," Chuck told Gus. "If you don't hear from us shortly, go after the firehouse." He said as they started falling back toward the south. The signal was lost as they continued, but the sense of someone's presence followed.

They neared the office doors when the empaths began to sense someone from the other direction, as well as from the rooms. "We're surrounded," O'Connor said.

"You know that lightning bolt I'm always looking for?" Chuck asked Logan.

"Yeah," Logan unhappily replied, understanding that they had just found it.

The presence from the north got closer, and then a man came into view from the end of the corridor.

As he approached, the group realized that this was a face they had not seen before. He was five feet and ten inches tall and had short dark-brown hair, almost black, and appeared to be of Japanese descent. He was athletic, with a medium build and had a noticeable difference in the color of his skin around the neck. The back was a darker tan color, and the difference in the two tones speckled together on the sides of the neck.

He wore the same clothes and gear as the last few Hunters, except for an additional device that encased his right forearm. It was cylindrical, looked to be made of either metal or plastic and had a dark gray color with a smooth surface. A horizontal slot was on the front, above the wrist.

Chuck raised his Glock, and Logan gathered his energy while Haley and Elizabeth turned their attention the other way. Their neck hairs stood from the unnatural vibes of the two Archons coming up through the floor opening.

"This is your one opportunity to surrender peacefully," Sahmbo calmly told the group. "Will you yield?" he asked as the office doors opened. There was a Proctor standing in the doorway closest to Chuck and three more Hunters in the other door near Logan. The two Archons had energy gathered and ready as they looked menacingly at the girls.

Chuck looked the Cetatian man in the eye and said, "If you're feeling froggy…then leap."

Sahmbo nodded and replied, "As you wish." The Proctor and three Hunters charged out of the doors at the Marshals. Haley and Elizabeth dove behind some crates as the Archons hurled mystical bolts their way, aiming their shots low so they wouldn't hit the Hunters beyond them.

Chuck turned to engage with the Proctor as one of the three Hunters ran right past Logan to assist the guard. The other two Hunters went straight for Logan.

Haley sent a volley of five blasts and then ducked back behind the crate. As she did, Elizabeth leaned out to the other side and tossed a mystical bolt. Haley then popped up above the top with another shot.

The Archons quickly hopped across a couple of ledges to the other side of the floor opening and took cover behind another crate. Elizabeth said, "We gotta keep the pressure on!" She moved forward and dove behind a crate near the edge. Haley followed suit and ran forward while she fired another five shots on the way. She took cover behind a support beam on the eastern wall as the Archons fell back further.

Chuck dropped the Proctor and pivoted in time to see the Hunter's punch in mid-swing. Almost faster than the eye could follow, Gentry grabbed the Hunter's right wrist with his left hand, continuing the pivot and redirected the Hunter face-first into the western wall.

Sahmbo raised his right arm to take aim. He knew that the Marshals would be quick enough to dodge his projectile, so he looked up and saw a clear shot at Elizabeth a little further down. From his gauntlet, the lead Hunter fired a disk that was two inches wide and a half-inch thick. Just as Gentry was gelling his other opponent, he saw Sahmbo fire and instinctively leaped in front of the disk to protect Elizabeth.

Four cables shot outward from the edge of the disc, wrapped around the Marshal and cinched tight, dropping him to the floor. The disk and cabled emitted an electromagnetic field, disrupting Chuck's energetic abilities and repelling the nanobots, which prevented them from breaking down the snare for mass. Sahmbo had hit his intended target.

Haley and Elizabeth crossed the opening in the floor and continued to pour it on, forcing the Archons back further. One of them spoke a word as he waved his hand, and three shards of red light flew toward Elizabeth. She ducked behind another crate as the shards buzzed by her head and hit the wall. The girls looked over to the shards, stuck there like knives for a second or two before fading away. They returned fire again, forcing the reptilians back further.

Logan gelled his opponents and turned around to see Chuck on the floor when Sahmbo knocked him unconscious with a kick. The anger apparent in his eyes, Logan said, "I'm gonna…"

"Do nothing," Sahmbo said definitively. "Nothing you've ever done has mattered," he added in a dismissive tone.

The Marshal's blood was boiling. He didn't even know why, but something about the way this man, this total stranger, said the words just got under O'Connor's skin. The Cetatian felt a tremendous gathering of energy from the Marshal and knew that he had Logan's complete and undivided attention.

So, the empath never felt the intense focus from the Hunter that had remained in the office with a rifle. Never noticed the barrel slide out the still-open door. He didn't sense the shift in vibration as the Hunter, halfway through an exhale, pulled the trigger. And since he didn't know it was coming, Logan did nothing to stop the round, leaving only his subconscious field to protect him. In a splash of green and purple light, the round bounced off his temple, tumbled and clinked to the floor, followed by the thud of an unconscious O'Connor.

In less than thirty seconds, Sahmbo had both Marshals subdued at his feet. The Hunter raised his arm and launched another snare disk at Logan as the sniper stepped out of the office. They looked to the south and saw the girls following the retreating Archons away from sight.

Another Hunter stepped out from the western door as Sahmbo, watching the exchange down the other end, said, "Get them to holding, immediately."

One of them nodded as the Hunter-Ralt pressed a button on his gauntlet. The snaring disks levitated, lifting the unconscious men. Chuck and Logan lifted into the air as the Hunters took them by the shoulders and led the pair away.

Haley was in the moment. Elizabeth was here, and they both had abilities. Fighting side by side, the farmgirl was actually enjoying the battle, practically forgetting how dangerous their situation truly was, and Elizabeth was feeling the same way. The two friends practically felt invincible while they pressed the invaders further back into the darker areas.

As they retreated, Haley and Elizabeth enthusiastically pursued until the empath realized something. The Archons were also enjoying this. With an expression of confusion, she looked at Elizabeth and said, "They're not scared."

The mystic's eyes went wide as she said, "Duh! I should have known." She looked back at Haley. "A trap!" Elizabeth motioned with her eyes to the north, and Haley nodded. The two started back toward the Marshals.

The Archons saw the girls quickly retreating and realized that they must have figured it out. Not about to let them get away, the two reptilians immediately started chasing the pair.

As Haley and Elizabeth ran toward the opening in the floor, they saw no one around. The empath reached out with her senses and gasped. She looked horrified as she said to her friend, "I can't feel them."

They looked over their shoulders to see the Archons coming, and Haley wrapped her arms around Elizabeth and engaged the thrusters, flying them down to the lower level.

When they touched down, Haley held up her phone and activated the portgate. "We don't want to go there," she said to Elizabeth while pointing at the map. "That's where the snake-thing is."

The Archons dropped down from the floor above and saw the portgate was still open. Wasting no time, they both dove through right before the vortex closed. Then Haley and Elizabeth stepped out from behind the gate as the mystic asked with a smile, "Do you think they'll like the snake-thing?"

"I hope not," replied a smirking Haley. But then her face dropped, "I can't sense the Marshal's. Not even Logan." She took a deep breath and said, "I don't know what to do."

"Me neither," sighed Elizabeth.

Haley tossed her phone to the ground, and a holographic map appeared. "This is where we could get out through the vents," she said. "We were supposed to meet Gus outside, but we have to get there first."

"We can make it!" Elizabeth said with a measure of confidence.

Haley nodded and said, "We could, but…"

"But what?" asked the mystic.

Haley pointed to the final generator. "Chuck said we might be able to get there by this hallway," she remembered while tracing her finger along the intended route. "We turn it off. The rest can't move here!"

Elizabeth looked at her friend, a little surprised. Then, the corners of her mouth slowly turned up into a smile, joined by an amber glow in her pupils.

Haley dropped her gaze to the floor. "I still can't do that," she sighed.

Elizabeth chuckled at Haley's comment, said, "C'mon," and they started back for the elevator.

CHAPTER 21
It's Electric

Sahmbo approached the intercom on the wall to contact Kone and update him on their progress. He was also considering the two young ladies who have been raising a ruckus. The Proctors had shoot-to-kill orders, but the Hunters were tasked with apprehending them as the killing of children was strictly forbidden by the Hunter's Code. Kone never assigned a duty to a Hunter that would conflict with their Code, although he had been pushing those boundaries in recent years. So, they've been ordered to, upon capture, turn custody of them over to the Cetatian State.

The Hunter-Ralt input his security code and opened a line.

The conference room was large and well lit. A large wooden conference table with marine-themed carvings around the edge was in the center, and Podmen from different areas of the world were present.

At the head of the table sat Kone. He was discussing the state of the world, the direction they intended to move it and the best ways to accomplish these goals. A tone sounded off, and Kone looked down at the table's surface. A holographic image appeared in the glossy finish, and Kone looked back up to the men around the table.

"Excuse me for a few moments, gentlemen," he said in his deep voice. Kone stood up, turned and walked through the door to his office. Upon entry, he shut the door and looked toward a large monitor built into the wall. It activated, and the face of Derek Sahmbo appeared.

"Two of the Marshals are in custody," the Hunter informed Kone.

"Excellent," Kone replied, "and the young ladies?"

"Still at large," Sahmbo replied.

"Let me know when you have them," Kone instructed the Hunter-Ralt.

"I will," he replied. And then he stated, "I have a concern."

Kone looked to the monitor with true curiosity as he did not often hear that from this man. "About what?" the Cetatian Uniralt asked.

"The girls' fate," Sahmbo answered. "I would prefer that they not be turned over to the Archons."

"I certainly understand that concern," Kone calmly said as he walked over to his desk and poured a scotch. "You've gone through the information and have seen the problem they could become."

The Hunter nodded.

"If your Hunters catch them before one of the Proctors kills them, they will be declared a danger to Cetatian progress. And if they can't be re-educated, they will eventually be sentenced to death," Kone answered as Sahmbo closely watched his eyes. "But they will not be handed over to the Archons. Their ways are far too cruel and heinous for a child to suffer. Even a human child."

The Hunter nodded, confident in the answer that he had seen, and he said, "It will be finished tonight."

The screen went dark, and Kone sipped the last of his scotch. In truth, he was indifferent to the suffering of a child, but he also understood that others were often squeamish concerning the young ones.

Sahmbo had noticed that the Archons, being a hive mind, tended to seek out an independent thinker for leadership and direction. Ahnk-Hume was the perfect choice for them since he was part of the Hive and therefore understood it.

Kone considered that when the Drakel rejoins the Hive, his emotions will stabilize, but he will no longer think so independently, and the Archons will seek out someone new. The Cetatian Uniralt knew exactly to whom they would look.

So, he intended to turn the two girls over to the reptilians, cementing the trust that he had been building. Kone looked forward to having an army of Archons at his disposal.

Archons, who provided one of the most incredible opportunities that Kone had never thought possible. Their blending of magick and technology allowed the wizards to maintain a binding spell on many unsuspecting immortals at once, leaving little to no opposition standing in the way of the remaining gods with whom Kone was aligned.

He smiled as he walked back out to the conference room, knowing that the combined forces of the Cetatians, the gods and the Archons would seize control of the First Density in one fell swoop. Once under Kone's command, he intended to take the combined might of the Human and Cetatian forces to overwhelm the Dvwargarian people in the Third Density. Then, the Alfan people of the Fourth Density. All the mortal races of Earth will be under his rule.

Kone confidently thought, *Moloch will be pleased.*

The doors slid to the side, and the girls stepped back into the vertical shaftway. Looking up to the door they needed to take, Haley wrapped her arms around Elizabeth and flew them to the corridor entrance.

They continued without much resistance, other than a few of the mindless beasts running around, but the girls dispatched them easily. Elizabeth asked Haley to tell her about the other generators and what they might expect. They chatted back and forth along the way yet managed to stay alert for hostiles while they discussed what they might do.

"It's the last one, so they're probably gonna have a lot of people there," Elizabeth said. "What can we do to make 'em look somewhere else?"

Haley shrugged. "I don't know."

"Maybe we'll get a good idea when we see the place," Elizabeth hoped.

As they continued through a couple new corridors, their coms beeped and displayed an air vent big enough for them to fit, showing them a way down to what was probably the washroom next to the final generator. Haley smirked as she asked, "Wanna play secret agent?" The empath knew the answer as she noticed a mix of excitement and nervousness. Something she felt from Elizabeth whenever the rebellious girl was about to pull one of her stunts.

With a smile and an intense look in her eye, the mystic said, "Let's shut 'em down and find our parents!"

They made their way to the vent opening and found that it was near the ceiling. Haley lifted them up, and Elizabeth climbed in first. It was dark in the airshaft, so Elizabeth held up her hand to gather energy and make an orb of light, but then the nanobots started moving, wrapping around her head and forming into a set of glasses. The inside of the lenses granted her night vision and a head-up display.

"This is awesome!" Elizabeth whispered while Haley crawled in behind her. Haley could use her thrusters to float, but Elizabeth had to crawl. They finally came to where a vertical shaft intersected with theirs. "This is the one," Elizabeth said, "but I don't know how I can get down without falling."

"I'll go first," Haley said, and you can stand on my shoulders."

Elizabeth looked over her shoulder to realize that Haley was wearing no glasses. "You can see in the dark!?"

"Yeah." She moved forward and dropped feet first into the new shaft. Using the thrusters, Haley lowered down, and Elizabeth dropped her feet onto the Haley's shoulders. Making barely a sound, they slowly descended all the way down as Elizabeth walked her palms down the inside of the shaft for balance.

The vent cover beneath Haley's feet was the in the ceiling of the washroom. She turned her senses outward, but there didn't seem to be anyone in the immediate area. Using her cling ability, Haley attached one foot to the cover and the other to the shaft wall along with her hands. She pushed down, breaking the cover free but keeping it attached to her foot.

"Ready?" Haley asked.

"You bet you're…"

"Hey!" Haley harshly whispered. She lowered until Elizabeth's hands were above her head as she hung on to the shaft opening for balance. Balance, the young mystic realized, that was coming easier.

"Let's do it," Elizabeth whispered.

"Okay…go!" and Elizabeth stepped off of Haley's shoulders to the front. Haley caught her and lowered her to the floor.

She released the vent cover from her foot, and they took a good look around to see a door on both ends of the room. One led to the generator and the other, unknown.

The girls carefully made their way to the door, and Haley floated up to look through the glass. "There're some guards and some workers, but not that many people," Haley said in surprise as she lowered back down to the floor. She grabbed Elizabeth and lifted her back up to the glass so they could both see.

"Not as many as before," Haley mentioned.

"We can surprise 'em," Elizabeth said. "If we hit it fast, we might get out of here before everybody comes running."

Haley checked behind them to make sure they were still alone, and then they took another look through the glass. Elizabeth was noting where the guards and technicians were located as Haley was taking a good look at the layout of the place.

Instead of various scaffolding, staging and platforms, this generator had a permanent catwalk structure around it. Three levels made their way around the giant cylinder, with stairs between each. There were two elevators, one on the eastern side and the other on the west, that went from the floor to the decking on top. The lift platforms themselves were ten feet wide, six feet deep and traveled inside a cage-like shaft.

There were four Proctors on the floor and another on the mid-level catwalk. Three technicians were seen moving about the walkways and one operating a console on the top decking.

They set it down on the floor, and Elizabeth said, "I think, when we go in, you should shoot for the guard on the walkway, and I start shooting the ones on the floor."

"Okay," Haley said.

"Once you stop that guard, help me with the rest on the ground. And then the workers should be easier."

"Then we break the fittings and get out," Haley said with a smirk. She thought about the intense beam of energy she unleashed with the tiger. *If I line my shot upright, I could use that to break two at once*, she thought.

The girls hopped up to take another look to see where everybody was and then dropped to the floor. "Ready?" the mystic asked as they both gathered energy.

"Oh yeah!" Haley replied with a confident smirk.

The door slid to the side, and they both launched a charged blast while entering the room. The Proctors were caught by surprise as a bobcat burst into the guard on the walkway while Elizabeth threw her large amber orb at two guards who were close together.

The mystic's blast was enough to gel both guards, and the girls turned their attention to the last two. They threw up protective fields as pistol bolts zipped in, then dropped their barriers to return fire, taking down the Proctors.

"Let's finish 'em!" Elizabeth said as they began firing at the technicians. The workers had no means of ranged combat available to them, so they were quickly taken down. Haley grabbed her friend, and they began to fly up toward the top.

Haley started gathering energy for a sustained blast but found that it just wasn't quite there. *I'll just do it like last time*, she thought as they rose to the top.

They came up to unexpectedly find a woman standing in the center of the decking. She was five-foot-nine, had long black hair and was thick of build, toned to athletic perfection. Her hair was braided back into a tail, and she wore the same tactical jumper as the Hunters. There was a familiar coiled object on her right hip and a katana sheathed on her back. Her face was tan, the back of her neck had a sea-green pigment, and the two tones were a speckled mix down the sides of her neck, which presented in a swirling pattern that Haley found to be reminiscent of henna. There was a vertical scar on her forehead above the left eyebrow, and she had a neutral expression on her face.

The only thing Haley could detect from the Cetatian woman was a slight sense of determination, but there did seem to be a weariness to the Hunter. Perhaps it was something about her eyes. "Wow!" Haley said. "You're really pretty."

The woman reached for the coil on her hip and spoke with a Spanish accent. "So," she said as the whip unrolled and electrified, "we meet again."

The Hunter's expression remained neutral, and her tone calm as she said, "Turn yourselves in. There is no need to harm you."

The girls glanced at each other, then with a scoff and a bit of a laugh, both said, "No!" in unison.

"Very well," the woman said as she drew a pistol with her left hand.

Haley and Elizabeth both fired a volley of blasts as the Hunter's whip rolled up in front of her, precisely snapping every orb from the air. The woman returned fire with her pistol, and the quick girls dashed to the side. Haley thought she felt a breeze as Elizabeth moved a little quicker than usual. The girls returned fire, but the Hunter easily snapped their blasts.

Having attached discs to the ceiling and walls upon arrival, the Hunter used her magnetic harness to suddenly start zipping around the decking. She hopped up about a foot off the platform and seemed to slide sideways through the air across the top of the generator, firing shots as she went. Both girls took a hit before they got their fields up, and the Hunter fired a few more shots.

As soon as she had the chance, Haley partially charged a shot and aimed for the ceiling. Upon releasing the blast, the Hunter remembered the falling platform and jumped backward while looking up to see what hazard the tricky farmer had unleashed. There was nothing, but Elizabeth used the ruse to finally land a shot.

The Hunter stumbled back with a grunt and quickly snapped away the incoming five shots from Haley. A return shot hit the farmer's field as Elizabeth threw three bursts of energy. The first two were energy orbs that the Hunter effortlessly snapped away, but the third was a gust of air, pushing the whip into the Hunter. She convulsed for an instant, but the whip shut down and recoiled itself to the woman's hip as she took a couple shots from Haley.

The woman tumbled over backward but regained her bearings as she sprang back to her feet and saw a glowing potato gun pointed in her direction.

"You're not in a shell," Haley shouted. "Please stop."

The Hunter replied by activating her magnetic harness and zipping upward. Haley fired as the woman moved to the side and then toward the Haley.

The Hunter dropped to the decking a couple of feet in front of Haley and twisted to the side, avoiding Elizabeth's mystical bolt. The woman pivoted the other way as she stepped forward, punching Haley in the gut. With a splash of blue, Haley was launched a few feet back and landed on her butt.

The woman spun again, dodging Elizabeth's blasts while moving toward the mystic. Haley regained her presence of mind and fired another volley of five blasts. The Hunter casually danced between and around everything being thrown at her. The woman leaped in with a sudden sidekick, knocking the rebellious mystic to the decking.

The Hunter then flipped backward, avoiding Haley's next shots and closing the distance. Almost instantly, the Cetatian was in front of Haley, and the girl took hits quicker than she could comprehend. The Hunter zipped up and out of the way as Elizabeth's shot flew by under her feet and landed on Haley, knocking her back to the decking.

The Hunter dropped down in front of the mystic, and Elizabeth took a swing. The Cetatian easily caught her by the wrist and looked at the knuckles, seeing scars from the restless girl's less-than-stellar moments. The woman then twisted Elizabeth around, putting the Elizabeth's right arm in a chicken wing. So, with her left, Elizabeth flicked the lighter.

A wave of fire rose up between them, startling the Hunter, who let go and leaped backward. Elizabeth spun around to let loose with a blast but received a lightning-quick jab to the forehead, knocking the girl down on her back.

Haley snapped back to her senses and got on her feet. She raised her arm cannon as the Hunter aimed her pistol toward the prone mystic. The empath finally had a good shot when she noticed something from the Hunter. A faint sense of conflict.

The dots of Haley's mental notes connected as her eyes widened with the sudden realization of just who she was truly dealing with. The detective's daughter decided not to fire but instead quickly dashed in, grabbing the woman's wrist in an upward motion. The pistol discharged harmlessly high…

And the dam broke.

Haley tumbled into a sea of turbulent emotion. Fear, dread and horror. She felt helpless. All sense of self-ownership stripped from her. At the mercy of whoever's whim rolled over her, adrift in the currents of cruelty.

A newly-orphaned Sabrina Carmen was just eleven years old when the three Proctors strapped her to the interrogation table. "Talk!" one of them shouted as he zapped her with an electric lead.

"I don't know anything!" Sabrina cried, which resulted in another zap. These Proctors weren't like the others that the young Sabrina had met. They knew that the girl had no information. They didn't care. It was nothing more than a sick, sadistic power trip. Drunk on the fear of someone who couldn't fight back.

One of them said, "I'm not convinced!" and smacked her on the forehead with a horsewhip, splitting the skin.

Sabrina's sense of self was utterly destroyed that night as those she thought to be trusted the most used their position of authority for kicks. She numbed herself to her empathic senses and her feelings in general. The Cetatian girl didn't even know she was an empath, but now all the senses came flooding back in full as the pair fell to the decking.

Haley landed in a sitting position while Sabrina unleashed a blood-curdling wail as she collapsed to her knees, then started sobbing heavily.

Tears were streaming down the cheeks of both empaths as Haley looked up and met the Hunter's gaze. "I'm sorry," she said sincerely in a cracked voice. "I wish you didn't have to feel like that."

Sabrina's eyes dropped back down as another wave of tears came gushing forward, and she buried her face into her palms, shaking.

Elizabeth wasn't sure what just happened, but she immediately hopped up and started throwing bolts at a coolant fitting. Haley stood up and wiped her eyes as Sabrina took her hands from her face and wrapped them around her own shoulders. She lowered her head, stared at the decking and continued to sob.

Haley turned around and started blasting one of the fittings while Elizabeth was finishing off the first. Then Haley thought she heard the faint sound of a tuning fork as the Hunter's feelings disappeared from her senses. Both girls instantly spun around to see nothing.

Sabrina was gone.

After a couple of seconds, they turned back around, quickly finishing the job, and the generator shut down.

"Wicked awesome!" exclaimed Haley as Elizabeth threw her fists in the air and shouted, "Yes!" The Archons would not have enough power to come to their universe.

The girls hugged each other in celebration when Elizabeth regained her good senses. "Let's get outta here!" she reminded Haley. The farmer tightened her embrace, flew them down to the floor, and they headed back to the washroom.

CHAPTER 22
Accept No Substitutes

They ran into the washroom and looked up to the vent. "Once we get up there, I gotta get you in first," Haley said.

Elizabeth looked up and around the vent for something which she could grab while climbing onto the farmer's shoulders.

"Meow," they heard from behind. It was a familiar voice with a downward inflection, making the cat's vocalization sound like a definitive statement. The girls turned around to see an orange and white shorthair with a crooked tail. "Meow," the cat said again.

"Nomad!" both the girls said in surprise. This cat had been seen all over town throughout the years and earned his namesake because of his tendency to wander. He came up to the girls as they both stooped down to pet him.

"Meow," he said happily while rubbing against their shins.

Haley picked Nomad up and snuggled the feline. The girls had known this cat before they even knew each other, and seeing him hear just brought a sense of relief. A sense of the normal world. The empath looked into Nomad's eyes and felt the giddiness from the affectionate cat. And she felt his resilience. This cat has faced many rough times, yet he's always persevered. Haley always found the way this cat pressed on inspiring, and his presence was a morale boost.

She snuggled him again as he purred, and Elizabeth reached up and scratched his head. Then Nomad hopped down and started walking toward the southern door. He stopped, looked over his shoulder at the pair and said, "Meow."

He walked up to the door and sat down as if he were waiting.

"Is Nomad pulling a Lassie?" Haley asked her friend.

"I think so," Elizabeth said and then she smiled. "Let's go find Timmy in the well."

"Nerd," Haley poked as they started following the cat.

"Lassie isn't nerdy," Elizabeth flatly replied as they continued down the new corridor. They noticed an opening on the eastern wall, an elevator shaft with no door. Upon looking into the shaft, the girls found that the lift wasn't on their level.

Haley flipped open her phone, and the com-system synced in with the controls. She was about to call the car when Nomad said, "Meow." The girls looked at him, and he was a little way further down the corridor. "Meow," he said as Haley detected urgency in the feline.

The young adventurers picked up their pace and caught up with him at a door. Nomad sat down. "Meow."

Haley could detect people inside. Some were focused but most felt stressed, so she conjured her helmet and carefully cracked the door open.

Elizabeth looked at the helmet and wondered if she had one as well, which prompted the bots in her PJs to motion, forming a helmet for her. The HUD displayed to her what Haley was seeing. There were rows of large transparent, cylindrical containers filled with clear fluid. Many of these vats had shells that looked fully developed, but most of them had new shells in various stages of growth.

Some of the vats drained, and the cylinders retracted into their bases as more Cetatian Proctors opened their new avatar's eyes and stood up. They stepped down from their vats and grabbed clothing from the bins that were lined up against the southern wall. They hopped around in an attempt to get dressed while running toward a portgate on the eastern end of the room.

The girls watched them all port away as a few lab technicians remained behind, continuing their work.

Haley shut the door and turned to her friend as their face shields flipped up. "Are you thinking what I'm thinking?"

"How'd you get your nickname?" the mystic asked in return with a smile.

"Breaking glasses," Haley stated with a smirk and both their face shields closed.

"Meow," Nomad added.

Haley cracked the door again to get one more good look at where everything and everybody was.

"Ready?" Elizabeth asked.

The door swung open, and the technicians looked up to see energetic blasts coming their way. The scientists dove for cover as the girls let loose. Haley was sending volleys of five blasts, shattering vats and damaging equipment.

Elizabeth saw one of the scientists running for the portgate and took him down with a bolt. She ran over to the gate and put her com to work as she threw more blasts around at the equipment.

The remaining lab tech knew there was nothing he could do, so he reached up, pulled off the visor, and his avatar gelled.

For the next couple of moments, they let their energy fly with reckless abandon, smashing every vat in the huge lab. The girls finally arrived at the back corner to find a large vat with a cloth draped over the top. Elizabeth pulled it back to reveal the contents, and when they saw Ahnk-Hume's replacement body, both their jaws dropped. Neither Haley nor Elizabeth could detect anything inside the empty vessel. No emotions. No energy.

"Whoa…that's scary," Elizabeth said.

They looked at each other, and both nodded as their energy gathered. The two friends released their charged blasts, shattering the cylinder, and then they unloaded on the cloned body.

It was resilient. A good barrage of blasts from the two damaged it beyond viability, but it didn't turn to gel. The young ladies looked at the body, and Elizabeth asked, "You don't think it was…a person, do you?"

Haley looked at the body for a moment, shaken and wondering if they had just killed someone, but then she relaxed a little and said with certainty as she dismissed her helmet, "No. It was empty."

Elizabeth also dismissed her helmet as they started looking around, breathing a little easier now that they can't keep coming in more shells. Haley looked at the portal and opened her phone. "You already got it!" she exclaimed to Elizabeth.

"Yeah," Elizabeth replied as she looked at her phone. "It says it was going to the…cafeteria?" She looked to Haley and said, "We can take them by surprise! This might be the last of them," then started for the gate.

"No," Haley blurted.

Elizabeth turned around with a bit of a surprised look on her face. "Huh?"

"No," Haley said again with more conviction. "We were over there earlier, but the elevator outside goes up toward the Town Hall." Elizabeth already realized where Haley was going as she continued, "Your mom and my dad have to be somewhere. And we haven't been there."

Elizabeth smiled but also silently lambasted herself for not thinking of that. "Let's go!"

They turned and ran for the door to find Nomad still there. "Meow," he said as he stood up and headed toward the elevator. Haley summoned the lift and it was waiting for them when they got to the shaft. Nomad walked right in, and the girls followed. With a mental command, the platform began to rise, and Haley tried turning her senses upward.

She felt sorrow and misery. A collective sense of hopelessness and fear. Haley remembered feeling that earlier when she was near the blast door and, according to the map, they were directly beneath that area. "Could it be them?" she wondered out loud while looking upward.

Elizabeth turned to her and asked, "You think you sense them?"

"Yeah…" Haley said, feeling overwhelmed that she might actually be about to see her dad. She felt the intense anxiety become strong and she stopped the lift on a doorless level.

The girls slowly leaned out into the corridor, looked around and then turned their attention toward the north. Nomad stepped out and turned in the same direction. Haley felt the fear clearly, and Elizabeth began to notice the tension in the air as well.

The townsfolk were completely disheartened.

Ed was looking a little off and Johnny, an EMT, was the first to notice. He was well known by everyone in the area. His endless charisma combined with his Jamaican accent made Johnny's bedside manner locally famous. He walked up to the State Trooper and asked, "Ed, you okay?"

The Trooper looked to Johnny. "Yeah…I'm alright."

The EMT noticed Ed start to lose his balance a time or two, and now he could see cracking in his lips. "When's the last time you had water?"

Ed hadn't had any since he got here, and there was none available. "I haven't, and it's not an option," the Trooper stated as he looked out the bars

into the larger room. "The only option we have is to find a way to get out."
Ed looked at the four Proctors, who were now posted outside the cell.
"Harry," he said, and the Marine made his way over.

"What's up?" he inquired.

"Any thoughts on how we might be able to get those guns from the guards?" Ed asked.

Harry glanced out to the men as he stroked his chin. Before he could really start sinking his mind into the question, one of the Proctors looked to the south. And then they all looked.

A second later, they all sprang into action, running toward the corridor. The Proctors went into the tunnel beyond where any of the townsfolk could see, and after a moment of commotion, everything fell silent.

Murmurs could be heard throughout the crowd as everybody started wondering and speculating on what was happening.

The chatter suddenly stopped when Haley and Elizabeth came running up to the bars calling for their parents.

"Haley!" Harry shouted in disbelief.

"Elizabeth!" Shouted Maggie with tears of joy to see her daughter seemingly unharmed, other than a bruise in the middle of her forehead. "What happened?" she asked, looking at the mark.

"I got punched by a ninja," she casually replied.

Haley opened her phone, but this was an old-fashioned lock with no electronics and had to be manually opened. Elizabeth had checked the guard's pockets a moment ago. Shaking her head in aggravation, the mystic said, "They didn't have any keys."

Haley looked at the latching mechanism and wondered if she had the oomph to break it. "Stand back," she announced. "I have an idea."

The folks took a couple of steps back as they wondered what the young farmer might have in mind. Haley raised her arm toward the lock when her dad said, "Haley…no." She looked up to her dad as he continued, "I'm sorry, but there's no way a potato is going to break that."

"But it's not a potato," she replied.

Confused, Harry asked his daughter, "What is it then?"

"It's a…" her face dropped as she tried to think of a way to explain this. "It's a…" Then, she lifted her head back up as a mischievous smirk grew across the right side of her face. That same smirk she would get as a toddler.

She turned her head up to her father and said, "It's a bad kitty!" She directed her attention back to the lock and gathered her energy.

"Whoa," Maggie said with wide eyes as she felt the vibes increase. The blue plasmatic light began to whisp along the barrel as a few of the people gasped, and Harry's jaw dropped.

The Marine spun around with his arms out, shouting, "Everyone, get back!"

Haley conjured her helmet as the group backed up, and when they were ready, she released her blast. The bobcat burst on the mechanism, damaging it some.

Gasps and shouts of surprise came from the crowd as Haley began charging up again. Elizabeth came by Haley's side, conjured her helmet and began gathering energy for a large burst.

Maggie's eyes slowly widened, and her opened-mouth smile grew larger as she witnessed Elizabeth utilize energy beyond anything she actually thought possible.

The two friends released their blasts together. The mangled latch snapped, allowing them to break the gate free and slide it to the side. The girls dismissed their helmets, Haley grabbed her father into a hug, and he was shocked by her strength. Maggie was similarly surprised by Elizabeth's incredible squeeze.

"I love you, Dad," Haley said as tears started to fall.

"I Love you, too," Harry said, hugging her tight in return.

Elizabeth and Maggie were also wet in the eyes as they shared an embrace for which they had both longed.

"Meow."

Harry opened his eyes and looked down at the cat. "Nomad?"

The firefighters and EMTs organized the crowd, and they all started following the two young adventurers into the corridor toward the elevator.

The Proctors' uniforms were on the floor, and Harry asked, "Where are they?" as he leaned down to collect the pistols.

"They're not really here. They're controlling the fake bodies from somewhere else. When you shoot them, they melt into a puddle and disappear." Haley explained as her father looked over the unfamiliar pistol. "Those shoot blasts of yellow energy."

Harry took a good look around and then said. "Everybody, stay behind me." The Marine aimed the pistol at the floor about seventy feet ahead, said,

"Fire in the hole!" and pulled the trigger. There was almost no kickback as a yellow bolt shot forward with a zipping sound and accurately hit the point that Harry had picked. The small amount of kick that he did feel was deliberate haptic feedback designed into the gun. He noticed two adjuster dials on the side, so he fired a few more rounds on different settings to find that one altered the power of the shots and the other the intensity of the kickback.

"Do you know where the other kids are?" asked a weakening Ed.

Haley pointed straight up and said, "I think they're near the top."

"How did you two do that?" Harry asked the young ladies.

Maggie spoke up next, "It's energy!" she said, excited by what she had seen.

"I don't know how to explain it," Haley said as she flipped open her phone to show her dad the map.

"Wow!" He looked at the screen in amazement, "Where did you get this?" her father asked, seeing that the elevator was going to need numerous trips to get everybody out.

"From the Marshals, but they…" As the empath thought about them, she noticed that she could sense Logan. "He's alive!" she suddenly shouted.

"Who?" Harry asked.

"Logan!" she happily explained. "He's one of the Marshals, and I can sense him. I couldn't for a while, and I was afraid that he might have been…" her eyes drifted as she paused, not wanting to even finish the sentence.

"How can you sense him?" her father asked.

"We're both empaths," Haley said.

He wasn't sure what to make of that but turned to show the map to the firefighters so they could plan the evacuation.

"Whoa!" Johnny shouted as he caught a stumbling Ed.

"We need to get him out now!" said one of the firefighters.

"Looks like this elevator goes up to the Town Hall," Harry said.

"He needs water," Johnny called out as he and Dr. Patel walked the dehydrated Stated Trooper into the elevator.

"Girls, you're going up too," Mary said.

"Wait," Harry said as he handed the phone back to his daughter. "We don't know who could be up there."

Elizabeth quickly put in, "That's why you want us up there," as an amber light pulsed in her eyes.

Harry's jaw dropped, Mary gasped, and Maggie inhaled sharply as her eyes figuratively lit up at the young mystic's display. Haley then dropped her head as she griped, "I still can't do that on purpose yet."

The Chief looked to one of his larger firefighters, "George, go with them in case there's trouble." George nodded and turned for the elevator. Harry handed him one of the pistols. The Chief continued, "Hank, Joey. Will you guys watch the back of the group?"

"You've got it," said Joey.

"Sure thing," said Hank.

They both received a pistol from the Marine, and then The Fire Chief looked to Harry, "Once you clear the area, I'll start sending everybody up.

Harry nodded and then stepped into the lift with the others. Haley sent a mental command through her phone, and the platform began its ascent.

She held her father's hand and squeezed. Harry looked down at her eyes as she smiled. They all rode the car upward in silence, reflecting on the happenings of this strange day. The lift slowed and then stopped as the door on the shaft wall behind them slid open.

The group turned around to see the tunnel under Town Hall. The walls of rock and dirt were perfectly smooth, and they were lined with the same metal bars as below the warehouse. A cylindrical object could be seen mounted to the ceiling and seemed to be tied in with the bar system lining the room. The tops of the chutes that lead down to the large cell were on the northern wall.

Haley could feel a mix of emotions. There was definitely an uneasiness, but a regular spectrum of emotions could be felt as well.

"I wonder what that is," Harry said, pointing at the object on the ceiling.

Haley held up the phone to scan the object, and it was identified as a port beacon. She handed the phone to her father so he could see, and then the empath turned toward a particular door.

Haley and Elizabeth headed for the door, and Harry followed. The empath could feel the emotions become stronger as she reached up for the handle.

"Stop," Harry said, and the girls turned to look. These two young ladies have always been a little adventurous, but he was surprised at how willing they were to just put themselves into harm's way to check on others. "When did you two become so brave?" he asked with a smile. Before an answer could be given, the Marine continued. "I'm very proud of you both, but get safely away from the door while I check."

Both girls nodded and took a few steps back. Haley conjured a pair of safety glasses and handed them to her father as he handed her the phone, "They'll record what you see," she explained.

"My daughter's done turned into James Bond," he said dryly as Haley and Elizabeth giggled. "A little further away," he said to the pair and the girls maturely complied.

Elizabeth handed George a pair of glasses, and he went to stand beside Harry. The Marine turned to check on the girls once more. The inside of Haley's barrel was emitting a blue glow, and Elizabeth had an amber orb of light in each hand. Many questions ran through his mind as he turned back to the door and focused on the moment. He and George nodded at each other. Then Harry tried the handle. It turned, and he slowly pulled the door open, just a crack.

He could see an imposter of Dr. Patel as well as a Joey and a Harry in Proctor's uniforms. And he could see the kids!

The children were mostly playing with various toys throughout the room, and he could see an ample supply of snacks and drinks in the corner. The Proctors were talking and interacting with the children, as was the false doctor. The place looked like a make-shift daycare center, and the three imposters were actually being nice to the young people, but four teenagers were in the corner, not looking too happy.

The others observed through their lenses until Harry shut the door. "Can we draw them out here?" Elizabeth asked.

The Marine considered the question and smiled.

Ahnk-Hume entered the shell lab, and his eyes went wide with fury at the shattered equipment before him. "No!" he screamed as his stomach sank, and he bolted for the back corner.

He was there in seconds, and his lips curled back as his brow furrowed and eyes widened. There, slumped over the vat base and onto the floor, was his replacement body. Completely unviable.

The Drakel seethed. He couldn't believe it. Ahnk-Hume's anger rose to new heights, and he actually became light-headed. The only thing he could think about was getting his hands on Haley. Getting his revenge.

His voice started as a low growl but ended in something more like a shriek as he screamed, "She shut me out again!"

The Archon shut off his implanted projector, and the avatar turned to gel. In the Second Density, he stood up from where he sat and immediately went to retrieve an item. Ahnk-Hume was so angry that tears began to form in his crazed eyes.

A moment later, he opened a case that contained two metallic bands. They were cylindrical, silver in color, and about six inches long. They were made with a mineral that would prevent Ahnk-Hume from phasing back to this plain, allowing him to remain in the First Density indefinitely.

He picked them up with his upper hands and slipped them over his lower wrists. He shuddered when they slid onto his forearms, as the resonance which allowed him to remain in the denser plain also made an Archon feel very uncomfortable in his own skin. But he was too angry to care.

He didn't even have the clarity of mind to realize that they could easily make another in less than a month. He growled as he began making his way to a portgate. There was only one thing on his mind, and that was the complete and total unmaking of Haley Starr.

CHAPTER 23
Earn Your Stripes

Chuck woke up first. Lying on the floor, the Marshal rolled to his back and sat up. He was still in the snare with his arms pinned to his sides, so taking a good look around, Chuck could see that he was in an eight-by-ten cell. The snare emitted a frequency that prevented him from utilizing his energetic abilities, but his physical regeneration was unaffected, leaving him with not even a bruise. He got onto his feet and shuffled over toward the bars.

Logan opened his eyes as he heard a Proctor's voice state, "Remain away from the bars."

"Or what?" Chuck dared to ask.

The Proctor immediately walked to the cell and jabbed Chuck through the bars with a baton that discharged an electrical shock, resulting in the Marshal collapsing onto the ground with a thud. "Ooph!" he blurted as he hit the concrete floor.

"Please, remain away from the bars," the Proctor firmly stated. Then, he turned and went back to his post by the door.

As Logan sat up, his temple started throbbing, making his stomach turn. "Well," he said with a groan, "at least I've got company this time."

"No talking either," the Proctor stated.

"Darn," Logan said flatly. He tried to focus on the snare, but this one was made specifically for him. It was constantly rotating through different disruptive frequencies, making it too complex for him to adapt to his own field.

Chuck was racking his brain, trying to come up with an escape plan, but he was at a loss for the moment.

Dismissing their helmets, Neil and Remy exited the southern end of the incinerator room. They had made contact with Gus and heard the news that Chuck had found both Haley and Elizabeth, although nobody's heard from them since.

But they had their objective. If Chuck's theory was correct, those who were somehow binding the immortals were in the firehouse.

Remy held up his phone and watched the screen as his com tried the codes on the security gate. After a couple of seconds, one of the codes blinked green, and the gate unlatched. "Yes!" he quietly exclaimed.

Neil followed the Marshal through the gate and into the elevator. He was thinking about how to undo the binding on the gods but also wondered how a binding of this magnitude could have even been cast. The mystic took a deep breath in an attempt to steady his nerves, wondering just how far in over his head he might be and hoping that he would be able to dispel such potent magick.

The imposters all looked to the door in surprise when it suddenly opened to see Harry leaning half into the room with an urgent look on his face. The Marine quickly pointed at the three shells and quietly motioned for all of them to come out the door as if he was trying to be discrete around the children. Then he stepped back out and softly shut the door.

A Proctor opened the door first to see Harry and George standing beneath the port beacon. George was pointing at it with his right hand and a worried look on his face while he was motioning with his left and said, Hurry up!"

The Proctor came out, followed by the other two. When they were halfway there, Harry and George pulled their pistols and fired.

Caught by surprise, the three imposters were quickly gelled while Harry and George watched, with revulsion, the strange sight of them melting away.

"How much weirder can today get?" George asked as the double doors to the third chute entrance opened. Johnny and Dr. Patel walked Ed out and toward the room with the children, followed by Haley and Elizabeth.

The girls ran ahead of the three men and pulled the door open as they brought the State Trooper into the room.

The kids all looked up when Johnny and Scott came in, setting Ed in a chair. "What's this?" fourteen-year-old Billy asked. He was the oldest in the room and had been trying to help keep the others calm.

"He's dehydrated," Dr. Patel said as Billy noticed the different clothing.

The teen went to the corner of the room and grabbed a couple of water bottles, and ran back over, handing them to the pediatrician. "You're…" he started to say.

"Yeah, he's the real Doc," Elizabeth said.

Dr. Patel saw to Ed while Johnny walked around the room checking on everybody. They had no doubt that this was the real EMT as nobody could act like the charismatic Johnny. Except Johnny.

The girls went back out to the larger room where Harry and George had just finished searching the guards' clothing. The two guards had bolt pistols on the lowest setting and nothing more.

"I don't sense anybody up there," Haley said as she pointed up to the building above them.

Harry looked at the earth ramp going up to the assembly room of the Town Hall. "Let's make sure."

He and George walked up the ramp with their pistols drawn and began to systematically search the area. They both stopped and stared for a moment at the strange stone gateway standing along the eastern wall of the assembly room. The rest of the building was clear. After a couple of moments, they met back at the ramp. "Let's start bringing them up," Harry said.

George went back down the ramp while Harry stood watch in the assembly room. Billy and the other three teens each carried a case of water out of the room. "Dr. Patel said to bring this down, too," Billy explained.

The teens placed the water in the lift, and Geoge went back to the room. Haley, Elizabeth and the teens followed, and they all gabbed another case of water and brought them to the elevator. Elizabeth then stepped inside the lift with George and sent a mental command to her phone.

"Haley, stay with your dad and everyone else. Stay in the room until we come back up," said George. The door slid shut, and the teens returned to the room as Haley ran up the ramp and, with enthusiasm, hugged her dad again.

"I've missed you all day!" she said with a smile as she closed her eyes and squeezed.

After a moment, they released their embrace, and Haley started looking around. Her attention immediately fell upon the stone structure. "A portgate!" she said, excited to tell her dad about them. She flipped her phone open and was about to sync into the system when the signal it was maintaining transferred to another gate within the complex. And then a vortex appeared.

He held still, so his head wouldn't throb. But the constantly changing frequency emitted by the snaring device was just too chaotic. Logan thought that he had found a vibe with which he could work, but it was gone as soon as he noticed it.

About thirty seconds later, he noticed it again. O'Connor focused in on this particular sensation, and after a moment, it became more prominent to his senses. He noticed it more clearly and realized it was coming up in regular intervals.

Logan started to count and found the pattern. There it was, now plain as day, every third and fifth second. "…three…five," he whispered. "…three…five…three…five," He fell into the rhythm as he harmonized his own vibration with the targeted frequency.

Chuck and the Proctor heard chunks of the snaring device smacking against the cement walls.

"What are you doing," the guard asked as he approached O'Connor's cell but was suddenly flung forward into the wall at the back of the larger room. The neck cracked, and he dropped into a heap of gel.

"What took you so long?" Chuck asked.

"Mine had a modulating frequency," he answered as he held his hand up to the side of his head. Logan winced when he ran his fingertip over the nasty welt. He gathered some energy and sent it into the injury. Unlike Haley and Chuck, Logan didn't have any regenerative abilities, but he could sooth the pain enough to get himself back to functional. "Give me a couple minutes. I gotta get past the bindings on the bars next."

"I'm not going anywhere," Chuck reminded him.

Logan started to tune into the bindings when his com beeped, causing him to lose his focus. He decided to check the phone, and O'Connor's expression became one of confusion as he said, "We've got an incoming signal."

"From who and how?" Chuck asked, just as confused.

"Unknown. Looks like it was an intercepted message," he said as the com-system isolated the signal and then opened it. "It's some kind of Cetatian computer code, and it…no way!"

"What?" But just as Chuck asked, the gates on both their cells unlatched and automatically slid to the side while the snare deactivated.

Logan walked into the cell and said, "Somebody sent us the keys,"

Chuck stood up and conjured his phone to try and see who just broke them out. "I would have thought Gus, but…we'll have to figure that out later." He then stepped out of the cell and found a set of keys in the guard's pocket. "Let's go."

As they opened the cell room door, their coms beeped again. Chuck looked at his screen, and a smile spread across his face. The latest code, combined with the other successful codes generated, gave the com enough data to finally crack a security system firewall and communication within the next few moments was likely.

The elevator door slid to the side, revealing a stairwell. Neil and Remy stepped out of the lift and walked up to a hatch in the ceiling. Remy slowly opened the lid and saw that they were in an office inside the firehouse. He then turned toward Neil with a grin and a thumbs-up. They stepped up and into the office, but aside from some heavy bindings on the walls, nothing else seemed unusual.

Approaching the door on the western wall, Remy slowly opened it and looked out to see a short hallway. To his right was the meeting room, and to his left was the garage. Seeing no one around, the Marshal made his way toward the left. He sidled up to the door at the end of the hall and looked through the glass.

None of the trucks were in the garage, but in the center of the open space was a crystal pedestal, and on this pedestal stood a simple-looking ceramic vase with a lid.

Evenly around this vase, three feet away, sat six wizards in chairs. They were wearing ceremonial robes, but they each had their bare feet in a tub of water on the floor.

Three feet behind each of them was a round, stone pedestal, three feet high and three feet wide. On top of these was a rectangular bar, made of iron, two feet wide and three inches thick. The bar bent around back to itself in the shape of a rectangle, standing upright at three feet high and two feet wide.

Each wizard had a copper wire wrapped around a submerged ankle. The line ran out of the tub and behind the wizard, over to the pedestal. The line went up and wrapped around the left side of the iron rectangle and then led back down to the wizard's other ankle.

On the right side of the rectangle was another copper line, but this one had many more winds around the bar. Both ends of this line ran upright like a pair of antennae, three feet above the iron rectangle.

Remy motioned for Neil to take a look. As the mystic peered through the window, his eyes widened with understanding. "That's genius!" he whispered.

Seeing the expression on Remy's face, Neil explained, "Those pedestals behind them, the wires…They're using those coils to boost their power."

"Like the coil for a spark plug?" Remy asked.

"Exactly," Neil said. "These guys don't have nearly as much power as I thought. It's just being amplified by the transformers."

"Oh," said Remy with a smile as he gathered his energy. "In that case, excuse me for one moment." And he waltzed right into the room, throwing a seismic blast.

A pedestal under one of the coils was shattered, as was the wizard's focus. Two jumped out of their chairs, and the others fell over from the startle when the coil tumbled to the floor. As the wizards, still trying to get their bearings, looked at the Marshal, Neil stepped in and threw a mystical bolt at the vase. Upon impact, an intense electromagnetic wave pulsed out from the vessel, which brought looks of panic to the wizards' faces.

"So," Remy started to ask with a smile, "how many of them are probably mad at ya?"

The wizards answered by gelling out.

Gus was standing on the bridge of the Wavelength, speaking to another man, when his com beeped. He cast it onto the main monitor to see that the local Cetatian portgate network had been cracked. The Marshal was quite pleased to see the new info as, every moment or so, another gate in the complex became visible on his system. He quickly singled out one particular gate, maintaining a constant connection to elsewhere.

He was about to shut it down, but before he could, Gus' face changed to one of confusion as somebody beat him to it. And whoever it was, they did it manually.

Harry was both concerned and intrigued as he watched a vortex form and widened in the archway. "I'm not doing that," Haley nervously told her father.

The Marine was starting to raise his firearm as a ten-foot-tall reptilian with four arms and a pair of wings burst out from the gate, throwing a mystical orb of red light and darkness.

Harry fired his shot, and the two bolts zipped by each other and landed. Ahnk-Hume winced as he took a round to the face, resulting in a black eye. The magick bolt hit Harry in the chest, knocking him across the room and into the wall, where he crumpled to the floor, unconscious.

"Dad!" shouted a horrified Haley. She popped her arm up and sent a burst of five shots at Ahnk-Hume.

The reptilian sidestepped while moving forward with a scowl on his face. Three of the blasts landed, shuddering the large reptilian man, but he didn't seem harmed by it as he still pressed forward.

The anger felt tangible to the frightened empath. The sheer hatred and bitterness were overwhelming as the Archon's vibes made her skin crawl. Ahnk-Hume dove at Haley, swinging all four fists down to the floor with a mighty slam as she dashed to the side.

Using the thrusters, Haley flew fast to the other end of the room and turned to shoot back, but Ahnk-Hume was following right behind her and grabbed her while she was turning.

"Ah!" she screamed as the reptilian, like an angry child throwing a tantrum, hurled her across the room. In a splash of blue and purple, Haley slammed into the wall and tumbled to the ground. Grunting while standing to her feet, she was suddenly grabbed again. Ahnk-Hume lifted her up with his upper-left hand and let go as his upper-right fist came swinging in, knocking her back out toward the middle of the room.

The rage was unbelievable. The Drakel was almost hyperventilating from his anger as he spat a word between each breath, "You will know pain!" He was drooling, and his eyes looked like the gaze of madness itself.

Haley was terrified by the giant reptilian walking right up to her. Her eyes darted over to her father on the floor, and she immediately burned with a rage of her own. She narrowed her eyes and kicked the thrusters into high gear, launching herself straight at Ahnk-Hume in an attempt to slam him in the face with her barrel.

The Archon caught Haley in the air and slammed her to the ground in another splash of blue and purple light. She made an "Ooph" sound on impact, but before she could register what was happening, Ahnk-Hume again sent her flying with a kick.

Haley landed on the floor near the wall and was seeing stars. She started to regain her presence of mind as the Drakel was walking toward her. She again saw her dad, still unconscious on the floor, and her blood began to boil.

"Did you really think you could overpower me?" Ahnk-Hume asked incredulously. The enraged Archon continued as he approached. "Did you think you could get away with destroying my replacement body?" His wroth rose, as did Haley's, while Ahnk-Hume spoke further. "Did you really think you could stop *us*?!" His breathing increased, and he growled, "What exactly were you thinking?"

Think now, be mad later, Haley suddenly remembered.

Summoning every ounce of willpower she could muster, the empath set her feelings to the side and tried to observe her current circumstance as if she were an outsider. She watched while Ahnk-Hume clenched all four fists and crouched with his rage boiling.

When Haley felt his rage pop, she dove to the side as Ahnk-Hume sprang into a lunge. She successfully dodged, and the Drakel slammed himself into the wall. Haley, trying to keep her feelings in check, quickly spun around to see the Archon stumble to the floor with an aggravated grunt. The empath sensed his rage increase again.

Haley reached a bit of a different state. The empath suddenly felt her emotions, all of them, simultaneously. Not at all chaotic or overwhelming, but they instead blended together in harmony, and she felt the intensity of each individual one as they all converged into a powerful calm. Haley had entered her flow state. She was in what Elizabeth called 'the sweet spot.'

Ahnk-Hume wasn't thinking clearly, but Haley was. And her next thought was a very simple question:

What would Dad do?

The Marine's daughter sent a mental command to her phone, hijacking anything that would function as a speaker, and the music began to play.

As Ahnk-Hume was standing himself up, he noticed the steadily increasing volume of the guitar fading in, which just irritated him even more. Then the instruments hit sudden, intense and deliberate beats when the enraged reptilian turned around to see Haley standing in the middle of the room.

She made a fierce blue glow appear in her eyes, and while a mischievous smirk spread across the right side of her face, the glow intensified, then faded as the intro to "Eye of the Tiger" continued to play.

He seethed beyond all sensibilities, "You wretched…impetuous…little…"

"You're really bad at this stuff," the empath casually interrupted as she sensed his blood boiling. When Haley felt it pop, she dodged and the Drakel dove harmlessly by. Haley spun around and released some blasts, hitting her mark, but the Archon's physiology and magick made him quite durable. He pivoted, teeth bared, and his eyes were wild with frustration.

"Are other reptiles embarrassed by the Archons?" she asked in an innocent tone. Then there was that emotional pop and Haley jumped up with her thrusters. As Ahnk-Hume's lunge carried him underneath her, she pounced. Her feet slammed into the back of his head, releasing the burst of energy, and she rebounded back up, charging her energy as she went. A bobcat was released at the apex, followed by a volley of four shots that all landed on the Drakel as she touched down.

Ahnk-Hume spun with a wave of his hand, and three shards of dark red light shot toward Haley. She threw up her protective field, blocked the incoming missiles and said, "You're not doing so good. Did you accidentally eat a positive feeling?"

Her taunts were driving him insane! He screamed in pure aggravation and then glared at the tiny little farmer.

She tilted her head. "Want some Repto-Bismol?" she cutely asked with a slight smile.

He roared, charging in with his upper left fist out wide, and Haley stood her ground, watching the telegraphed haymaker. Haley engaged her thrusters last second to move with the punch, just enough to let Ahnk-Hume feel a good sense of connection from the swing. It still hurt, but she used the thrusters to control her trajectory. Haley exaggerated her crash into the stone-faced base of a support column and then dropped to a knee on the floor.

"Ow," Haley moaned while she watched the reptilian from the corner of her eye, continuing his rage with a charge.

Harry thought he heard his favorite song as he felt the soreness in his upper body. He opened his eyes to see Haley crash into the column and the giant reptilian about to crush her. He was instantly on his feet and running for her but then stopped, stunned by what he saw next.

Overflowing with madness, Ahnk-Hume dove at Haley. She jumped straight up with her thrusters before the Archon slammed through the stone facing and into the lally column, shuddering the building. Haley came back down with a pounce and rebounded off Ahnk-Hume's back. The reptilian convulsed with the impact, and Haley ascended back up, leaning backward as her feet came over the top of her head.

She was gathering energy while she turned upright and her feet touched down. Wisps of blue and purple began to roll across her body as a dazed Ahnk-Hume stood up. He stumbled a little when he turned to face Haley. Energy arched from her as she held her potato gun level with the Archon. He began to gather his energy, but Haley released hers.

A wide sustained beam of blue shot from her barrel, the ghost-like images of all types of cats racing forward within. The blast hit Ahnk-Hume, knocking him past the column and slamming him into the wall. He convulsed until the blast ended, then slid down to the floor. The reptilian could barely comprehend what was happening at that moment.

He was slowly lifting his head when he heard Haley say, "This spud's for you!" Ahnk-Hume focused his eyes in time to see the potato just before it hit. The tuber knocked the back of his thick skull into the wall, and as his head bounced forward, an ethereal bobcat burst in his face. Ahnk-Hume slumped over, unconscious.

Harry's jaw could've hit the floor as he stared with amazement, trying to process everything he had just seen. Haley turned to see him standing there. "Dad!" she shouted with excitement and rushed in, hugging him tightly. He wrapped his arms around his daughter and picked her up, squeezing just as tight.

After she hopped down to her feet, Haley asked with a giant smile, "Did you see that?"

"Yeah…what was that?" Harry asked, still in disbelief.

"That was my first flip ever!" she beamed as Harry began to chuckle. They looked at each other, sharing a warm smile.

Ahnk-Hume blinked his eyes open, not yet certain where he was. An instant later, his mind snapped to the present, and, despite the pain, the Archon sprang into action.

Haley's eyes widened with shock as she felt the sudden rush of anger and hatred. She spun around, raising her arm cannon, but was suddenly shoved aside by Harry as Ahnk-Hume dove at them.

He took a step toward Ahnk-Hume while thrusting his right fist forward. Harry, this Marine, this father protecting his daughter, drove his knuckles between the charging Drakel's eyes and against the thick reptilian skull. His feet slid back a few inches from the impact, and Ahnk-Hume dropped to the floor. Out cold.

Harry's hand was already swollen from the fractures, but he didn't care one bit. He looked down at this being who tried to harm his Haley as she came back over to him. "Dad?" she called out, looking at his hand. The Marine wrapped his left arm around Haley's shoulder, pulled her in close and kissed the top of her head.

Haley started to look around as she felt a shift in energy. She sensed a presence, and it seemed to increase, then coalesce in the center of the room as a ghostly image of a woman took form.

The Starrs watched as she manifested, Harry utterly confused and Haley sporting a huge smile. The apparition became solid, and she looked to the empath with a smile of her own and a tear of joy running down her cheek.

"Bast!" Haley shouted as they ran toward each other and hugged for the first time. The goddess then stood straight, looked over to Harry and winced upon seeing his swollen hand. "This is my dad."

She approached the Marine, holding her hands out, palms up, toward his right arm. "May I?" She asked.

Harry didn't know what to make of it, but Haley certainly seemed to trust this woman. He nodded, and Bast could sense his apprehension, but as she ran energy from her hands to his, the swelling quickly reduced, and the throbbing ache diminished. A few seconds later, his hand was fine, and the soreness from Ahnk-Hume's mystical bolt vanished.

Harry held up his hand as he painlessly moved his fingers. "Thank you," he said, the shock still obvious in his voice and on his face.

"Oh," Haley said, "There's a tiger down there. We fed him, but he needs help."

Bast closed her eyes and sent her consciousness through the complex. Now that she was fully manifest, the mystical bindings and barriers were nothing to the goddess, and she easily dispelled them as she went. Bast saw Dr. Patel and Johnny tending to the children and a stable-looking Ed sitting upright in his chair.

She saw the first group of townsfolk who had come up in the elevator. She saw Elizabeth and Maggie, who were riding the elevator back down and noticed her presence as she passed by. She saw the Marshals, who also noticed her presence, joining up with the rest of the townsfolk below. She saw her cats. And she saw Aastik.

"Oh my…" said Bast with a horrified look on her face. She furrowed her brow, and a golden light began to shine from her eyes. A few seconds later, she nodded as if satisfied with what she had done.

The front doors opened, and in came Gus, firearm up and an Air Force Colonel at his side, who was also armed. Five more men came in behind them. Gus had made the call.

The Colonel looked at Ahnk-Hume, then over to the portgate and back to Gus. "So, this is an Archon," he stated more than asked as he motioned to the reptilian.

"Yessir," Gus replied in an upbeat manner as he placed two sets of cuffs on Ahnk-Humes wrists. "These cuffs are made with that mineral I told you about. It will keep him from phasing back to the Second Density," Gus explained while clicking them closed. "I never thought we'd see the day where we actually have him in custody." He stood up in time to catch an enthusiastic hug from Haley.

"Hey," he said with a smile, returning the hug.

"I'm sorry to tell you that you still don't have him," the Colonel said to Gus in his gruff voice. "He will be detained by the United States Air Force." He then turned to look Gus directly in the eyes as he firmly added, "In *this* universe."

"You want him," said Chuck as he walked up the ramp with Trooper Weathers and some townsfolk, "you can have him!" He turned and looked to a younger version of Colonel Decker when Haley's arms wrapped around the Marshal, who was next up in her hugging spree. And Haley was ready to give more hugs when Elizabeth, Maggie and Nomad walked up the ramp.

Chuck approached the Colonel and said, "I'm Marshal Chuck Gentry. This is Trooper Ed Weathers, and have we got an incident report for you!"

Then the portgate activated, and everybody looked. "Who's using the line?" Chuck asked Gus.

"I don't know," the Texan replied while looking at his phone screen, utterly confused.

"I'm doing it," Bast stated as the vortex opened to fill the archway. Then Squeaks, Lulu, and three other cats that Haley had not seen came sauntering out of the vortex, followed by a Bengal tiger.

Gasps of shock could be heard from some of the people as the great cat limped into the Town Hall. Decker and the other Airmen in the room immediately raised their weapons.

"No!" shouted Bast, stepping between them and the tiger with her arms out.

"Ma'am, step out of the way," one of the Airmen ordered.

"She knows what she's talking about," Chuck shouted as a golden glow appeared in the goddess' eyes. She turned toward the tiger and said, "Please, come." The tiger started limping toward the woman as everybody watched. Bast leaned down, looked into his eyes and connected. Then, she stood up, and the tiger brushed against the goddess' legs, and as he did, the wounds closed and sealed. The vigor returned to the great cat right before everyone's eyes. A few quiet gasps and whispers of wow could be heard from the people.

"Pleased to meet you too, Aastik," Bast said with a warm smile. She turned, started walking toward Ahnk-Hume, and Aastik walked alongside. Bast motioned to the Archon on the floor, and Aastik stepped right up to him, sat down and stared.

With a tiger keeping the Drakel under guard, Bast walked over to the EMTs and offered the use of her healing abilities.

"This way," an Airman said, walking with Remy and Neil. They weren't in the room more than fifteen seconds before they were pulled into hugs by Haley. When Neil was released, he was then pulled into another from Elizabeth and then Maggie.

Everyone got their bearings, and proper introductions were made as more of the townsfolk continued their way out from beneath. Although from another universe, Harry immediately recognized Remy as a fellow Marine. Logan continued to operate the elevator while the firefighters and military men worked together, guiding the people in an orderly fashion. Then, an armored truck arrived.

Ahnk-Hume slowly opened his eyes and groaned. The lump on his forehead throbbed, and he felt nauseous. When his vision came into focus, he looked up from the floor to see the stern visage of Aastik staring back at him. The great cat growled, baring sharp teeth, as he inched his face closer to the reptilian's, and Ahnk-Hume froze in terror.

"I think he's got the message," Bast said. "Let these men do their jobs."

Aastik stood up, walked over to Bast and sat as the Air Force took Ahnk-Hume into custody.

Haley held her dad's hand, and they watched the airmen escort Ahnk-Hume into the back of the large truck. Harry pulled her in tight when they heard a sudden sound of joy.

"Squeaks!" an excited little girl shouted as she picked up her cat.

Haley smiled at the reunion, feeling the relief and giddiness of the pair. She sensed so much tension being relieved as the townsfolk made their exodus from the underground facility.

"Meow," Nomad said, and Haley stooped down to pick him up. He wriggled around in her arms with happiness as she giggled. The rugged old cat settled and purred for a moment. Then he hopped down and turned to leave.

"Nomad," Bast called.

The cat stopped and looked back toward the Egyptian goddess.

"Come with me," she offered. "We have something to discuss."

Nomad walked over to Bast, and she stooped over to pick him up. The tired cat settled into her arms and purred. Haley, Harry and Neil were now talking with Elizabeth and Maggie when they saw Bast walking toward them.

The five looked to Bast as she approached, "You both have amazing daughters," she said with admiration to Harry and Maggie. "I must be going now," Bast continued, looking over to Neil and then down to Haley and Elizabeth, "but I'll keep in touch," she finished with a genuine smile.

Haley held Nomad one more time, then the two girls and goddess exchanged hugs. Bast picked Nomad back up, walked over to Aastik, and they all waved goodbye. Bast, Nomad and Aastik faded from view.

245

EPILOGUE

It was approaching nine o'clock. After a tour of Gus' ship, they had gathered in a small conference room on board the Wavelength and were debriefed by Decker. Haley and Elizabeth were now standing at the top of the ramp in the chilly evening breeze, looking down at the military vehicles and state police cruisers parked around the Wavelength, which was no longer cloaked. Just inside the cargo bay, Neil, Harry and Maggie were speaking with Colonel Decker, and the Marshals conversed with Trooper Weathers.

After a few moments, they all converged into a single group and continued chatting for a bit, but it was getting late. It was time to start saying their goodbyes.

Haley ran to her father's truck, grabbed a bag and trotted back over to the group. She came up to Gus first and gave him a big hug. After they let go, she reached into the bag and produced a word puzzle book. "You seem like you like to discover things," she said.

"Thank you," Gus responded with a smile.

"And thank you," Haley replied with another hug.

She turned and saw Remy as she reached in the bag, "Think fast!" Haley shouted while tossing him a tennis ball. The Marshal snagged it from the air with a grin as he jogged over and wrapped her up in a hug.

"Thank you," Haley said as she squeezed.

Next, she turned and saw Logan walking by. She ran over to him, and he felt her getting closer. O'Connor turned around and wrapped the incoming Haley in a big bear hug. He picked her up and squeezed as she laughed. He set Haley down, and she looked up into his eyes while gathering energy into her own. A fierce blue light appeared as her fellow empath's eyes, in unison, glowed green. They shared a smile, one more hug and said goodbye.

Logan turned and walked halfway up the ramp when Haley said, "Hey!" Logan looked back, and she tossed an object to him. The Marshal reached up and caught the potato as Haley said, "For luck."

Logan thought back to this morning when Haley did the exact same thing right before they left. He held the potato up and looked in her eyes with a warm smile, nodded, turned and continued up the ramp.

Haley then saw Chuck, walked over and hugged him. She was squeezing him tight when he said, "It was good to meet you, Kid." After a brief pause, he added, "Again."

Haley snickered, released her hug and reached into the bag. She pulled her arm back out and held up a video game controller as she said, "You helped teach me how to control myself."

"We hot-heads gotta stick together," he playfully replied with a grin. They hugged again, and Chuck said, "Hopefully, we'll meet again one day." Then he suddenly pulled her into a noogie. "So, I can do this!" Everybody outside could hear Haley having a case of the giggles.

Colonel Decker shook Harry's hand and said, "You'll be hearing from me." He and Ed went and stood beside Chuck and Haley as they finished their goodbye.

Haley waved, then Chuck turned to walk up the ramp with Trooper Weathers and Colonel Decker. Haley, Elizabeth and the others went over to Harry's truck and climbed in.

Maggie sat in the back seat with one arm over Elizabeth's shoulder and the other over Haley's. Trinket climbed into Haley's lap, and Neil was putting on his seat belt as he said with a sigh, "What a day."

Harry placed his key in the ignition and said, "Strangest day I've ever known." He turned the engine over, put the truck in gear and rolled out from between a cruiser and a Humvee.

"Life is strange," Maggie stated.

"Life is weird," Elizabeth added.

"Life," Haley said as she stared out the window at a clear sky, "is what we choose."

All the information that the Marshals had acquired on the Cetatians, the underground facility and the Archons were on a simple-looking phone in the Colonel's hand.

"There are still six other Archons here," Gus reminded. "They can be nasty."

"We'll definitely be keeping tabs on all of them," the Colonel said as he watched the screen react to his mental commands. He placed the device in his pocket and said, "Thank you for helping to protect our timeline."

Haley and Harry stood in front of the headstone of Heather Starr. The farmgirl had a nanotech jacket blocking the chilly evening breeze as she and her father held hands and remembered their precious time with this amazing woman.

They prepared to go, and Haley set her hand on the edge of the headstone. "Thanks for all the help today, Mom," she said with a mist in her eyes.

Haley took her father's hand and squeezed as they started down the path toward the road. The pair walked in silence, just happy to have each other safe when the breeze at their backs suddenly increased to a gust, then it eased off just as quick, and a whisper could be heard in the air as it settled.

"I'm proud of you," said a woman's voice. A voice they recognized.

"Heather?!" Harry said as he looked around with a tear in each eye.

Haley looked over her shoulder, an expression of shock on her face. She lowered her eyes as a single tear rolled down her cheek. With a sad smile, she looked back over her shoulder toward the starry sky and said, "I love you, Mom."

Haley hugged her father tight and said, "I love you, Dad," as he squeezed her back.

"I love you, Haley," Harry said to his daughter.

They just finished their first lesson together. Elizabeth thought about the events of the day and how she saw things so differently than just a few short hours ago. Now here she was, practicing energy with her mother and grateful for the time with this woman she so often tried to avoid.

She went to her room and stretched her arms out with a yawn, pulled them back in and then reached straight up into the air for another stretch while her mom started dinner. Elizabeth could smell the clam chowder on the stove, a favorite for both of them.

Her stomach rumbled, and she smiled, thinking, *I guess we're more alike than I wanted to admit.*

Elizabeth decided to try picking up another one of her mother's practices. She sat down on her bed, closed her eyes and prayed. She began a new path that would start to ease the constant restlessness in her stomach. She found her mother. She found her focus. And now, Elizabeth began to find her relationship with God.

"So, do you think they're the same ones we know?" Remy asked as they started the ship's systems.

"Probably not, but pretty close," Chuck said.

"Is that even possible?" Logan asked Gus.

"Yeah, but extremely unlikely," Gus said. "Obviously, there must be versions of us that, for lack of better description, closed the loop. But the odds of that being us would be like winning the cosmic lottery."

"Hang on," Chuck interjected. "If I'm understanding this correctly, wouldn't this entire thing have had to been started by a version of us coming here who never met Beth and Haley?"

Logan started nodding. "That makes sense, but who would have saved your butt from the robot?" he asked Chuck.

"How would you have gotten out of those caverns?" Chuck asked in return.

Logan shrugged, "You had a plan, didn't you?"

"Yeah, but it was a longshot," Chuck reminded, "And one we thankfully didn't have to take, or you would have been in there for a couple days at least."

"Well, who's to say that the original group that came here was even us," Remy threw in for consideration.

"Don't know," said Chuck.

With a shake of the head and a sigh, Logan said, "The multiverse is weird."

Walking up to Gus, Chuck asked, "Ready to find your universe?"

An anxious look appeared in Gus' eyes as he wondered if they would ever find where he originally came from. He slowly nodded as Chuck set his hand on his friend's shoulder and looked him in the eye.

"We'll find it," Gentry reassured the ship's captain.

Logan and Remy hopped into the pilot seats, and Gus asked, "Everybody ready?"

"Yes, sir," they all happily responded.

"Take us up," said Gus.

Outside, a soft low hum could be heard coming from the ship. The men from the Airforce, alongside some State Troopers, watched as it lifted straight into the air without causing any disturbance.

Colonel Decker observed the advanced craft as it moved higher, then the ship forward and away.

Chuck looked at his phone, smiled and selected a song.

It was a short walk between their house and the graveyard. Haley and her dad were halfway home when Harry pointed to the sky. Music began to play from the speakers of Haley's bandana as the Wavelength flew by. They saw a vortex open up ahead of the ship. It expanded wider, the ship flew through, and the vortex collapsed in on itself. They were gone.

The Starrs looked each other in the eyes, and Haley lifted her arms. Harry bent down, wrapped her in a hug and lifted her up as she laid her head on his shoulder. The sleepy empath felt the rhythm of Harry's steps while he continued walking home. Haley closed her eyes and peacefully dozed off as Jonny Cash's version of "Won't Back Down" played softly beneath her ears.

More than a year before it would release.

Kone was at his elaborate conference table when the six remaining Archons were escorted into the room. With the connection between their worlds severed, they were the last, and they felt alone. Nervous, they entered the room, wondering what fate now awaited them, to find six empty seats at the large ornate table.

"Welcome," Kone said to them as he motioned toward the unoccupied places, "Please, sit." The reptilians walked around the table and did so as three of Podmen entered the room, followed by Sahmbo and a couple of Commandos and a General.

"You six are the last of your kind," Kone began as he walked to the head of the table, "My condolences," the Cetatian Uniralt added, then sat in his chair as Sahmbo came around to stand behind Kone's left shoulder and Commando Conrad to his right.

"But I believe you have survived long enough for fortune to smile upon you once more," Kone continued with a smoothly spoken confidence. "While I would have preferred that your kin could have joined us, you six will be able to see the plan that Ahnk-Hume helped form come to fruition."

The Commando clicked a button on a device he was holding, which brought the large monitor on the wall to life, and Kone directed their attention to the screen.

As the Cetatian Uniralt laid out a revised version of the plan, the Archons went from nervous to curious and then to downright enthusiastic. Kone turned to the Commando on his right and said, "Please inform them of the new timeline."

Peter Conrad, Kone's top strategist, was about six foot three with a buzz cut and a sense of confidence that would make anyone think twice about messing with him. "A year," he said with complete certainty.

"Two decades ahead of our original schedule," Kone stated. "Gentlemen," he announced in his deep voice with a slight smile, "Prepare for the new millennium."

Based on the video game of the same name that has not yet
been made at the time of this publishing…

The multiverse is weird.

Haley Starr created by Sonnet Stevens and Ethan Sasportas.

Special thanks to:

Christina Adcock.

Connor Cryan-Sasportas.

Logan Cryan-Sasportas.

Chuck McDonald.

Joshua Stevens.

Sonnet Stevens.

Yeshua.